DEAD MAN'S GOLD

**Center Point
Large Print**

DEAD MAN'S GOLD
The Loner

J. A. Johnstone

CENTER POINT PUBLISHING
THORNDIKE, MAINE

This Center Point Large Print edition
is published in the year 2010 by arrangement with
Kensington Publishing Corp.

The text of this Large Print edition is unabridged.
In other aspects, this book may vary
from the original edition.
Printed in the United States of America.
Set in 16-point Times New Roman type.

ISBN: 978-1-60285-662-2

Library of Congress Cataloging-in-Publication Data

Johnstone, J. A.
    Dead man's gold / J. A. Johnstone.
        p. cm.
    ISBN 978-1-60285-662-2 (library binding : alk. paper)
    1. Large type books. I. Title.

PS3610.O43D43 2010
813'.6--dc22

2009038307

DEAD MAN'S
GOLD

Prologue

A castle outside Seville, Spain, 1668

Albrecht Konigsberg tried not to think about the fact that the torturers would be coming for him soon. He might have prayed, except that the men who were about to kill him considered themselves to be doing the Lord's work. If they were right, then God would not listen to his prayers anyway, because he was a heretic.

Even knowing that, Konigsberg slipped to his knees beside the bed in his cell and sent a prayer heavenward, asking for deliverance.

He was still kneeling there when footsteps began to echo in the long corridor leading through the vast underground dungeon.

A bitter laugh came from Konigsberg's lips. So much for his prayers being answered. He hadn't expected anything else, really. He was a German, he was a Jew, and he was a man of science, rumored to be a descendant of the great astronomer Regiomontanus. To these Spaniards, any one of those things might have been enough to condemn him. Taken together, they were damning beyond redemption.

He stood up and faced the cell door. He would not force them to drag him out like a coward. He would go to meet the inquisitors on his feet. He would die a man, even though he was a heretic in their eyes.

But when a key rattled in the lock and the door swung open, it wasn't the priests or the torturers who stood there. It was one of the guards, a man named Alphonso.

"German!" he said. "I would have a word with you."

"What do you want, Alphonso?" Konigsberg asked. "I have nothing with which to bribe you. The Church has taken everything I own."

The guard came closer and tilted his head to one side. Greed lit up the eyes in his brutal face. "It is rumored that you know a secret . . . a secret that is very valuable."

"I know nothing," Konigsberg replied with a shake of his head. "If I did, would I not try to trade it for my life?"

"I will help you escape, if you take me to the treasure," Alphonso went on, as if he hadn't heard a word that Konigsberg said.

"Are you not listening to me? I know no secret! I know nothing of any treasure!"

Alphonso smiled and pointed a blunt, dirty finger toward the stone ceiling. It was a moment before Konigsberg realized that the guard was really pointing toward the heavens.

"The Twelve Pearls," Alphonso said.

Konigsberg's breath hissed between his teeth. He had to restrain himself from leaping forward, grabbing the guard's tunic, and shaking him. "What do you know of the Twelve Pearls?"

"I know that *you* know their secret."

Konigsberg never would have thought of it that way. No wonder he hadn't realized what Alphonso was talking about. The guards must have gossiped among themselves, taking a thing that had only scientific importance, and inflating it until it was supposed to be the key to some sort of fabulously valuable treasure.

Sensing that this would be his only chance for freedom, for life itself, Konigsberg put a sly smile on his face and said, "What if I do know the secret of the Twelve Pearls?"

"Is it worth your life?" Alphonso demanded. "The torturers will be here soon." The guard lifted his ring of keys and jingled them. "But I can let you out. You'll be gone when they get here."

Suddenly, Konigsberg worried that this was a trick of some sort. A test for the heretic.

"What about you?" he asked. "They'll know you did it. They'll torture and execute you in my place."

Alphonso shook his head. "No, I'm leaving with you. They're not watching your cottage anymore. Take me there and give me the secret, and then we will go our separate ways." He paused. "I have a cousin, the master of a ship sailing tomorrow for the New World. I intend to be on that ship. With the wealth that you will give me, I will be an important man in New Spain!"

The fool. The utter fool. But like most poor men, he had a dream, and that dream told him that if he could do one certain thing, achieve one certain end, then he would be rich and all his problems would be solved. It didn't matter what that thing was; it was probably different in every dream.

And like all dreams, it never came true.

"All right," Konigsberg said. He had nothing to lose. "But let us go quickly."

Alphonso nodded eagerly. He led the prisoner out into the corridor and then locked the cell door behind them. When the torturers arrived and found the cell locked and empty, they would be puzzled, until they figured out that Alphonso was gone, too. Then they would understand, and they would come looking for the guard.

As Alphonso led Konigsberg through the rat's warren of passages underneath the castle, he said quietly, "I heard the priests talking about how they searched your cottage, German. They found nothing save some journals. You hid the secret of the Twelve Pearls well, I think." Alphonso laughed. "Are they real pearls, German?"

"You'll see," Konigsberg said.

But you won't understand.

They came to a narrow flight of stairs, dimly lit by a candle in a wall sconce. When they reached the top, Alphonso unlocked another door and led the way into a chapel. It was a small room, but richly furnished. Konigsberg saw a golden candlestick inlaid with gems that had to be worth a small fortune. There were other things there in the castle that were equally valuable, but Alphonso would never dream of stealing them, because they belonged to the Church.

He wouldn't hesitate to steal from a German Jew, though. That was entirely different.

Konigsberg had no doubt that Alphonso planned to kill him as soon as he had turned over the secret of the Twelve Pearls. Then he would flee to the harbor at Cadiz and his cousin's ship bound for the New World.

As they went past the table where the candlestick sat, Konigsberg snatched it up.

"Here now!" Alphonso said. "You can't take that! It belongs to the Church!"

Konigsberg's lips curled in a snarl. "I'm a heretic, remember? I need something to pay my way, to help me escape." And to recompense him for the tortures he had already suffered, he thought. A shudder ran through him as he remembered the pain that had been inflicted on him in numerous sessions.

Alphonso hesitated, then shrugged. "Your immortal soul is damned anyway, I suppose. Come!"

They reached a small door leading out of the castle's rear wall. The guard unlocked it, and the two men stole into the night. No one had seen them. They had made their escape, and Konigsberg breathed deeply of free air once again. It smelled wonderful.

Alphonso's hand closed around his arm. "Now, take me to your cottage," he ordered. His other hand caressed the handle of the knife at his hip. "Give me the secret of the Twelve Pearls."

"Of course. A bargain is a bargain."

Konigsberg's cottage was on top of a hill, well outside the city. He had settled there for a reason. The view of the night sky was unobstructed. He remembered all the pleasant hours he had spent with his telescope in front of the little, thatched-roof cottage.

He wondered how the view of the stars would be from the New World. Perhaps he would find out. Alphonso had planted that idea in his mind, and with luck, it would take root and grow.

They reached the cottage an hour later. The door hung crookedly from its hinges where the men who worked for the inquisitors had wrenched it open. A goat came trotting out as Konigsberg and Alphonso walked up. It bleated at them and ran off. Konigsberg knew the inside of the place was probably unfit to live in now, but that didn't matter. He didn't plan to stay there.

"The books that the priests found," he said to Alphonso. "What did they do with them? Did they burn them?"

"Of course! They were sinful, the work of a heretic."

Konigsberg laughed. He reached down to the stone in front of the door. "Help me pry this up."

"What?"

"The secret lies underneath it."

That was enough for Alphonso. He bent down, and his strong back and arms did most of the work as the two men pried up the stone, revealing a small cavity underneath. Konigsberg went to his knees—so oddly like prayer, he thought—and reached into the dark hole. He brought out a small wooden chest. Inside it, wrapped in oil-cloth, was the only truly important book he had. The other journals he had left lying around on purpose, so that if the priests ever searched the cottage they would have something to find and destroy in a fury of self-righteousness. Now, Konigsberg clutched the box and its precious contents to his chest.

"Is that the treasure?" Alphonso asked eagerly.

"No, that's still in the hiding place," Konigsberg said. "You can get it if you'd like."

Instantly, Alphonso was on his knees beside the hole. He bent over and reached down into the cavity.

Konigsberg picked up the candlestick he had set aside and brought it crashing down with stunning force on the back of Alphonso's head. The unexpected blow drove the guard to the ground with a grunt of pain and surprise. Konigsberg struck again before his victim could regain his senses. The candlestick was heavy, especially its base. He smashed it down on Alphonso's head again and again and again, until the man's skull had been beaten into a shape that didn't resemble anything human. Blood and brains leaked into the hole that had hidden the secret of the Twelve Pearls.

Konigsberg straightened from his work. Earlier tonight, he had been prepared to die. Now, through a miracle—divine intervention? —he was not only free, at least for the moment, but he had recovered his life's work.

The inquisitors and their torturers would try to find him, he knew. Every hand would be against him. But he would cling to his freedom as long as he possibly could, and perhaps where one miracle had occurred, so could another. He would make his way to Cadiz, find that ship, tell Alphonso's cousin that Alphonso had sent him . . . If word of his escape and Alphonso's death had not yet reached the port . . . if the ship sailed in time . . .

Well, in that case, Konigsberg thought as he hurried through the night, the box in one hand and the candlestick in the other, then he would know that every now and then, God heard the prayers of a so-called heretic after all.

God . . . or possibly the Devil . . .

Chapter 1

New Mexico Territory, 229 years later

The man who called himself Kid Morgan reined the buckskin to a halt as he topped a ridge dotted with gnarled mesquites and clumps of hardy grass. This was a dry, rugged land, inhospitable to men and animals and hard on vegetation.

The Kid leaned forward in the saddle and watched as a wagon raced from right to left across the flats in front of him. A couple of hundred yards back, three men on horseback galloped after the vehicle, steadily gaining on it.

The Kid's eyes narrowed. The riders weren't shooting at the wagon, just chasing it. He didn't know what was going on, and these days he made it a policy to mind his own business. Over the past year, he had experienced quite a bit of tragedy and strife in his life, and now he wanted nothing but to be left alone. To drift aimlessly, not caring about anything. He wasn't looking for trouble.

Although a person wouldn't know that to look at him. The walnut grips of the Colt .45 holstered on his right hip showed signs of considerable use. Saddle sheaths were strapped to both sides of the buckskin's rig; the stock of a Winchester repeater stuck up from one of them, while an old Sharps Big Fifty was snugged in the other one. In addition to the three guns, The Kid carried a Bowie knife in a sheath attached to his belt on the left side, angled slightly so that he could reach across his body and draw it in a hurry if he needed to.

Yeah, he was armed for trouble, and the eyes under the shade of the broad-brimmed brown hat were keen, always watchful for any signs of danger. But just because he was alert didn't mean he was going to go rushing blindly into every ruckus that came his way.

He kept telling himself that, anyway.

The wagon was just about even with him. Two men swayed back and forth on the driver's seat as the vehicle careened along. The terrain looked absolutely flat from up there on the ridge, but The Kid knew that it was rougher than it appeared when you were actually down there driving a wagon over it. The man handling the reins lashed at the rumps of the team with the trailing ends of the lines, trying to urge the horses on to greater speed.

He might as well give up, thought The Kid. That wagon wasn't going to be able to get away from men on horseback. It just wasn't fast enough.

The pursuers still hadn't opened fire. Evidently they just wanted to overhaul the wagon and stop it. The Kid had no idea why. None of his affair, he told himself again. He lifted the buckskin's reins, poised to turn the horse away and ride back down the far side of the ridge when the wagon jolted particularly hard over a rough spot, and the driver's hat flew off.

Long red hair that was bright in the sunlight spilled down the figure's back.

"Well, hell," The Kid said softly.

So that was a woman at the reins, he thought . . . although it might be a man with really long hair; it was hard to be sure at this distance. But he knew in his gut it was a woman, just as he knew that now he couldn't ignore what was going on, couldn't just turn and ride away.

Couldn't because the beautiful blond ghost who haunted him wouldn't want him to.

He reached for the Winchester and pulled it from its sheath. Working the rifle's lever to throw a bullet into its firing chamber took only a second. Kid Morgan brought the Winchester to his shoulder, nestled his cheek against the smooth wooden stock, and rapidly cranked off three rounds, placing them about halfway between the wagon and the three riders, who had closed to within fifty yards.

Those horsebackers might not hear the shots over the pounding of their mounts' hoofbeats, but they couldn't miss the way dirt and rocks sprang into the air where those slugs smacked into the ground in front of them. The Kid knew by the way they reined in so sharply that they had seen the bullets hit. One of the men hauled back on the reins so hard his horse stumbled and went down in a welter of kicking legs. Dust billowed around the fallen man and horse.

The other two men yanked their mounts around and pulled rifles from saddle boots. If they had simply turned and ridden away, The Kid would have let them go. But they clearly wanted to make a fight of it. He heard the sharp crack of shots and then the whine of a bullet passing over his head.

They had called the tune, he thought. Let them dance the dance.

Shooting uphill or downhill, either one, was tricky, which was why the first hurried shots from the riders on the flats were high. The Kid didn't give them the chance to correct their aim. Rapidly, but without rushing, he fired four shots of his own. One of the men hunched over in the saddle but didn't fall. The other twisted around and then, as his horse bolted, toppled off the animal's back. His foot hung in the stirrup, though, so the horse dragged him as it continued to run back the way it had come. His foot didn't come loose for a couple of hundred yards. When it did, he lay there motionless on the sandy ground.

The wounded man who was still mounted didn't try to keep the fight going. Instead he turned his horse and kicked it into a run after the one that had dragged off his companion. The Kid's eyes narrowed as he lowered the Winchester and watched the man flee. He might have been able to hit the hombre again, even at that range, but he didn't attempt the shot.

Maybe that was a mistake. Letting an enemy go usually was, thought The Kid. But that hombre didn't know who he was. Besides, the man was wounded and might not live.

The wagon had kept going without slackening speed. It was vanishing in the distance to the east, its location marked by the plume of dust raised by its wheels and the team's hooves. The Kid glanced in that direction, then clicked his tongue at the buckskin and heeled the horse into motion.

The horse that had fallen had managed to get back to its feet and apparently was unhurt. It was wandering around aimlessly near its former rider, who still lay on the ground. The Kid headed for that man first, because he might be alive and pose a threat. The one who'd been shot and dragged was dead, more than likely.

The Kid held the Winchester ready for instant use as he approached the fallen man. When he was close enough, he brought the buckskin to a stop, dismounted, drew the Colt with his right hand and used the left to slide the rifle back in its saddle sheath. He kept the revolver trained on the man as he walked over to him.

When he was still several yards away, The Kid could see that the man's head was twisted at an odd angle. He must have landed wrong and broken his neck, The Kid thought. He stepped closer, saw the glassy, lifeless eyes, and knew that the man was dead. The hombre wore range clothes and had a hard-featured, beard-stubbled face. Might have been an outlaw, might not have been. The Kid didn't know, had never seen the man before. But the other two had been quick to shoot at him, and those hadn't been warning shots, like the first ones he'd fired. He had no doubt that the trio had been up to no good by chasing the wagon.

A whistle brought the buckskin to The Kid's side. He mounted up and rode across the flats to check on the other man. As he had thought, that one was dead, too, drilled through the body by one of the slugs from The Kid's Winchester. A bloody froth drying around the man's mouth told The Kid that he'd ventilated at least one of the man's lungs.

This fella had the same hardcase look to him, The Kid noted. He supposed that they'd intended to rob the pilgrims in the wagon.

The buckskin pricked up his ears and tossed his head. That caught The Kid's attention. He turned to look and saw that the horse was reacting to the approach of the wagon, which was rolling steadily toward him at a much slower pace than it had been making earlier. The people on it realized that they weren't being chased anymore and had turned around to see what was going on.

Curiosity like that could get folks into trouble, The Kid reflected. It would have been smarter for them just to be thankful that someone had stepped in to help them and keep going.

He hoped they didn't want to spend a lot of time being grateful. He wasn't looking for gratitude.

The wagon came to a stop beside the other dead man. The passenger climbed down from the seat and knelt beside the corpse, probably checking to make sure the man was dead.

The Kid put a foot in the stirrup and swung up onto the buckskin. He thought about waving to the people with the wagon and then riding on without talking to them.

The driver hopped to the ground, and strode toward him. Now that The Kid was closer, there was no mistaking the fact that the slender but well-curved figure of the driver belonged to a woman. The long red hair swayed around her face and shoulders in the hot wind that blew across the flats.

The man he had once been had prided himself on being a gentleman. There was enough of that left in Kid Morgan to keep him from turning his back on the woman and riding away. Instead, he hitched the buckskin forward at a walk to meet her.

She moved like a young woman, and as he came closer, he saw that estimation was correct. She was in her mid-twenties, he guessed, with a lightly freckled face that was attractive without being classically beautiful. She wore trousers and a long-sleeved shirt, and The Kid was somewhat surprised to see that she had a gunbelt strapped around her

21

waist. It was unusual enough to see a woman in pants; to run across one who was packing iron was even more uncommon.

She stopped and put her hands on her hips, which meant her right hand was pretty close to the butt of the holstered revolver she wore. He supposed that she didn't fully trust him, which probably wasn't a bad attitude. While civilization had spread across much of the land, there were still some wild places left, and this remote area of southern New Mexico Territory certainly fit that description. Outlaws still roamed here, Mexican banditos sometimes raided across the border, and occasionally even bands of bronco Apaches from the mountains south of the Rio Grande ventured this far north in search of plunder. It was smart to operate under the assumption that anybody you met might mean you harm.

He reined in and held up a hand to show her that he didn't. With a polite nod, he called, "Hello."

She didn't return the greeting. Instead, she asked bluntly, "Is that other man dead?"

"He is," The Kid replied.

She glanced over her shoulder at the man who'd been on the wagon with her. He still knelt next to the first dead man. Then she looked at The Kid again and said with an intensity he hadn't expected, "Good. I wish you'd gone ahead and killed the third one, too."

Chapter 2

The Kid couldn't keep his eyes from rising in surprise. She saw that and said, "You must think I'm a bloodthirsty bitch."

"No, ma'am," The Kid said. "I don't know you well enough to venture an opinion either way."

"You don't know how they've been dogging our trail, either, making life miserable for us. Now Fortunato is just going to send more men after us, once the one you wounded gets back and tells him what happened."

"Could be, ma'am." The Kid reached up and tugged on the brim of his hat. "Good luck to the both of you."

He started to turn the buckskin away, when she cried, "Wait!"

The Kid paused.

"Don't you want to know what it's all about?"

"No offense, ma'am, but I figure that's your problem, not mine." The Kid had just spent several months taking care of personal business that had turned bloody and heartbreaking. He wasn't in the mood to take on anybody else's trouble.

"You mean you're going to just ride off and . . . and leave us here?"

"You don't have to worry about those men anymore. The one who was wounded won't bother you again. He looked like he was hit pretty hard.

You should have time to get where you're going."

"How do you know that? You don't know where we're going."

"No, I don't," The Kid admitted. She was a stubborn woman, and he was losing his patience. "And I don't care, either."

He pulled the buckskin's head around a little harder than he intended and immediately felt bad about taking his anger out on the horse. The buckskin was a damned fine animal.

"They're going to try to kill us again, you know!" the woman shouted at The Kid's back. "Fortunato doesn't want us to find it before he does!"

He knew what she wanted. She wanted him to stop and ask who Fortunato was, and what they were looking for, and why Fortunato wanted to find it first. There had been a time when he would have been very curious if he had found such a puzzle facing him. Not now, though.

The woman cried out suddenly, not in anger but in pain, and a second later, The Kid heard the faint boom of a high-powered rifle. He whirled the buckskin around and saw the woman staggering to one side, her right hand clutching her upper left arm. A crimson stain appeared under her fingers, spreading as blood welled from her arm.

The Kid's head jerked toward the east, where some low hills rose. The sun was quartering down toward the western horizon, and its rays struck a reflection from something in those hills. A pair of field glasses, maybe . . . or a telescopic rifle sight.

The Kid sent the buckskin racing toward the woman. She was still stunned from being wounded. He didn't know how bad the injury was, but he knew the next shot from that distant marksman might be fatal. He brought the horse to a sliding stop beside her, leaned down, and wrapped his left arm around her. She cried out again as he lifted her off her feet and set her in front of him.

Then he was galloping toward the wagon, and as he approached he shouted to the woman's companion, "Get back on the wagon! Get it moving!"

Those hills were close to a mile away. That had been one hell of a shot to come as close as it had to killing the woman. The Kid knew instinctively that that had been its intent. She had said that this fella Fortunato would try again to kill them. The Kid wondered briefly if Fortunato himself was the one who'd pulled the trigger.

The woman's traveling companion was an older man. He had taken his hat off, and his white hair shone in the sun. The Kid shouted at him again to get on the wagon and get the vehicle rolling, and this time the man gave a little shake of his head and reacted, as if he hadn't fully understood the first time. He clapped the hat back on his head, ran to the front of the wagon, and clambered up on the seat.

The Kid's back was to the rifleman. His skin

crawled. He knew that if he was targeted and the bullet found its mark, he would never hear the shot. The bullet would travel faster than the sound of its firing. But all he could do was keep going and wait for the dreadful impact of the lead, if such was his fate.

He reached the wagon. The old man was slapping the reins against the backs of the team and shouting at the horses. They broke into a run, which rocked the old-timer back on the seat as the wagon jolted into motion. He regained his balance and started slashing at the horses' rumps again as The Kid rode past.

The Kid thought about veering in close to the wagon and transfering the woman to the seat, but decided that was too dangerous. If she slipped, she might fall under the wagon wheels. Anyway, she was probably safer right where she was, with his body serving as a shield from any bullets that came their way.

He looked back as the buckskin pulled slightly ahead of the wagon. No matter how high-powered that rifle was, they had to be at the very outer edge of its range. At distances like that, a couple of hundred yards could make a big difference.

The Kid remembered his father, Frank Morgan, telling him about an old friend of his, a buffalo hunter named Billy Dixon, who had made a mile-long shot during an Indian fight down in Texas twenty-some-odd years earlier, shooting a chief's horse right out from under him at that range. But that had been a spectacular shot, a once-in-a-lifetime shot, and probably more than a little bit of luck had been involved, too.

Despite the fact that he thought they were probably safe now, The Kid kept the buckskin running and waved for the old man to keep the wagon moving, too. He didn't slow down until they had put another five hundred yards behind them. Even then he just slowed down and didn't stop, even though he was sure they were out of range of the rifleman in the hills.

When he looked back, he saw the sun glint on something again. He knew it was probably a foolish thing to do, but he lifted a hand in a mocking wave of farewell.

Then he turned back to the woman and asked, "Are you all right?"

She didn't answer him. Her head lolled loosely on her neck. The Kid bit back a curse. His left arm was still tight around her, just under her breasts, and he could feel her heart beating so he knew she wasn't dead. She must have passed out, he thought. He needed to find some place where they could stop safely and he could take a look at that wounded arm to see how bad it really was.

The arid flats stretched for a couple of miles, but he saw more hills and some green where they ended. There might be a little shade and some water, and both of those things would be welcome.

He kept moving at a steady pace, staying a short distance ahead of the wagon. As he rode toward the hills, he thought about how his desire to avoid other people's trouble had gone by the wayside. There had been a time, before he was the man he was now, when he truly *didn't* care about what happened to anybody else. That was before he had met his real father, who had started him on the path to growing up, and before a beautiful blonde named Rebel had come into his life and finished the job of turning him into a decent hombre.

Rebel was gone now, although there were times when he still seemed to see her, to hear her voice, even to feel the soft caress of her hand against his cheek. But the lessons she had taught him remained. She had never turned her back on people in trouble.

And she wouldn't let him do it, either, no matter how much he wanted to just be alone, to drift and not care.

He saw some trees at the base of the nearest hill and knew there must be a spring there. All the waterholes in this part of the territory were spring fed, except for a few *tinajas* that caught the occasional rain, and they were dry a lot more often than not. As they came closer, he saw grass growing. The horses would welcome some graze. The woman and the old man could camp there tonight, he thought.

The spring bubbled out of a rocky outcropping at

the bottom of the hill and formed a pool about fifteen feet wide. The horses headed straight for it once they smelled it. The Kid reached it first and waited for the wagon to get there. When it did, he motioned for the old man to stop short of the water.

"Set the brake!" he called to the old-timer. "I want to check the water before we let the horses drink, and I need help with the girl."

The old man nodded and hauled back on the brake lever. The horses in the team pulled against it but were unable to reach the water. The old man scrambled down from the wagon and hurried over to The Kid.

"Help me put her on the ground," he said as he carefully lowered the young woman. The old man was too frail to take her in his arms—he probably didn't weigh any more than she did—but he was able to steady her long enough for The Kid to throw a leg over the saddle and slide down from the buckskin's back. He got one arm under her shoulders and the other under her knees and lifted her, carrying her over to the grass alongside the pool so he could place her there carefully on the ground.

Then he stepped over to the pool, hunkered on his heels, and cupped a handful of water in his palm. It didn't smell of alkali, and when he tasted it, it was clear and cool and sweet.

With a nod, he told the old-timer, "All right, let the horses drink." He straightened, went to the buckskin, and led him over to the pool as well. "Not too much," he cautioned the old man. "That's not good for them."

"I know a thing or two about horses, young man," the old-timer said. He was short and slender. Startlingly blue eyes were set deep in a lined and weathered face. He wore a broad-brimmed black hat with a low, round crown, a white shirt, and black trousers.

"No offense," The Kid said. He went back to the young woman and knelt beside her.

The old-timer came over to join him. "Is she all right?"

"That's what I'm about to find out. Why don't you find a rag and get it wet? We'll need to wash the blood away from the wound."

"All right." The man went back to the wagon as The Kid took hold of the woman's sleeve and ripped it away from her shoulder.

He was pleased to see that there weren't any entry and exit wounds on her arm. Instead, there was just a bloody furrow on the outside of her upper arm. The bullet had nicked her, creating a messy but not serious wound. It had traveled far enough before striking her that it had lost some of its power, which helped. All he really needed to do was clean the wound and bind it up. He had a flask of whiskey in his saddlebags. That would do for swabbing out the bullet crease, even though it would burn like hell.

The Kid turned his head to see how the old man was coming along with the chore he'd given him. Because of that, he didn't see the young woman move. He sensed it, though, and a second later he felt the hard jab as she dug the muzzle of her pistol into his belly.

"Don't move," she said, "or I'll blow your guts out."

Chapter 3

"Annabelle, no!" the old man called from the wagon. "That's the young man who's helping us!"

"I'll kill you, Fortunato," the redhead muttered. Green eyes filled with hatred glared up at The Kid when he looked at her.

He shook his head and said, "I'm not Fortunato." He hoped that gun didn't have a hair trigger.

"You'll never get the Konigsberg Candlestick," the young woman called Annabelle went on. "Or the secret of the Twelve Pearls, either. I'll kill you . . . kill you . . ."

Those striking green eyes suddenly rolled up in their sockets as she passed out again. Her arm fell to the side, and the gun slipped out of her fingers when the back of her hand hit the ground.

The Kid heaved a sigh of relief.

"You have to forgive her," the old man said as he bustled back over to them from the wagon, carrying a piece of cloth he had soaked with water from a canteen. "She's out of her head from being shot. Will she be all right?"

"I think so," The Kid replied as he took the wet cloth from the old man and began washing away the blood around the wound. "There's a whiskey flask in my saddlebags. Reckon you can get it?"

The old-timer frowned. "You need a drink at a time like this?"

The Kid pointed to the bullet crease on the young woman's arm. "It's to clean the wound," he said, even though he was a little annoyed by having to explain himself.

"Oh. Oh, yes, of course. I'll see if I can find it."

While the old man was digging through the saddlebags, The Kid asked, "What's her name?"

"Annabelle. Annabelle Dare."

The Kid grunted. "Pretty name. She your granddaughter?"

"No. My, ah, daughter."

That struck The Kid as odd. He would have said there was too much differences in their ages for Annabelle to be the old-timer's daughter. She must have come along late in life for the couple.

"What about her mother?"

"I'm not married."

"All right." None of his business, The Kid told himself. Of course, he had tried to stick by that notion earlier, he recalled, and they could all see how *that* had worked out. "Have you found the whiskey yet?"

"Right here," the old man said as he brought the flask to The Kid, who took it and unscrewed the cap.

The Kid nodded toward Annabelle Dare and suggested, "Why don't you get up there by her head and hold her shoulders? She's liable to jump a little when I pour this Who-hit-John over that wound."

"All right." The old man got in position and put

his hands on Annabelle's shoulders. He might not be strong enough to hold her down completely, but at least his grip might help steady her a little.

The Kid grasped Annabelle's arm with his left hand and turned it slightly, so that he could get to the wound better. Then he poured the whiskey onto it, making sure to saturate the furrow thoroughly.

Annabelle reacted instantly, letting out a small cry of pain. Her back arched, but the old man's grip was strong enough to keep her from thrashing around. Her breath hissed between clenched teeth. Her eyelids fluttered.

The Kid wiped away the mixture of blood and whiskey that ran out of the wound. With a long sigh, Annabelle relaxed slightly, and The Kid realized that the pain must have eased somewhat. After a moment, her eyes opened.

"Should I move that gun out of your reach," he asked her, "or do you know who I am now?"

"I don't . . . know who you are."

"But you know I'm not Fortunato."

"Of course . . . you're not . . . Fortunato. What do you . . . mean by that?"

The old man leaned in and said, "A few minutes ago, you mistook our young benefactor here for that Italian brigand."

"Really?" Annabelle murmured.

"Yeah, you threatened to blow my guts out," The Kid said with a smile. "You sounded like you meant it, too."

"Oh, my God." She closed her eyes. "I . . . I'm sorry. I must have been out of my head."

The Kid nodded. "Getting shot will do that to some people. You lost some blood, too. Though not enough to worry about."

She opened her eyes and looked around. "Where . . . are we?"

"Some hills near those flats where Fortunato's men were chasing you," The Kid told her. "I reckon you're safe here for the moment. They can't cross those flats without us seeing them."

"Fortunato won't come after us this soon, anyway," Annabelle said. Her voice was a little stronger now. "You killed two of his men and wounded another. As far as I know, he doesn't have anyone else with him except a servant." A bitter edge came into her tone. "But it won't take him long to recruit some more gunmen to send after us."

The Kid sensed that she was still waiting for him to ask for an explanation. Maybe he was just contrary, but he didn't do it. Instead, he told the old man, "I'll need some clean cloth to bind up this wound."

He nodded. "I'll see what I can find."

While the old man was doing that, Annabelle said to The Kid, "You haven't told me who you are."

"Just a fella with a bad habit of sticking his nose in where it doesn't belong."

"Well . . . I'm glad you stuck it in today."

"Is that your way of saying thank you?"

"I suppose we do owe you our thanks. If you hadn't come along and helped us, we might be dead now." A shudder ran through her. "Or worse, Fortunato's prisoners."

The Kid sighed. She wasn't going to stop until she got what she wanted. He asked, "Who is this Fortunato hombre?"

"Count Eduardo Fortunato. He's an Italian nobleman."

"The old fellow called him a brigand, so I figured he was an owlhoot of some sort."

"Oh, he's a criminal, all right," Annabelle said. "Being of noble birth doesn't necessarily make a person honest. He's looted art treasures from all over the Continent." She added condescendingly, "I'm referring to Europe."

"Oh," The Kid said.

He didn't mention that as a younger man, he had spent several months touring Europe one summer, visiting every museum and historical site and soaking up the culture. That was the accepted thing for wealthy young Americans of a certain class to do. His late mother, Vivian Browning, had had her feet planted firmly on the ground and was as unpretentious as could be, but she had also believed that it wouldn't hurt anything for her son to be exposed to some of the finer things in life.

"Fortunato will resort to any means to get what he wants, including murder," Annabelle went on. "It's

36

rumored that he was involved in a robbery at the Louvre several years ago. The men who actually carried out the theft all wound up dead, and the paintings they took were never recovered. I'm certain they're hanging on the walls of Fortunato's villa."

"Sounds like a pretty bad hombre," The Kid said, not mentioning that he had been to the Louvre himself. She probably wouldn't believe him, anyway. "What's he doing over here in the States?"

"Have you ever heard of the Konigsberg Candlestick?" Before The Kid could answer, Annabelle waved a hand dismissively. "No, of course you haven't. It's a very valuable artifact that was stolen from a castle in Spain more than two hundred years ago. The castle was being used by the Spanish Inquisition as a place to hold prisoners and conduct trials. The candlestick was in a chapel inside the castle and was the property of the Catholic Church. It was stolen by an escaping prisoner and never seen again, although there were rumors that the prisoner fled to the New World, taking the candlestick with him."

The old man came up with several strips of clean cloth. The Kid nodded toward him and said to Annabelle, "So you and your pa are on the trail of this fancy candlestick, is that it?"

Annabelle frowned. "My what?"

"Your father. The old-timer here."

Her frown deepened as she shook her head. "He's not my father."

The old man sighed and said, "I'm afraid I may have misled you slightly, my son."

"He's Father Jardine," Annabelle said. "He's been sent by the Vatican to recover the Konigsberg Candlestick . . . and another artifact the prisoner may have taken with him."

The Kid sat back on his heels in surprise. "If he's a priest, then who are you?"

"Dr. Annabelle Dare."

The Kid raised his eyebrows. "Doctor?"

"Ph.D in History from Yale University, thank you." She moved her injured arm slightly and winced. "I believe you said you were going to bind up this wound?"

"Yeah. See if you can sit up."

With Father Jardine's help, Annabelle did so. Her face paled in pain, making the scattering of freckles across her nose more noticeable. The Kid knelt beside her and wrapped the makeshift bandages around her arm, pulling them tight enough to make her wince again.

"Do they have to be that tight?" she asked.

"The bleeding's stopped. You don't want it to start up again."

"No, I suppose not." She moved her arm a little, as if checking to see how bad it was going to hurt. Then she said, "You still haven't told me your name."

"It's Morgan."

"Is that your first name or your last name?"

"Doesn't matter. Some people call me The Kid, or Kid Morgan, so I guess you could say it's my last name."

Actually, he had given himself that name, taking the inspiration for it from a dime novel. He had assumed that identity to conceal who he actually was, and in time, the pose had become the reality. He had no intention of going back to being the man he'd been before.

"Kid Morgan?" Annabelle repeated, and the mocking tone in her voice put The Kid's teeth on edge for a second. "That sounds like the name of some sort of desperado or gunfighter."

The Kid shrugged and didn't say anything.

"Wait a minute," Annabelle said as wariness sprang up in her eyes. "Are you an outlaw, Mr. Morgan?"

He knew what she was worried about. She had been so anxious to blather on about wicked Italian counts and valuable old candlesticks that she might have revealed too much to the wrong man. After all, they had never seen him until an hour or so earlier and had no idea what he was capable of. He might kill them both and go after the Konigsberg Candlestick himself, or he might try to sell them out to Fortunato . . .

"I'm not an outlaw," he said. Whether or not she wanted to believe him was up to her.

Evidently she did, because she looked relieved. Then she said, "Then you must be a gunfighter."

The Kid didn't deny it. That was the reputation Kid Morgan had, and he supposed there was some truth to it.

Annabelle leaned forward suddenly and clasped his arm with her right hand. "If you're a gunfighter, Mr. Morgan . . . Kid . . . then I want to hire you."

"Hire me? To do what?"

"To kill Eduardo Fortunato," she said.

Chapter 4

The Kid felt a cold surge of anger inside him. This was the sort of thing that his father had been putting up with for years, he thought. Just because Frank Morgan had a reputation for being fast on the draw, most people believed that he could be hired to gun down anyone. That he was just a killing machine, a handy tool for whoever had the right price.

"You've got me mixed up with somebody else," The Kid said tightly, making an effort to keep his anger under control. "I'm not an assassin."

"But . . . I thought—"

"You thought wrong."

Annabelle shook her head. "Then I apologize. I meant no offense, Mr. Morgan. The way you helped us made me think you were the kind of man who seeks adventure, and then when you admitted that you're a gunfighter as well . . ." She shrugged her right shoulder, being careful not to move the left one and make her wounded arm hurt worse. "It was a natural enough mistake."

If she wanted to believe that to make herself feel better, The Kid didn't care. He stood up. "This'll be a good spot for you to camp. I'll help the padre tend to the horses, and then I'll be moving on."

Her eyes widened. "You're not going to stay here tonight, too?"

"No, I reckon I'll get on about my business . . . which doesn't include killing Italian noblemen."

Annabelle's mouth tightened into an angry line. "I suppose I deserved that," she snapped. "You can at least help me to my feet and give me back my gun before you go."

"I said I'd help with the horses, too," The Kid responded as he reached down, grasped her upraised hand, and pulled her to her feet. Then he picked up her gun and extended it to her butt-first. It was a double-action Smith & Wesson .38, he noted with approval, small enough for a woman to handle without too much trouble, especially if she practiced with it, but a heavy enough caliber to have some stopping power, too.

She took the weapon and slid it back into its brown leather holster. Then she stood and watched in silence as The Kid helped Father Jardine unhitch the team from the wagon. They hobbled the horses to keep them from wandering off, but the animals could still drink freely from the pool and graze on the grass that grew on its banks.

"You must forgive Annabelle, my son," the priest said quietly when he and The Kid paused on the other side of the wagon. "She means well, she truly does, but she has little patience and our mission is very important to her."

"What's in it for her?" The Kid asked. "If you recover this fancy candlestick for the Church, what does she get out of it?"

"It was her research that led me here. Tell me, Mr. Morgan, have you ever heard of the Jornada del Muerto?"

The Kid nodded. "It's a stretch of badlands north of here a ways, isn't it?"

"That's right, but its name means Journey of the Dead Man."

"So?"

"Have you any idea how it got that name?"

"Not really," The Kid replied with a shrug. "I suppose it's because the place is so hot and dry, it'll kill you if you try to cross it."

"Many years ago . . . two centuries ago, in fact . . . one such man *did* try to cross it. Unwisely, as it turned out, because he died before he reached the other side. His name was Albrecht Konigsberg."

The Kid smiled. "The man with the candlestick?"

"Exactly. He escaped from the Inquisition in Spain and came here to this land. I suspect that he stole the candlestick thinking that he could use it to pay his way to the New World. It was made of gold, after all, and decorated with fine gems. Somehow, though, he managed to hang on to it. Annabelle set out to trace his movements. She spent three years in Mexico doing so, pouring over endless piles of old government and Church documents. She was able to find a record of his arrival in Vera Cruz, and from there she traced him to Mexico City, where he was able to take on a new identity and serve as an advisor to the viceroy in charge of what was then New Spain. Konigsberg was a scientist, you see, an astronomer and astrologer who knew a great deal about the stars. But eventually his past caught up with him. Agents of the Inquisition found him, and he had to flee, taking the candlestick with him once again."

"So he ran north," The Kid guessed, "into what's now New Mexico Territory."

Father Jardine nodded solemnly. "Yes. He hid himself again by assuming a new identity as a trader known as El Aleman. However, his enemies ferreted him out after a time and he was forced to flee yet again. This time, his luck finally deserted him. With an Indian servant, he started across what is now known as the Jornada del Muerto but never reached the other side. There is a story about how an Indian near death stumbled into a mission and told stories of his master, a German who possessed a great treasure and hid it somewhere in the wasteland. But this was during the time soon after the Pueblo rebellion, when there was still much trouble with the Indians, and the priests and the soldiers at the mission had no time to see if the man's story was true. Eventually it was forgotten. But the story was still there, in the faded records of the mission that now reside in Mexico City."

The Kid ran a thumbnail along his jaw. "So when Miss Dare figured all this out, she got in touch with the Church authorities and told them she thought she knew where the candlestick ended up?"

"That is right. And the Vatican . . . sent me. The loss of what has come to be called the Konigsberg Candlestick has never been forgotten . . . or forgiven."

The Kid thought they might have picked somebody more suited to come all the way to New Mexico Territory and search for the missing artifact, but he supposed Father Jardine might be tougher than he looked.

"I reckon this Count Fortunato must have some spies who heard about the whole thing?"

"Fortunato has spies everywhere, even, although I hate to say it, in the Holy City."

"And he wants it for himself."

Father Jardine spread his hands. "For some men, their greed is so overpowering that it blots out everything else, including whatever decency they might have."

The Kid nodded slowly. "You've got your work cut out for you, then."

"Indeed we do. I hope you have a better understanding now, my son, of why Annabelle sought your help in this matter."

"I reckon so, but it doesn't really change anything—"

Annabelle came around the wagon, her eyes alight with suspicion. "What are the two of you whispering about around here?" she demanded.

"I was merely thanking Mr. Morgan for his kind assistance so far," Father Jardine said blandly. He smiled at The Kid, clearly leaving it up to him what he would do next.

The Kid didn't have to think very long about that. "Good luck to both of you," he said. He walked around the wagon to where the buckskin stood with his reins dangling, contentedly cropping at the grass.

"You're really leaving?" Annabelle said as she and the priest followed him.

"Yep." The Kid glanced at the sky as he picked up the reins. There was only about an hour of daylight left. "If you haven't been standing guard at night, it'd probably be a good idea if you started. There's more out here to worry about than just Fortunato."

"You mean mountain lions, things like that?"

The Kid swung up into the saddle. "Yeah, and some two-legged predators, too. There are still owlhoots and banditos in these parts."

"I thought the West was civilized now."

"You thought wrong," The Kid told her.

With that he turned and rode away, heading higher into the hills, leaving Annabelle to glare after him.

The whole thing was like something out of a storybook, he thought that night as he stretched out on a flat slab of rock, lying on his belly with the Winchester beside him.

The Spanish Inquisition, for God's sake!—so to

speak. A golden candlestick studded with gems, a desperate escape, a dying man with a fabulous story . . . The Kid was a little surprised that the candlestick wasn't supposed to have a curse on it. That was about the only thing missing from that loco yarn.

Although, he mused, if the story was true, Albrecht Konigsberg had wound up dying in a terrible wasteland and being immortalized by having it named after him—the Dead Man. Maybe that was curse enough.

Even though several hours had passed since sundown, the rock slab still retained some of the day's heat. It was warm underneath The Kid, but not all that comfortable. It was perfectly positioned, though, for him to keep an eye on the campsite a couple of hundred yards below him at the bottom of the hill. Annabelle and Father Jardine had built a pretty big fire, and he could see them moving around it. They might as well have erected a giant arrow pointing to them. Anybody out on the flats, or even in the hills on the far side, could see that fire and know exactly where they were.

Earlier, The Kid had ridden well out of sight, then stopped long enough to build a small, almost smokeless fire to boil some coffee and cook his supper. He had eaten and put the fire out before darkness settled down over the landscape. Then he had mounted up and moved back down to this place so that he could keep an eye on the two pilgrims.

Somebody needed to look out for them, that was for damned sure. Like he had told them, Fortunato wasn't their only problem. He didn't think they stood a chance in hell of going up into the Jornada del Muerto by themselves and coming out alive. The Kid had never been through there himself, but he recalled hearing his father talk about it. Hard country, Frank Morgan had said. And if that's what the man called The Drifter thought, then, brother, that country was *hard!*

Chances were, Annabelle Dare and Father Jardine would die of thirst or be killed by outlaws even if Fortunato and his men didn't catch up to them. Unless somebody went along with them who knew what he was doing.

"Damn it, damn it, damn it," The Kid said under his breath. He was talking himself into it. He had ridden away from their camp knowing that he was going to watch out for them tonight, but now he was persuading himself to make it a full-time job.

If he did, he'd just be beating Rebel to the punch. If he tried to abandon them, he knew good and well he'd have her ghost whispering in his ear.

He saw a shadow move, out on the flats. His hand went to the rifle next to him, drew it closer. A savage grin tugged at his mouth.

Come on, he thought. *Let's see who you are before I kill you.*

Chapter 5

The six young warriors crowded behind Manuelito. He hated his name because it meant Little Manuel. Not only was he big, especially for an Apache, but he had nearly forty summers and was a war chief.

None of the other warriors ever made fun of his name, though. They knew that to do so was to invite swift death. Manuelito was known throughout the Apache strongholds in northern Mexico as a man who could kill quickly and without remorse.

Unfortunately for his people, there weren't too many like him anymore. So many of the chiefs had given up the fight and surrendered to the white men. Even Geronimo's fangs had been pulled, and now he lived on a reservation somewhere, at one of the white men's forts. Some of those who had gone with him years earlier on raids across the border into the United States refused to believe that the great Geronimo could be brought so low, but Manuelito knew it was true. Only a few of the old, canny fighters such as himself were left.

But there were still young men who wished to fight, hungry for the glory of battle as young men always were. Manuelito had led six of them across the border a week earlier with no firm destination in mind. They would just look around and see what they could find.

A couple of days earlier, they had found an iso-lated ranch defended only by a man and two boys. Those defenders had died easily, leaving the woman and the girl-child for Manuelito and his companions to enjoy. After a day, the minds of both females were broken, and it was not nearly as pleasurable raping them when they no longer knew what was going on, so Manuelito had told two of the young warriors to go ahead and cut their throats. They had left the ranch house burning behind them with the corpses still inside it.

Since then, the Apaches had come across nothing else to entertain them, until that afternoon when they heard shots in the distance. More than likely, gunshots meant white men, although it could be Mexicans. Manuelito didn't care. He would kill either one, without prejudice. If they were not Apache, they were enemies.

When night fell, they saw the fire. White men, then, thought Manuelito. Mexicans were not so stupid as to announce their presence like that. The war party left its horses out on the flats and approached on foot, stealing silently through the darkness.

As they drew closer, Manuelito could make out the wagon, and then the two people moving around it. One was an old man, to judge by the way he walked and his white hair. The other was a woman.

But what a woman . . .

Tall and shapely, unlike the squat Apache women

he was accustomed to, and with hair like fire that cascaded down her back. Manuelito had heard of redheaded white women, but he had never actually seen one until now. As he watched her, he felt his lust growing. He would take her first, after they had killed the old man.

Or perhaps it would be better to let the old man live for a while, so that he could watch. The flame-haired girl was probably his daughter or grand-daughter, and it brought a grunt of satisfaction to Manuelito's lips to think of the old man being forced to look on while they all took the girl, one after the other. Then they could kill both of the foolish whites. It would be a good night's work.

Manuelito turned to the young warriors and issued his orders in swift, harsh Spanish. Some of them might not like it that he was claiming the red-headed woman for his own first, but none of them would challenge him. Manuelito was certain of that. He motioned for them to follow him.

The Apaches lay on their bellies and crawled forward until they were just outside the circle of light cast by the fire, so close that they could almost reach out and touch the two whites, who were completely unaware of the danger. Manuelito had been watching closely. He knew the girl and the old man were alone. No one else was in the camp.

"I'll take the first turn standing guard, Father," the girl said.

Manuelito understood the white man's tongue,

although he would not speak it. The words tasted like ashes in his mouth. So the white-haired man was the girl's father, as he had thought. Now that he had gotten a closer look at them, the old man seemed almost too old for that, but Manuelito didn't waste any time worrying about such things. He was more interested in the gun the flamehair wore in a holster on her hip. Was it possible she actually knew how to use it? Manuelito had never encountered a female who carried a gun like that. Even if she could handle the weapon, he wasn't particularly worried. He knew he was faster than any white woman.

The Kid figured the lurking shapes in the darkness were Apaches. He was sure neither white men nor Mexicans could move with such stealth. He could barely make them out, and he was looking for them.

Several years earlier, he and his father had run into some trouble from renegade Apaches in New Mexico Territory. Obviously, there were still a few hold-outs in the mountains south of the border who hadn't given up the fight against the white men.

The Kid waited. It would be better if he knew exactly how many enemies he was facing before he opened fire. He also didn't want to reveal his position by shooting too soon. He watched the figures as they crawled along the sandy ground toward the fire. Finally, he decided that there were half a dozen of them, give or take one. Formidable odds, but he had the high ground and he had fifteen rounds in the Winchester. It was time for him to take them by surprise and start picking them off.

Just as Manuelito to was about to leap up and rush at the redheaded woman, screaming a war cry that would paralyze her with fear, one of the young men jumped to his feet and sprang forward, no doubt allowing his lust to get the better of his common sense. He had to be crazed by the sight of the redhead, otherwise he never would have gone against Manuelito's orders.

Manuelito surged up and yelled piercingly, and so did the rest of the war party. The young man who had disobeyed orders was reaching out for the woman, but Manuelito was only a step behind him. Manuelito was so close that when the rifle cracked and the young warrior's head exploded from the slug that bored through it, the spray of blood and brain matter splattered all over the side of Manuelito's face. As he stumbled to an abrupt halt, more shots rang out.

This was not good.

The Kid didn't have time to think, only to react. He tracked the Indian for a split-second with the rifle, then stroked the trigger. The Winchester cracked and bucked against his shoulder, and the Apache flopped at Annabelle's feet, drilled through the head.

By the time the warrior hit the ground, The Kid had already shifted his aim and fired again. His second shot wasn't quite as accurate as the first. The bullet grazed the shoulder of the big Apache who'd been right behind the one leaping at Annabelle and knocked him sideways and down. That left five members of the war party still on their feet. As The Kid came up on one knee, he tracked the rifle from left to right, spraying bullets at them as fast as he could work the lever. He hoped Annabelle and Father Jardine had the sense to get down and stay down.

From the corner of his eye, he saw that that wasn't the case, at least where Annabelle was concerned. She had drawn that S&W .38 from its holster and slammed out three shots of her own. The Kid saw blood spurt as those slugs punched into the chest of one of the warriors and knocked him backward.

The Kid's fire had cut down two more of the Apaches. That left just two on their feet, and The Kid accounted for one of them by sending a bullet into his belly. The remaining warrior turned and ran like the Devil himself was after him.

The Kid turned his attention back to the second man he'd shot, the one he'd only grazed. With a grimace of disgust, he saw that the big Apache was gone. He must have scrambled up and dashed off into the shadows, too. He hadn't been wounded so badly that he couldn't move fast.

Holding the revolver level and ready to fire, Annabelle hustled Father Jardine behind the wagon. They crouched there, shielded to a certain extent by the vehicle in case the two surviving Apaches fired at them from the flats.

"Stay where you are!" The Kid yelled to them as he stood up and leaped off the slab of rock. He landed on the hillside and started half-running, half-sliding down the slope toward the camp.

With a clatter of rocks, he reached the bottom of the hill and ran behind the wagon to join Annabelle and the priest. Annabelle stared at him, but The Kid noticed that Father Jardine didn't seem particularly surprised to see him again.

"Have you got a shovel?" The Kid asked.

Annabelle's eyes widened even more. "A shovel?" she repeated. "What are you doing here? Why do you want a shovel?"

"Saving your lives, to answer the first question," The Kid replied curtly. "And that's why I want the shovel, too. We need to get that fire put out, and the fastest way to do it is by throwing sand on it."

"Let me," Father Jardine said as he reached inside the wagon and pulled out a short-handled shovel. He ran out into the open and started throwing sand on the flames.

"Blast it, Father, I intended to do that!" The Kid said.

"You and Annabelle have guns, Mr. Morgan. I

don't. If those savages shoot at me, you can return their fire."

The Kid had to admit that made sense. Anyway, no shots came from the flats during the two or three minutes it took for Father Jardine to shovel enough sand on the fire to smother all the flames. The big Apache was wounded and probably in no mood to fight at the moment, and the other one had been just about scared out of his breechclout and leggings. A welcome darkness closed in thickly over the camp as the last of the flames sputtered out.

"Thanks, Father," The Kid said. "You should be safe now, but come on back over here behind the wagon just in case."

"I can't," Father Jardine said as he set the shovel aside and straightened.

"Why not?"

"I have work to do," the priest said.

And with that, he walked over to the nearest of the fallen Apaches, dropped to his knees beside the warrior, and began to pray.

Chapter 6

The Kid heard the swift, softly spoken words, recognized them as Latin, and figured that praying was what Father Jardine was doing. He had taken Latin in college back east, of course, and after a moment he was able to recall enough of what he had learned so that he was certain the priest was performing the last rites.

"You're wasting your time, padre," The Kid said as he walked out from behind the wagon. "Those Apaches are heathens, at least by your lights. For a couple of hundred years, missionaries have been coming out here to try to convert them, but none of them have been very successful."

"That won't stop me from asking for forgiveness for them," Father Jardine said.

"Well, then, how about this? Some of them might still be—"

Before The Kid could finish his warning, one of the fallen Apaches reared up with a harsh cry of mingled pain and hate and raised a knife. The Kid saw starlight wink off the blade as the warrior tried to lean over and plunge it into Father Jardine's back.

Before the knife could fall, The Kid swung up the Winchester's barrel, put the muzzle against the side of the Apache's head, and pulled the trigger. The shot blasted away a good chunk of the warrior's skull and hammered him to the ground.

"Like I was saying," The Kid continued as the echoes of the shot rolled away across the flats, "some of them might still be alive."

Even after that, he thought for a second that Father Jardine was going to argue. But then the priest sighed and stood up.

"Very well. I'll let you attend to *your* work first, Mr. Morgan."

"That'd be a good idea," The Kid said.

Annabelle followed him as he checked on the rest of the warriors. All four of them were dead.

"What are you doing here?" she asked. "I thought you abandoned us."

"I just rode up a ways into the hills where I could keep a better eye on you. I had a hunch something like this might happen tonight."

"Did you know those Indians were following us?"

"Nope. Like I said, I just had a hunch. There are so many different ways a couple of pilgrims like you two can run into trouble out here, I figured it was bound to start catching up to you."

Father Jardine said, "You may think you're insulting us by calling us pilgrims, Mr. Morgan, but I assure you, I'll wear that name proudly. All of us are pilgrims on the journey upon which the Lord has set our steps."

"No offense intended, padre, but I don't want it to be a dead man's journey, despite the name of the place you're headed for."

Annabelle mulled over what The Kid had said a moment earlier, and then spoke, "Let me get this straight . . . You rode off and used us as bait in a trap, hoping that someone would attack us?"

"Not hoping, no," The Kid replied with a shake of his head. "I just wanted to be ready in case there was trouble."

"So you *don't* intend to abandon us, after all. You're going to come with us and help us."

The Kid's jaw tightened. He wished Annabelle hadn't put it quite so bluntly, because part of him felt like a fool for going along with her. But he knew it was hopeless to argue not only with his own instincts, but also with the spirit of his late wife as well.

"Yeah," he said. "I reckon I'm coming with you."

And he hoped he wasn't making one hell of a mistake.

The Kid fetched his horse from up the hill while Father Jardine continued praying over the dead Apaches. By the time the Kid finished unsaddling the buckskin, the priest had picked up the shovel again and was digging in the hard ground. The Kid heard the rasping sounds as the blade bit into the dirt and gravel.

"What are you doing, padre?" he asked.

Father Jardine paused in his work and looked up. "Why, I'm digging graves, Mr. Morgan."

"For those savages?" The Kid gestured toward the dead Apaches.

"They're still the Lord's children, whether they knew Him or not, and deserve a decent burial. The Apaches *do* inter their dead, do they not?"

The Kid thought about it for a moment, then shrugged and shook his head. "To tell you the truth, Father, I don't know. But if you leave those bodies where they are, the scavengers will take care of them."

"I won't hear of it."

The Kid sighed and walked over to Father Jardine. "Give me the shovel," he said. "Dr. Dare, do you know how to handle a rifle?"

"I do," Annabelle replied.

The Kid handed the Winchester to her. "Keep an eye on the flats. You ought to be able to see fairly well now that your eyes have had time to adjust to the fire being out. If you see anything moving around out there . . . shoot it."

"Without knowing first who or what it is?"

"I was under the impression you and the padre don't have all that many friends out here."

Annabelle gave an angry sniff. "Meaning that anyone who approaches the camp is an enemy?"

"That's a pretty good bet," The Kid said. "Anyway, the chances of somebody bothering you again tonight are pretty small. You said it would be a while before that Count Fortunato came after you again, and I reckon those two Apaches won't be looking for any more trouble right away. I hit one of them, and I don't know how bad he was hurt."

While Annabelle stood watch, The Kid took over the chore of digging a grave. Only one grave, though, he explained to Father Jardine, not five. That was as far as he would go to humor the priest.

With a sigh, Father Jardine agreed. "All right. As you said, Mr. Morgan, they *are* heathens."

Digging in the hard, rocky ground was tiring and time-consuming. The Kid paused after a while to set aside his hat and take off his buckskin shirt. Nights in this part of the territory were cool, even during the summer, but The Kid was working up a good sweat. He would put the shirt back on as soon as he finished digging, to make sure he didn't catch a chill.

When he judged that the hole was deep enough and wide enough, he tossed the shovel aside, pulled the shirt on over his head, and went to the nearest corpse. He bent over, grasped it by the feet, and dragged it to the grave. He sensed Father Jardine watching his actions with disapproval, but that didn't stop him from dumping the body into the hole unceremoniously. The Kid wasn't interested in deliberately offending the priest, but he wasn't going to change his ways too much to placate Father Jardine, either.

When he had dragged all five corpses to the grave and tossed them in, he asked, "Do you want to say words over them now, or wait until I've covered them up?"

"It would be more fitting if the grave was covered," Father Jardine replied stiffly.

"All right." The Kid picked up the shovel again.

Getting the dirt back in the hole was a little easier than taking it out. The Kid worked steadily until he had a mound of sandy dirt and gravel that marked the final resting place of the five Apaches. Then he stepped back to lean on the shovel and catch his breath.

Father Jardine brought a Bible from the wagon. As The Kid stood there next to Annabelle and listened to the priest reciting the Latin words, he realized that Father Jardine hadn't been checking to see whether or not that hombre out on the flats was dead. He'd been praying over Fortunato's henchman. He probably would have insisted that they bury both of those men, too, if it hadn't been for the fact that Annabelle was wounded and they'd had to light a shuck out of there.

When Father Jardine was finished with the ritual, The Kid took the Winchester back from Annabelle. "Both of you better turn in and get some rest," he told them. "I'll stand guard the rest of the night."

"You most certainly will not," Annabelle said. "I can take my turn."

"As can I," added Father Jardine.

"You've already been awake all night,"

Annabelle went on. "If you stay up the rest of the night, you'll be utterly exhausted tomorrow."

The Kid grunted. "Wouldn't be the first time I've been tired."

"Yes, but it would be the first time you were that tired while we were depending on you to help keep us safe," she pointed out.

The Kid couldn't argue with that logic. He said, "No more fires, all right?"

"It'll be awfully cold by morning."

He nodded toward the recently-dug mass grave. "Not as cold as those fellas over there are."

Annabelle glared at him for a couple of seconds, then nodded. "You're right, of course. It was foolish to announce our presence like that, wasn't it?"

"Yep."

"No more fires. Except during the day when they can't be seen as easily?"

He nodded. "And I'll show you how to build one that won't give off much smoke, so you won't likely be noticed that way, either."

"All right. That sounds like a good idea."

"I'll stand the first watch and wake you up after four hours."

"What about me?" Father Jardine asked.

"You let Dr. Dare and me worry about it tonight, padre," The Kid said. "You can have a turn tomorrow night."

He figured he would try to find some other

excuse by then to keep the priest from standing watch. He wasn't sure Father Jardine would be able to pull the trigger, even if an Apache bent on scalping him was standing right in front of him. There was just too much goodness in the man. At least, that was the way some people would look at it.

The Kid didn't believe in that "turn the other cheek" business anymore. His days of being that meek were long since over.

The way he saw it, the meek never inherited anything except trouble.

Chapter 7

Annabelle climbed into the wagon to sleep, while Father Jardine spread a bedroll underneath the vehicle. As The Kid stood nearby watching the preparations, he frowned.

"You have a hair rope, padre?" he asked.

"What?"

"A rope made of horsehair, just like it sounds," The Kid explained.

"We only have the ropes we used with the horses." Father Jardine shook his head. "I don't know what they're made of."

The Kid had placed his saddle on the ground. He had a lariat made of braided rawhide, the sort that the Mexicans called *la reata,* but he also had a coil of hair rope that he carried. He fetched it and played it out from its coil as he walked around the wagon, until he had a circle of rope completely enclosing the vehicle.

By starlight, The Kid saw Father Jardine smile. "Is this supposed to be some sort of talisman to ward off evil spirits, my son?"

"You could call it that," The Kid said dryly. "A rattlesnake won't crawl over a hair rope because the fibers tickle his belly too much. If you ever woke up with a nice fat diamondback rattler curled in your blankets with you because he was looking to get warm, you'd think he was an evil spirit, all right."

"Oh. I'm sorry. I didn't mean—"

The Kid waved a hand. "Forget it, Father. Just get some sleep."

Father Jardine crawled into his blankets. The Kid walked over to a rock next to the spring-fed pool and sat down with the rifle across his lap. He sat still and quiet and sent his senses out to search for any sign of danger in the night. Everything seemed peaceful. Within a few minutes, he heard soft snores coming from the priest.

There was silence from inside the wagon. The Kid thought about Annabelle Dare sleeping in there, if indeed she was actually asleep. He caught himself wondering how much of her clothing she removed before she turned in, then forced that thought out of his head. He hadn't been a widower all that long and had no right thinking such things. Anyway, Annabelle Dare was opinionated almost to the point of obnoxiousness. She was clearly accustomed to always getting her own way, and she really wasn't all that pretty. She was just . . . striking-looking, that was all.

Maybe there would come a time when he was ready to move on with his life, when he could look at a pretty woman and have those sort of thoughts without feeling that it was wrong. But not yet. Not yet.

Right now, all he really wanted where Annabelle

was concerned was to keep her alive until she and Father Jardine could finish this loco quest they were on. If they succeeded, she could go back to Harvard or Yale or wherever she came from, and he wouldn't ever have to think about her again.

Time passed as the stars wheeled through their courses overhead. The Kid felt a little drowsy from time to time, but he was able to shake it off without any trouble. When he judged that four hours had passed, he went to the back of the wagon, stepped over the horsehair rope, and said quietly, "Dr. Dare."

He heard the sound of a gun being cocked, then Annabelle mumbled, "Who . . . ?"

The Kid stepped quickly to the side, just in case her finger got a mite too heavy on the trigger. He said, "Damn it, Doctor, there's a time and a place when you need to wake up with a gun in your hand. This isn't one of them."

"Oh. Mr. Morgan." He heard her moving around. A moment later she stuck her head out the back of the wagon. "I'm sorry. I was sound asleep, and I didn't know at first who you were."

The Kid nodded. "Your turn to stand guard, just like you wanted."

"Yes, of course." She climbed out of the wagon. "If you could give me a moment first . . ."

"Sure, go ahead."

He waited while she went off into the brush that

grew along the base of the rocky outcropping. When she came back, he handed the Winchester to her.

"Everything's quiet," he told her. "The padre's still asleep." The Kid could hear the snores coming from under the wagon.

"That's good. I'm glad we didn't disturb him."

The Kid motioned for her to follow him and led her over to the rock where he'd been sitting earlier. "This is a good place. You've got a good view of the flats, and it's just uncomfortable enough so that you won't be too tempted to doze off again."

"All right. Thank you for the advice."

"Here's another piece. That Smith and Wesson of yours is a double-action. You don't have to cock it before you shoot. But you know that, or you seemed to when you were gunning down that Apache."

Her breath hissed between her teeth. "Are you trying to remind me that I killed a man tonight?"

"First time?"

"Yes, of course."

"Well, I hope it's the last, too. But in case it isn't, it won't hurt you to get as good with that gun as you can. Maybe we'll work on it some on the way."

"You're going to teach me how to be a gun-fighter like you?" Her voice held a tone of mockery.

"Not like me, lady. You don't want to be like me."

He started to turn away.

"Wait," she said. "I heard you talking to Father Jardine earlier. The business about the rope and the rattlesnakes. You were nice to him, when he was a little condescending to you. I appreciate that. He really is a good man."

"He's a priest. That's what you'd expect, I reckon."

"You know a lot about surviving out here on the frontier, don't you?"

"I've had to learn," The Kid said. He didn't say anything about the tragic circumstances that had forced him to pick up a lot of his survival skills in a hurry.

"But I've noticed . . . there are times when there's something about the way you speak, the way you carry yourself . . . Are you an educated man, Mr. Morgan?"

The last thing he wanted to do was to tell her all about the life he had led back east, when he was still a pampered, pompous ass. Yeah, he was educated, all right, but he had also been ignorant of the things that mattered most in life. It had taken Frank Morgan and Rebel Callahan to educate him about those.

"No, Doctor," he said. "I don't know a damn thing except how to kill my enemies before they kill me."

With that, he turned and walked back to the wagon. He took his bedroll and spread it out on the ground inside the big circle of rope, placed his saddle where he could use it for a pillow, and stretched out to sleep. The ground wasn't too comfortable, and The Kid had trouble forcing thoughts of the conversation he'd just had with Annabelle Dare out of his head.

He was asleep in minutes, anyway.

The sky was gray with the approach of dawn when The Kid woke up. He opened his eyes first, without moving otherwise. His head was turned so that he could see Annabelle sitting on the rock. He watched her for a moment without giving away the fact that he was awake.

Her head was up, and it turned frequently from side to side as she looked around, evidently alert for any sign of danger. That was good to see. If he was going to travel with them, he had know whether or not he could depend on her. From the looks of it, she could stand a turn on watch. They'd have to wait and see about everything else.

Oh, and she could get her gun out fairly quickly and defend herself in a fight, he reminded himself. But that had been an instinctive reaction, and the Apache had been only a few feet away when she shot him. He would find out how fast and accurate she really was once they'd had a chance to practice a little. He wouldn't truly know how she would react in a fight until the time came again—which he was sure it would, if they were heading into the Jornada del Muerto.

The Kid sat up, which drew Annabelle's attention to him as she saw the movement in the dim light. He pushed his blankets aside and climbed to his feet, walked over to her.

"Everything quiet?" he asked.

"Yes. I haven't seen or heard anything except some sort of night bird a little while ago."

The Kid frowned. What Annabelle had heard might have been a night bird . . . or it might have been something else.

"Give me the rifle," he said, his voice flat and hard. "Then go get under the wagon with Father Jardine."

"What's wrong?" she asked. "Do you think—"

"I don't know. Just give me the damned rifle."

"You're a rude man, Mr. Morgan," she said, but she handed over the Winchester and stood up.

"Under the wagon," The Kid said again. "Where'd you hear that bird?"

She gestured vaguely toward the hills. "Up there somewhere."

"If you hear any shooting, stay where you are and keep the padre under there with you. Don't come out until I tell you to."

He set off up the hill, moving swiftly in a crouching run and veering from side to side. The light at this time of day wasn't good for shooting, just like twilight, but if anybody was up there waiting to bushwhack them, chances were the bastard's eyes would be adjusted to the dimness by now.

The Kid used every rock, every bush, every scrubby little tree he could find for cover. He climbed all the way to the slab of rock where he had watched over the camp the night before, without running into any trouble along the way. He paused there to listen.

Somewhere far away in the distance, he heard the drumming of hoofbeats.

The tension that filled The Kid eased a little, but only a little. His gut told him that someone had been spying on them, and more than one someone, at that, otherwise there wouldn't have been any need for signals passing between them.

The two members of the Apache war party who had survived the fight? Maybe. Indians often signaled with animal noises like that. It might have been some of Fortunato's men, too, although The Kid considered that less likely. And it could even have been someone else, some enemies Annabelle and Father Jardine hadn't encountered so far. The Kid wondered just how many people actually knew about this golden candlestick they were after. Something like that might be valuable enough to tempt any number of thieves and owlhoots.

But right now, The Kid didn't see or hear anything out of the ordinary, so he suspected that whoever was watching them was gone. He didn't know what the purpose had been in spying on them. He was sure he would find out sooner or later.

"What was it?" Annabelle asked when he returned to the camp.

"Nothing," The Kid said. No point in worrying her when he didn't really know anything. "I reckon it was just a bird, like you said." He handed the rifle back to her and went on, "Keep your eyes open. I'll get started on a fire so we can cook some breakfast." He looked toward the north. "We'll put some miles behind us today."

Chapter 8

"What is it, Arturo?" Count Eduardo Fortunato asked as he sat up on his cot and rubbed the sleep out of his eyes.

"The savages are back, Your Excellency."

Fortunato looked up at his dour-faced servant, who stood there in a nightshirt holding a lantern. "They found the woman and the priest?"

"I assumed you would want them to make their report to you, sir," Arturo replied in his usual irritatingly smug tone. "So I have no idea what they found."

Fortunato grunted and swung his legs off the cot. Arturo was an insolent bastard. Fortunato's ancestors would have had a servant like that flogged. In this day and age, of course, one could not do that, which was a shame, in Fortunato's opinion. Although he was quite fond of all the modern comforts and conveniences, in some ways it must have been better in the old days.

"Don't just stand there," he snapped. "Help me dress."

Arturo set the lantern aside on a folding table. Its yellow glow filled the large tent. The count had brought along as much as he could pack in a wagon—well, as much as Arturo could pack, anyway, since Count Fortunato himself did no physical labor except the occasional killing—so the tent was well furnished with a roomy, comfortable cot, a dining table, a writing table, and a folding chair with attached cushions. There was also a large trunk that contained the count's clothes, as well as several smaller cases that held his guns, a saber, and a pair of dueling swords.

A few minutes later, Fortunato pushed aside the canvas flap over the tent's entrance and stepped out. Arturo followed him, carrying the lantern again. The count was a stocky, middle-aged man, with thick, sleek hair that was still black as midnight and a ruggedly handsome face with deep-set dark eyes that could burn with passion or glitter with icy hatred, depending on the circumstances.

Two men stood in front of the tent, half-breed Yaquis in boots, leggings, and long tunics belted around their waists with colorful red sashes. Blue headbands held back their long, raven-black hair. They were half brothers as well as half-breeds, Fortunato knew. They shared the same father, a Mexican bandito who'd had a habit of raping and enslaving Yaqui women he captured. The brothers had been raised among their father's band of cutthroats. Their mothers had been discarded somewhere along the way; neither of them really remembered much about that.

Fortunato knew these things because the man who had helped him find and hire the brothers had insisted on telling him all about their dreary history. Fortunato didn't care, but it was easier to listen to the man, rather than risk offending him. That individual was a high-ranking officer in the *Rurales* with connections to numerous bandit gangs in the northern part of Mexico. In theory, of course, the *Rurales* were supposed to hunt down and capture or kill such criminals, but it was so much easier—and so much more profitable—to cooperate with them whenever possible.

For a man with the sort of money that Fortunato was willing to spend, the *Rurales* would do almost anything, including telling him where he could find a pair of trackers like the Yaquis who stood before him.

"Did you find the woman and the priest?" he asked them in Spanish. Fortunato spoke five languages fluently, as well as a smattering of several more.

One of the Indians pointed across the flats to the west. "They are camped where you believed them to be, where the fire was," he replied in guttural tones that were unpleasant to Fortunato's ears.

"What about those shots we heard earlier?" The distant reports had been very faint, which told Fortunato they came either from far out on the flats or even from the hills on the other side.

The Yaqui who had spoken shook his head. "We know nothing of them. The camp was quiet when we got there. We climbed into the hills above it and watched for a time. The fire was out then, and the people slept, except for a guard."

"A guard?" Fortunato repeated sharply. "Who was it?"

"The woman."

"What about the priest?"

"We did not see him. The other man slept near the wagon."

The other man . . . Now they were getting to what Fortunato really wanted to know. He was intrigued by the stranger who had interfered that afternoon and prevented his men from capturing Dr. Dare and the priest. Fortunato wanted to know who he was.

"Describe the man you saw."

"It was dark. We could not see much. He seemed to be young. He had a big hat and wore a buckskin shirt."

Fortunato nodded and turned. He went over to the wagon and kicked the leg of the man who was sleeping underneath it.

"Braddock! Come out of there."

The gunman crawled slowly and painfully out from under the wagon. "Yeah?" he said in a surly voice, then amended, "I mean, yes, sir? What can I do for you, Count?"

Braddock's midsection was heavily bandaged. Arturo had tended to his wound and pronounced that he would live . . . probably.

"The man who shot you and killed Davenport and Crimmons . . . you said he was young and wore a buckskin shirt?"

"Yeah, from what I could see." A whining note

came into Braddock's voice as he went on, "You gotta remember, Count, it all happened pretty fast, and he wasn't that close to us."

"Close enough to shoot you when you and Davenport missed him," Fortunato said.

"Sorry," Braddock muttered.

Fortunato waved a hand. "Never mind. It appears that this man has now joined forces with Dr. Dare and the old man. Your orders remain the same. As soon as it's light enough to see, you will start back to El Paso and find more gunmen to send out here to me."

"I'm hurt, boss," Braddock protested. "I got a bullet in my gut."

"Nonsense. Arturo said the wound was merely a deep graze. The bullet did not remain lodged in it."

"Well, it *feels* like it's still there. I . . . I ain't sure I can ride that far."

Fortunato rubbed his chin. "I suppose we could allow you to remain here for a few days to recuperate . . ."

"That'd be mighty good, Count," Braddock said eagerly. "I'll be right as rain in no time, you'll see. I just need to rest up a mite."

"Of course, the rest of us will have to push on and take the wagon with us, as well as all the supplies and the water."

Braddock's face fell. "But . . . but you can't do that! You can't leave me out here with nothin'!"

"Those things belong to me, Braddock,"

Fortunato said in a chilly voice. "I plan to take them with me when I set out after my quarry."

"All right, all right." Braddock muttered something under his breath. Fortunato assumed that it was an obscenity, even though he didn't hear it clearly. "I'll head for El Paso first thing in the mornin'."

"Dawn is less than an hour away. You might as well start getting ready to depart now."

"Yeah, I reckon so."

"You won't have any trouble finding more men?"

Braddock shook his head. "If there's one thing that ain't in short supply along the border, it's men who're good with their guns and willin' to use 'em if the price is right. How many fellas you want me to send to you?"

"Well, three wasn't enough, obviously. Suppose we double it to six?"

Braddock's head bobbed up and down. "Yes, sir. Six it is. And what about me?"

"You can consider your employment concluded once you've performed this task for me. You'll be free to remain in El Paso or move on or whatever else strikes your fancy."

"Find me a whorehouse and lay up for a few weeks while this bullet hole in my side heals up," the gunman said. "That's what I'll do."

Fortunato took a coin from his pocket and held it out. It was a fifty-dollar gold piece.

"Perhaps this will help." He wasn't frugal when

it came to spending what was necessary to get what he wanted in life. Even though he was loathe to reward failure, this bonus would help insure that Braddock would carry out the mission Fortunato had given him.

Braddock took the coin and rubbed it between his fingers. In the gray light of pre dawn, a sly, greedy smile appeared on his lips.

"And in case you're thinking of taking my money and failing to perform the task I've given you," Fortunato went on, "remember our two Yaqui friends. If the men you're supposed to send to me do not show up within, let us say, four days, then you can be sure that some dark night, those two will pay you a visit . . . and they will be the last visitors you ever have, Braddock."

"You can't hold me to that." The whining tone was back in the gunman's voice. "I ain't responsible for what other hombres do."

"Then I suggest you choose wisely. Pick men who can be trusted to do what they say they will do." Fortunato's voice dropped to a soft, dangerous purr. "Because I assure you, I *always* do what I say I will do."

"Yeah. Yeah, I get it." Braddock tucked the coin away in his pocket. "Is that all, Count?"

Fortunato nodded and made a gesture of dismissal. Braddock turned away and said, "Hey, Arturo, how's about gettin' some coffee on to boil?"

Fortunato strolled back to his tent. He was tired—he never slept well under primitive conditions—but his brain was full of activity.

He thought about the Konigsberg Candlestick and how valuable it was supposed to be. In truth, however, its monetary value meant little or nothing to Fortunato. He had inherited more wealth than he could ever spend. He wanted the artifact because it was reputed to be very beautiful, and after being lost for two hundred years, it was a real rarity as well. Nothing pleased Fortunato more than possessing something the likes of which no other man on earth possessed. Whether it was a painting, a piece of sculpture, or a beautiful woman, as long as he was the only one who had it, that was what really mattered to him.

He wondered briefly if Dr. Annabelle Dare was a virgin.

Then there was the secret of the Twelve Pearls. To this day, no one knew exactly what it was, but Albrecht Konigsberg had taken it with him when he fled Spain for the New World. This was known because Konigsberg himself had boasted of it and traded on its supposed worth to get what he wanted. Of course, the German could have been lying . . . but with the instincts of a born hunter, Fortunato did not believe that to be the case.

Now, after years of searching, he was on the trail of both the Konigsberg Candlestick and the secret of the Twelve Pearls. Rather, he was on the trail of

Dr. Dare and the priest, and from the information Fortunato had bought in Mexico City, he was convinced they knew where to look. He could not allow the Church to beat him to the treasure. He would never get his hands on it if that happened. Because of that, he planned to make Dr. Dare and Father Jardine his prisoners, so he could force them to lead him to what he sought.

In a moment of rage over having what he wanted almost in the palm of his hand, only to have it snatched away, he had taken one of his rifles from its case that afternoon and loosed a shot at the man who had interfered. That shot had missed its target and wounded Dr. Dare instead, and in that moment as he watched through the telescopic sight, Fortunato realized that he had almost made a terrible mistake. He wanted the woman and the priest to live . . . for now.

But as for the stranger who had dared to interfere in his plans . . . that man would die, and Fortunato would take great pleasure in his death.

Chapter 9

The hills ran north and south, so The Kid kept them on his left as he led the wagon northward that day. By mid-morning, he spotted a blue-gray line on the horizon ahead of them that marked the location of more hills angling from the southeast to the northwest. He wasn't sure, but he thought that beyond those hills, they would come to the valley of the Rio Grande. They would have to cross the river somewhere, because they were west of it and the Jornada del Muerto lay to the east.

He dropped back alongside the wagon. Annabelle had had a spare hat among their supplies and she wore it to protect her head from the scorching sun. She wore a fresh shirt, as well, since the one she'd had on the day before had been ruined by the bloodstain and the fact that The Kid had ripped the left sleeve off to treat her wound. He had changed the dressing on the injury that morning before they broke camp and was pleased with the way it looked. There didn't seem to be any infection around it.

"Why didn't you just take the train from El Paso to Las Cruces?" The Kid asked. "It's not far from there to the Jornada."

"We didn't come through El Paso," Annabelle replied. "We bought this wagon and outfit in Chihuahua and then swung around El Paso because we were afraid Fortunato might have spies there waiting for us. We were trying to give him the slip, in case he was already on our trail." She made a face. "Clearly, we were unsuccessful. We spotted him following us a couple of days ago and hoped that we could stay ahead of him until we found the treasure, but that doesn't look like it's going to be the case."

"You don't know that," The Kid said. "In hot, dry country like this, if he has a wagon he can't move much faster than you can. There's only so much a team of horses or mules can do under these conditions. If he pushes his animals too hard, he'll find himself stuck."

"I'm sure he has a wagon. I can't imagine Count Eduardo Fortunato traveling without his creature comforts, even in a godforsaken wasteland like this one."

Father Jardine said, "No land can be godforsaken, my child. Only those unfortunates who choose to forsake Him."

"Maybe so, but it's still a wasteland out here." Annabelle looked around. "Why would anyone choose to live in such a place?"

"You may have noticed, it's not real crowded," The Kid said with a smile. "But don't sell it short. Every place has its charms, I guess. Even the desert can be beautiful under the right conditions."

"You'd know better than I would, if this is your home."

The Kid didn't really have one of those anymore, not since Rebel died, but he didn't bother explaining that to Annabelle. It was none of her business, and he didn't know if she would understand, anyway. Most of the time, he wasn't sure that *he* understood.

In the middle of the day, The Kid found a spot under the overhang of some rocks that provided shade from the sun. He watered the horses from one of the barrels lashed to the wagon, which they had topped off before leaving the spring that morning. Then he called Annabelle over and showed her how to make a tiny fire from dried mesquite branches that gave off almost no smoke. He boiled coffee and fried some bacon, since they had plenty of supplies and could replenish them in Las Cruces tomorrow or the next day.

"Who taught you how to build a fire like that, Mr. Morgan?" Annabelle asked. "I'm just curious. You don't have to answer if you don't want to."

"I don't mind," The Kid said. "My father taught me."

"When you were a boy?"

"When I was younger than I am now," The Kid said. As a matter of fact, he had been almost a grown man before he ever met Frank Morgan or knew that the notorious gunfighter called The Drifter was really his father. But Annabelle didn't need to know that, and these days, The Kid made it a habit to keep private as much as he could about himself. The less folks knew about you, the more difficult it was for them to hurt you.

"Is your father the one who taught you all these things you know about getting along in the wilderness?"

"Pretty much," The Kid admitted.

"I suppose it's good, that a father can pass along such things to his children."

He looked up at her from where he hunkered next to the fire, tending to the bacon. "What about your pa? He ever teach you anything?"

Annabelle sniffed. "My father was too busy being a professor of antiquities and ancient languages. He didn't have time for his children, especially his daughters. They couldn't follow in his footsteps, you see."

"But you did, anyway."

"Yes."

"Didn't make him change his mind about you, though, did it?" The Kid guessed.

"I wouldn't know. He passed away a month before I received my doctorate."

"Oh. Sorry."

She shook her head. "It was a long time ago."

Couldn't have been that long, he thought, since she was only about twenty-five or twenty-six. But despite the momentary lapse he'd just made, he tried not to pry in other people's lives, just as he didn't want them prying into his.

He could be thankful, though, that Frank had always had faith in him, even when he didn't deserve it. And probably the last thing in the world that Frank had wanted was for his son to follow in his footsteps.

That was what had happened, though. The world was a funny old place.

After the three of them had eaten, The Kid drank the last of the coffee in his tin cup and then said, "Why don't we see just what you can do with that gun, Doctor?"

Annabelle frowned at him. "What do you mean?"

The Kid stood up and pointed. "See that little rock over there, sitting on that bigger rock? Let's see how many shots it takes you to hit it."

Annabelle squinted. "What rock? That little-bitty one? It must be fifty feet away! Handguns aren't that accurate."

The Colt flickered into The Kid's hand in a draw so swift that the eye couldn't follow it. The gun roared, and the rock he had pointed out to her flew into the air, splitting into two pieces under the impact of the bullet.

"Just a matter of knowing your weapon," The Kid drawled as he pouched the iron.

For a moment, Annabelle stared at the spot where the small rock had been, then turned her head and glared at The Kid. "You're just showing off," she accused.

"Showing you what can be done," he said. "There's a difference."

Father Jardine pursed his lips. "I'm not sure you should be doing this, Doctor. This isn't just . . . target practice. Mr. Morgan wants to teach you how to be a more efficient killer."

"Again, no offense, padre," The Kid said, "but getting your hands on that artifact you're after might depend on how good Dr. Dare is with her gun. Both of your lives might depend on it, as well."

"Don't worry, Father," Annabelle said. "If it's Mr. Morgan's goal to turn me into a gunfighter, he's going to be disappointed. When this is over and we have the Konigsberg Candlestick and the secret of the Twelve Pearls, I'm going straight back to Yale."

The priest sighed. "Very well. I suppose that if you're going to carry a gun, it's best to be proficient in its use."

"Amen, Father," The Kid said. He held up both hands, palms out. "Didn't mean anything by that."

Annabelle pointed to the spot where the smaller rock had been balanced on the bigger one and asked, "What am I supposed to shoot at now? You ruined the target."

"Hang on. I'll find something else."

The Kid walked over to the rocks and found another one about the size of his fist. He placed it on top of the bigger rock.

"There," he told Annabelle. "Shoot at that. Just let me get out of the way first."

She waited until he came back to her side, then drew the Smith & Wesson .38 and held it out in front of her as far as she could reach. Her arm was as stiff and straight as a board.

"See, there's your first mistake," The Kid said before she could pull the trigger. "You're too stiff. Loosen up a little. Bend your elbow. Not much, just slightly."

"Like this?"

"No, that's too much." The Kid took hold of her arm to position it and show her what he meant. "Like that."

He realized after a second that he still had hold of her arm and could feel the warmth of her flesh through the shirt sleeve. He let go and stepped back.

Annabelle peered over the barrel of the gun with her right eye and screwed her left eye shut as tightly as it would go.

"No, that's going to throw your aim off," The Kid said. "Keep both eyes open."

She bared her teeth at him. "Are you going to let me shoot or not? This was your idea, you know."

He stepped back and spread his hands, then crossed his arms over his chest. "Go ahead."

"Fine." Annabelle turned her attention back to the target, and a second later, she pulled the trigger. A shot blasted from the .38.

The rock didn't budge. There was no sign that the bullet hit anything else, either.

Annabelle lowered the gun and frowned. "Where did it go? I didn't see it hit anything."

The Kid waved a hand toward the flat. "It landed a few hundred yards out yonder. You were way high. That's because you jerked the trigger too hard, and you were aiming too high to start with." He nodded toward the rocks. "Want to try again?"

"Yes, I most certainly do." Annabelle aimed and fired again. This time the slug plowed into the ground about halfway between where she stood and the rock she was aiming at. "Oh!"

"You corrected too much. Try this. Don't aim."

"Don't aim?" she repeated. "How can I hit anything if I don't aim at it?"

"You're not hitting it when you do aim at it," The Kid said. "*Point* the gun. Just point it, like the barrel was your index finger. And then squeeze the trigger, don't jerk it."

"I don't think it'll work, but . . . all right."

Annabelle did like he told her, taking a casual stance as she pointed the gun and fired. The bullet hit the big rock about a foot and a half below the target and whined off.

"Oh, my goodness!" Annabelle cried as her eyes widened. "I almost hit it!"

"Almost will usually get you killed out here," The Kid said. "Try again."

She frowned at him. "You could tell me that I did a good job, you know. It wouldn't hurt you."

"When you were back there at Yale, did your teachers tell you you did a good job every time you answered one question on an examination?" The Kid pointed at the rock. His meaning was clear. The target was still there.

Annabelle muttered something under her breath, shook her head, and pointed the Smith & Wesson at the rocks again. This time her shot was a foot low and a little off to the right.

"Turn your body," The Kid suggested. "Again, not much. All these adjustments need to be slight, because the gun will magnify them."

"Fine." She shifted her stance.

"Take a deep breath and hold it," The Kid said. "Not long, just for a second while you pull the trigger."

"All right." She pointed the gun, took a breath, held it, squeezed the trigger.

The little rock leaped in the air.

"I hit it!" Annabelle cried. She turned to The Kid and smiled. "I hit it! Did you see that?"

"Yep. Get to where you can do that ninety-nine times out of a hundred, and you might survive your next gunfight. Assuming, of course, that there is a next one."

Her face grew serious. "With Fortunato after us, I'd wager that there will be."

"You'd bet a hat."

"What?"

"That's what folks out here sometimes say when they're sure of something. I'll bet a hat."

"Well, I'm not betting this hat," Annabelle said. "It's the only one I have left, and I don't like the sun on my head."

The Kid laughed. He couldn't help it. "Want me to find you another rock to shoot at?"

"Yes, please."

He glanced over at Father Jardine, who was sitting on the lowered tailgate of the wagon. The priest still wore a look of disapproval on his lined and weathered face. The Kid could tell that he was just aching to quote some Scripture, probably "Thou shalt not kill."

The Kid remembered some words from the Good Book, too, about the Lord helping those who helped themselves. Out there on the frontier, helping yourself usually involved gunsmoke.

"Here you go," he told Annabelle a moment later as he balanced a slightly smaller rock on top of the bigger one. "Take a shot at this."

Chapter 10

The rest of that day passed without incident. The Kid kept a close eye on their backtrail but saw no signs of pursuit. Annabelle was adamant that Count Fortunato was still behind them somewhere.

"He won't give up," she said. "I've heard enough stories about him to know that. He's like a bulldog once he gets his teeth into something."

That night was quiet. The Kid and Annabelle took turns standing guard again. The Kid couldn't think of a good excuse to deny Father Jardine's request to take one of the shifts, so he said bluntly, "I'm sorry, padre, but if there's any trouble, I have a hunch you might hesitate before you pull the trigger. That could cost all of us our lives."

"Very well," Father Jardine replied stiffly. "It's true that my beliefs would never allow me to kill as swiftly and without remorse as you, Mr. Morgan."

The Kid felt a surge of anger. If the priest wanted to talk about remorse, The Kid was old friends with that emotion. But instead of saying anything, he just gave Father Jardine a stony nod and moved to the edge of the camp with the Winchester, where he could keep an eye on things.

They arrived at Las Cruces late the next day,

crossing a long wooden bridge over the Rio Grande just west of the settlement. Annabelle was still a little leery of going into a town.

"Fortunato could have spies there, waiting for us," she said as she drove the wagon toward the cluster of frame and adobe buildings.

"He's already dogging your trail," The Kid pointed out. "It's not like he doesn't know where you're going."

"But how *could* he know? That's what's puzzled me all along."

"How many people in Mexico City knew where you were headed?" The Kid asked.

"Not many. A few church and government officials. We had to have their help while we were trying to track down Konigsberg."

"Well, there's your answer. An hombre who has as much money as this fella Fortunato and doesn't mind spending it to get what he wants can find out almost anything. He probably just started bribing folks in Mexico City until somebody told him where you and the padre had gone."

"You seem to think money is the answer to everything, Mr. Morgan."

"No, not everything," The Kid said with a shake of his head as he thought about all the things money *couldn't* buy. "It won't stop a bullet, or bring back somebody you've lost."

He knew that all too well.

Annabelle frowned at him and looked puzzled, as if she wanted to ask him what he meant by that. He heeled the buckskin to a faster pace and rode ahead. The last thing he wanted was to have to answer a bunch of nosy questions from some doggone curious female.

Las Cruces was a good-sized settlement. The railroad tracks ran along the western edge of town, so The Kid came to them first. He crossed the tracks and looked toward the depot, a large adobe building with a red tile roof a couple of blocks to his right. The street that dead-ended at the train station appeared to form a dividing line of sorts, with the respectable businesses and residences, along with the churches and the school, to the north of it, and the saloons, cantinas, gambling dens, and whorehouses to the south.

It was a common enough arrangement in frontier towns, The Kid knew. If there was no natural boundary to set the high-toned folks apart from their more rough-hewn fellow citizens, they would come up with an arbitrary one.

The Kid turned in the saddle and waved the wagon on. It bumped roughly over the railroad tracks. As Annabelle drove up alongside The Kid, he pointed out a large emporium to her and said, "Take the wagon over there. We'll stock up on supplies, then go down to the public well there at the end of the street and top off the water barrels."

She nodded. "All right. Then what?"

"Well, we could push on toward the Jornada and make camp somewhere, but there's only a couple of hours of daylight left. By the time we pick up those supplies, there'll just be an hour or so. Doesn't hardly seem worth it."

"Are you suggesting that we spend the night here in Las Cruces?"

"I reckon it would make the most sense. You could get a good night's sleep in a real bed for a change."

Judging by the look on her face, Annabelle didn't like the idea very much. She turned to the priest and asked, "What do you think, Father?"

"Mr. Morgan is right," Father Jardine said, although he sounded like it pained him a mite to admit that. "We should make a fresh start in the morning."

"All right . . . but I think we should guard the wagon overnight."

The Kid pointed to a livery stable and wagon yard across the street. "The outfit will be fine over there," he said.

"You don't understand. If Fortunato has agents here, they could sabotage the wagon and hold us up long enough for him to catch us."

If it hadn't been for the things he'd seen so far, The Kid might be starting to think that Annabelle was a little loco on the subject of Fortunato. She seemed to believe that the count or his men were lurking behind every rock and bush, ready to jump them.

But he recalled those men who'd been chasing the wagon and the long-range shot that had creased Annabelle's arm, and he couldn't guarantee that she was overstating the threat. Maybe she was right.

"Tell you what," he said. "I'll stay with the wagon. You and the padre can get rooms in one of the hotels and get a good night's sleep."

"That hardly seems fair," Annabelle protested.

"I can bed down just fine in the wagon, so if anybody tries to bother it, they'll get a mighty big surprise."

"Well . . . it *would* feel nice to sleep in an actual bed again."

The Kid smiled. "It's a deal, then. Come on, let's see about getting those supplies. That way, we'll be ready to pull out first thing in the morning and won't have to wait."

Annabelle had tucked her long red hair up under her hat, but there was no disguising the curves of her body. The sight of a woman wearing men's clothing and packing a gun drew some curious looks from the people in the street as she drove the wagon over to the general store and parked it in front of the high front porch that served as a loading dock. The Kid saw the stiff set of her face and knew she was doing her best to ignore the stares.

Annabelle and Father Jardine climbed down from the seat. "I'm going to walk over to the church," the priest said, nodding toward a large adobe building topped by a bell tower.

"All right, but be careful," Annabelle said. "Don't tell anyone who you are."

Father Jardine just smiled. "I agreed not to wear my cassock in an attempt to conceal my identity, Doctor, but obviously, that ruse failed. I see no need for further deception."

"Just humor me, Father, all right?"

The priest sighed and then nodded. "Very well. It will be as you wish."

Father Jardine ambled off toward the church. The Kid and Annabelle went into the store.

The place was fairly busy. They had to wait to be helped by one of the aproned clerks behind the counter in the rear of the store. While they were standing around, The Kid consulted with Annabelle about exactly what they would need, so they had a list worked out by the time it was their turn. The clerk used a stub of a pencil to scrawl their order on a piece of butcher paper, then set about gathering up the supplies.

Feeling eyes on him, The Kid glanced over and saw a couple of little boys standing in front of a glass-fronted candy case, stealing glances at him and whispering to each other. He smiled at them, and that emboldened one of the youngsters enough for him to come a couple of steps closer and ask, "Mister, are you a gunfighter?"

"What makes you think so?"

The boy pointed at the revolver riding in the buscadero holster on The Kid's hip. "My pa says that men who carry a six-shooter like that are gunfighters."

"Well, I wouldn't want to go against anything your pa told you," The Kid said, still smiling. "I'm not really a gunfighter, though." He lowered his voice to a conspiratorial whisper. "I just pretend to be one."

"But . . . ain't that dangerous?" the boy asked with wide eyes.

"Not if you pretend good enough." The Kid took a couple of pennies from his pocket and held them out on the palm of his hand. "You and your pard have some licorice on me."

"Gee, thanks, mister!" Both boys snatched a coin from The Kid's hand. They turned eagerly toward the candy counter, but the one who'd been talking glanced back and asked, "What's your name?"

"Morgan," The Kid said.

"Thanks, Mr. Morgan!"

A minute later, as the youngsters scampered out of the store trailing long strings of licorice they had bought with the pennies The Kid had given them, Annabelle commented, "That was nice of you."

"You sound surprised."

"You put up a hard façade, Mr. Morgan. It's nice to know that there are at least a few tiny cracks in it."

The Kid didn't think it was so nice. In fact, he told himself that he was going to have be more diligent about being a hardcase. He didn't want anybody thinking that he was turning soft, even his traveling companions.

A few minutes later, the clerk set a couple of wooden boxes on the counter. "Here you go, folks," he said. "These are the supplies you wanted."

"Much obliged," The Kid said. "How much do we owe you?"

"Three dollars and six bits."

The Kid reached for his pocket. Annabelle said, "Wait a minute. I can pay for this."

"No need," The Kid told her. "If I'm going to be traveling with you, I can pay my share of the freight."

The fact of the matter was, he could have bought and sold their whole outfit thousands of times over. He didn't have that much cash on him, of course, but there was plenty of money in bank accounts in Boston, Chicago, Denver, San Francisco, and Carson City. Of course, the name on those accounts wasn't Kid Morgan, but he could put his hands on the funds any time he wanted them, just by sending a few wires to the attorneys who handled his legal and business affairs. His father Frank, who was equally wealthy because they had shared in the inheritance from Vivian Browning, had the same sort of set-up.

That was just one more thing he had learned from Frank Morgan, The Kid thought with a faint smile.

He handed a five-dollar gold piece to the clerk, collected his change, and then tried to pick up both boxes. Annabelle took one of them out of his hands.

"The least you can do is let me help carry them out," she said.

"All right," The Kid said as they took the boxes and turned toward the open double doors that led out onto the general store's porch.

They stopped short as three men suddenly appeared in the doorway, blocking it. "Morgan? Kid Morgan?" one of them challenged in a loud, harsh voice.

"Oh, hell," The Kid said softly, under his breath. He knew all too well what was coming next. Those varmints wanted to prove that they were faster on the draw than he was.

And there he stood, his hands full of flour, salt, sugar, and a side of bacon instead of a six-gun.

Chapter 11

"Mr. Morgan?" Annabelle said, her voice taut with worry.

"Move off to the side, Doctor," he told her. His eyes never left the three men as he spoke. He was at another disadvantage there, because they had the light from outside behind them. The late afternoon sun wasn't as bright as if it had been midday, but even so, the men in the doorway were little more than silhouettes to The Kid.

He kept his eyes on them anyway, watching for any telltale twitches or other involuntary movements before they slapped leather.

Annabelle hadn't moved. She asked, "Is there going to be trouble of some sort? Should I try to find the local authorities?"

One of the men laughed. "You do that, missy," he said. "You go find the local authorities."

Annabelle stiffened and took a step toward them. "How dare you mock me!" she said. "I'll have you know that I'm a doctor!"

"Good. Your friend there's gonna need a saw-bones when we get through with him."

"More likely an undertaker," added one of the other men.

"Dr. Dare," The Kid said between clenched teeth. "Annabelle. *Get the hell out of the way.*"

"Oh!" she said. But she moved; that was the

102

important thing as far as The Kid was concerned. Carrying the box she had taken from him, she edged away, if not completely out of any possible line of fire, at least farther away from it.

"I just came in here for supplies," The Kid told the men in the doorway. "I wasn't looking for trouble."

"You found it anyway, mister. We been hearin' all over the territory about this gun-thrower who calls hisself Kid Morgan. That'd be you, right?"

The Kid knew there was no point in denying it. "I'm Kid Morgan," he said.

"My name's Culhane," said the man in the middle of the trio. He nodded to the man on his right. "Jericho." And on his left. "Mawson."

"Can't say as I'm happy to make your acquaintance."

"Reckon not, since we're the men who're gonna kill you."

At first, The Kid had heard a lot of scurrying around behind him. He knew the clerks and the other customers were hunting cover. Now an uneasy silence hung over the store. The Kid didn't hear anyone moving around.

"Doctor," he said.

"Wh-what is it, Mr. Morgan?"

"You see anyone else besides me and these three hombres in here?"

"No," Annabelle said. "Everyone's hiding. It's like the store is empty except for us."

103

"Good." The Kid addressed the three men in the doorway. "Culhane, you and your pards just back on out of here, and nobody has to die."

"You got that wrong," the gunman called Mawson said. "You have to die, Morgan, if we're gonna be famous."

"Famous for gunning down a man when the odds are three to one in your favor? A man who has his hands full and can't even reach for a gun?"

"People will forget the details," Culhane said. "They'll just remember that we're the men who killed Kid Morgan. And you can drop that box any time you want to. In fact, you'd better do it right about—"

The Kid saw the tiny, almost imperceptible lift of their shoulders as they tensed to draw. At that same moment, a side door into the store opened and the little boy who had talked to The Kid earlier ran in, saying, "Mr. Morgan! Mr. Morgan!"

The Kid didn't drop the box of supplies. He threw it at the three gunmen, sending it sailing through the air toward them. Instinct made them duck away from it, even though it didn't reach them but crashed to the floor in front of them.

By the time the box hit the floorboards, The Kid's Colt was in his hand, spewing flame. It roared and bucked against his palm. His first shot punched into Culhane's chest, knocking the gunman back a step. The Kid had no way of knowing which of the three men was the fastest on the draw. It was just a gamble, no matter what he did. But Culhane was a loudmouth, so he got the first bullet.

A shaved instant of time later, The Kid's second bullet broke Mawson's shoulder and spun him half around. That was the moment The Kid realized he had made a mistake. He should have started at one end or the other. Now he had to backtrack to kill Jericho, and if the man was fast at all—

He was. The gun in Jericho's hand blasted. He had gotten a shot off, which was more than Culhane or Mawson had managed. The Kid heard the wind-rip of the slug past his ear as he shifted his aim and fired again. Jericho doubled over as the bullet ripped into his gut. He stumbled forward and forced his head up as he tried to lift his gun for another shot. The Kid put a round between his eyes. Jericho's head jerked, and he collapsed.

The only one still on his feet was Mawson. His right arm hung useless at his side. He had dropped his gun. But his left hand darted behind his neck and came out with a knife that was hidden in a sheath that hung down his back. He screamed a curse as he threw the knife at The Kid.

Twisting to the side, The Kid fired instinctively at Mawson as the spinning blade flickered past his eyes. He heard it thud into something behind him. Mawson toppled to the floor, blood spurting from his neck where The Kid's bullet had torn it open. His bootheels drummed against the boards as he died.

The whole thing had taken about five seconds, even though to The Kid's danger-heightened senses it had seemed considerably longer. As the deafening echoes of the shots began to die away, he glanced over at Annabelle, who'd had the good sense to drop the supplies and hit the floor when all hell broke loose.

"Are you all right?" he asked her.

She looked up at him, swallowed hard, and nodded.

The Kid turned his head to look the other way and smiled at the little boy, who stood there with his eyes so wide it seemed like they were about to pop out of his head. Part of a licorice whip still dangled from his grubby hand.

"How about you, son? You're not hurt, are you?"

The boy found his voice after a couple of seconds. "N-no, sir, Mr. Morgan."

"Stay right there," The Kid told him and strode forward to check on the three would-be gunfighters.

It was easy to see that Mawson was dead; a huge pool of blood surrounded his head. The Kid had put a bullet in Jericho's brain, so he knew Jericho wasn't a threat anymore. That left Culhane, who had landed with his head on the porch and the rest of his body in the store. The

Kid saw the lifeless eyes staring upward and knew that Culhane was dead, too.

He had killed three men in less than five seconds. That was just going to add to his growing reputation, and someday, some other hombre who fancied himself fast on the draw would throw down on him because of it. But the alternative would have been to stand there and let those three bastards kill him, and The Kid was damned if he was going to do that.

As he walked toward the back of the store, he saw Mawson's knife stuck in the side of a cracker barrel. It was still quivering a little bit. The Kid broke open the Colt and started thumbing fresh rounds into it from the loops on his gunbelt as he walked over to the little boy. When he had finished reloading, he slid the gun back into leather and knelt in front of the wide-eyed youngster.

"What can I do for you, amigo?"

The boy had to swallow again before he could answer. "I . . . I heard some men talking," he said. "They were sayin' they were gonna come over here and . . . and shoot you, Mr. Morgan." He pointed a shaky finger at the ventilated corpses. "It was them right there."

The Kid nodded. "I figured as much. Did you come to warn me?"

"Yeah." The little boy looked miserable. "I should'a come right away, but Billy McLaughlin's got a new puppy, and he was showin' it to me . . .

and I . . . I sort of forgot for a minute. I'm sorry!"

"That's all right," The Kid told him. "I understand how it is with puppies. What's your name, son?"

"Jamie, sir."

"Well, Jamie, some fellas would've been too scared to even think about coming over here to warn me. They'd be afraid that they'd wind up in the middle of a gunfight."

"The way I almost did!" Jamie said.

"Yeah," The Kid agreed. "The way you almost did. I just want you to know I appreciate what you did, and I'm glad you weren't hurt."

"You killed those three men!"

The Kid nodded solemnly. "Yeah, I did. They didn't give me much choice in the matter."

"I never saw anything like that before! You must be the fastest draw in the world!"

"Nope. There are men who are faster."

"That don't seem possible."

"Take my word for it," The Kid said. He straightened. Folks were coming out of hiding in the store now. Annabelle had come up behind him and stood there with the box of supplies she had picked up. "You'd better run along home now. And don't be surprised if your ma's a mite put out when she hears about this. Mothers are like that about their young'uns being in a place where a lot of bullets are flying around."

"Okay, Mr. Morgan." Jamie paused. "I really am sorry I didn't come and tell you sooner."

"It's all right."

The Kid watched the youngster hurry out of the store through the side door, since Culhane's body still blocked the front door.

That didn't stop the man who appeared in the doorway and stepped over the corpse. He carried a shotgun and looked around the inside of the store with angry dark eyes.

"What the hell's going on here?" the newcomer demanded. He wore a gray suit and hat. A badge was pinned to the lapel of the coat.

The Kid lifted his hands so that the lawman could see they were empty. Never give a man holding a shotgun an excuse to get nervous, he thought.

"Take it easy, Sheriff," he said. "The shooting is all over."

"I'll decide when things can be took easy and when they can't," the man snapped. "What happened here?"

The clerk who had filled the order for The Kid and Annabelle spoke up from behind the counter. "It wasn't this fella's fault, Sheriff Lipscomb," he said. "He and the lady were minding their own business when Culhane and those two cronies of his came in and started threatening them. They were going to kill Mr. Morgan here."

Several other customers who had seen the whole thing—or at least all of it until the shooting started—chimed in to support what the clerk said. Sheriff Lipscomb lowered the greener and came further into the store. He checked the bodies, then frowned at The Kid.

"You shot all three of them?"

"Seemed like the thing to do at the time," The Kid said.

"And how many shots did they get off?"

The clerk answered that question. "One! I was peeking around the end of the counter and saw it. Slickest thing ever, Sheriff, the way Mr. Morgan drew his gun and shot them."

Lipscomb grunted. "Yeah. Slick. Your name's Morgan, eh?"

"That's right."

"Can't be Frank Morgan. He'd be a lot older than you, if he's even still alive."

"He's still alive," The Kid said. "You can count on that."

"Then you must be the one I've heard some talk about. Kid Morgan, or something like that."

The Kid nodded.

"Did you come in here to buy supplies?" the sheriff asked.

"That's right."

"Well, here's what you do. Take your supplies and get the hell out of my town."

The words were flat and hard, the sort that brooked no argument. The Kid gave him one anyway. "My friends and I were going to spend the night here."

The sheriff shook his head. "Your friends are

welcome in Las Cruces. You ain't. I want you gone before the sun sets." He nodded toward the bodies. "You see, Culhane had more friends than just Mawson and Jericho. I don't want any more gunfights around here."

The Kid had heard his father talk about things like that. Lawmen across the West disliked and distrusted Frank Morgan on sight, simply because of his reputation, even though Frank had never started a fight and had gone out of his way at times to avoid them.

But that didn't make any real difference. Violence followed him anyway.

It was starting to dog The Kid's trail, too.

"All right," he said. "I'll go."

"And so will we," Annabelle declared with an angry glare directed toward the local lawman. "If you're not welcome, Mr. Morgan, then neither are we, regardless of what this gentleman says."

"I don't mind if you stay here tonight. We can meet up again tomorrow—"

"Nonsense."

The Kid was relieved. He didn't really like the idea of having Annabelle and Father Jardine that far out of his sight overnight. He didn't know if Fortunato was really as dangerous as Annabelle seemed to believe, but there was no point in taking unnecessary chances. It would be better if they all stuck together.

"Fine," he said as he bent to pick up the supplies

that had scattered from the box he'd tossed at the three gunmen. "I reckon we'll push on, even if it is late."

He was confident that he could find an acceptable place to camp for the night. They would have to be more watchful than ever, though. If Culhane had friends who might be upset about his death, as Sheriff Lipscomb had implied, then those hombres might decide to come after the man who'd killed him and try to even the score.

So there might be a few more people who wanted him dead, The Kid thought as he left the store with Annabelle and placed the supplies in the wagon.

That number seemed to be growing all the time.

Chapter 12

Father Jardine was nowhere in sight. The Kid nodded toward the mission at the other end of the street and said, "He's probably still down there visiting with the local priest. Why don't you go get him?"

"You could come with me," Annabelle suggested.

The Kid shook his head. "I'm not sure the padre would think that a killer like me was fit to set foot inside a church."

"I thought everyone was supposed to be welcome in a church."

"Maybe that's the way it's supposed to be. Doesn't mean that's always the way it is." The Kid nodded toward the wagon. "Anyway, somebody ought to stay here and keep an eye on your outfit and the supplies."

"Isn't it *our* outfit now, since you've joined forces with us, Mr. Morgan?"

The Kid grunted. "Not hardly. I'm just along for the ride."

Annabelle didn't say anything to that. She just gave The Kid a look he couldn't read, then started down the street toward the church.

He leaned against the wagon. Quite a few people were gathered around the general store, having been drawn by the sound of shots, and most of them were looking at him and trying not to stare. The Kid felt their eyes on him. He knew what they were saying as they whispered among themselves.

Gunfighter, I hear . . . Killed three men, just like that . . . Wonder how much blood he's got on his hands?

The Kid was learning to ignore reactions like that. As long as he was Kid Morgan, that was the way people were going to act around him.

Sheriff Lipscomb stepped out onto the porch a moment later. "You haven't left yet?" he asked curtly when he saw The Kid.

"It's only been a few minutes, Sheriff. The lady's gone to fetch our other friend. He's down at the church."

"As soon as they get back, I want you out of town."

"We'll leave . . . as soon as we've topped off our water barrels at the well." The Kid wasn't about to start into the Jornado del Muerto without those barrels being full to the brim. "No law against us using the water, is there?"

"It's a public well," Lipscomb replied, although he sounded like he wished he could refuse to let The Kid and his companions draw water from it. "Undertaker ought to be here soon."

The Kid nodded. Lipscomb had dragged Culhane's body into the store, so that his head wasn't on the porch anymore. The Kid figured most, if not all, of the customers had cleared out, not wanting to share the store with three corpses.

"I imagine there's always a lot of work for the undertaker wherever you go," Lipscomb went on.

"I get it, Sheriff. You don't want me around. I said we're leaving, but I won't be rushed."

Lipscomb shifted the shotgun that was now tucked under his arm. "As long as you get out, that's all I care about. This is a nice, peaceful town most of the time. I'd like to keep it that way."

Yeah, thought The Kid, so nice and peaceful that gun-wolves like Culhane and his friends were allowed to walk around unmolested, with guns on their hips, looking for trouble. While *he,* who had done nothing but defend himself, was being run out of town at the point of a shotgun.

Well, nobody had ever claimed life was fair, The Kid reminded himself. He knew that was true from his own bitter experiences.

He glanced along the street and straightened from his casual pose against the wagon when he spotted Father Jardine hurrying toward him. The priest was alone, though. The Kid didn't see any sign of Dr. Annabelle Dare.

As Father Jardine came closer, The Kid saw that he wore a scared expression on his weathered face.

"Father," The Kid said as he stepped forward to meet him, "what's wrong?"

"Men at the church," Father Jardine panted, slightly out of breath from moving so fast. "They have Dr. Dare!"

The Kid stiffened. "What happened? Were they Fortunato's men?"

From the store's front porch, Sheriff Lipscomb asked, "Who's Fortunato?"

Father Jardine ignored the lawman and shook his head in reply to The Kid's question. "From some of the things they said, I believe they're friends of men called Culhane and Mawson and Jericho." An accusatory frown creased the priest's forehead. "Men who, according to them, you killed a short time ago, Mr. Morgan."

The Kid's hand instinctively started toward his gun. Father Jardine caught the movement, and his frown deepened.

"That's what got Dr. Dare into the trouble she's in," the priest snapped.

"And it's what'll get her out of it, too," The Kid said. "What do they want?"

"They said that you should come down there and face them. If you do, they won't harm Dr. Dare."

"What did they do, sneak in the back of the church?" The Kid had been watching the front, and he hadn't seen anyone except Annabelle go into the sanctuary in the past few minutes.

"That's right. They had their guns drawn. They threatened me and Father Horatio and took Dr. Dare prisoner."

"Did they hurt her?"

"Not that I could see, although they were handling her rather roughly."

The Kid's jaw tightened in anger when he heard that. He took a step toward the church.

"Hold it!" Sheriff Lipscomb said. "Where do you think you're going, Morgan?"

"You heard the padre. If I don't go down there, those hombres are liable to hurt Dr. Dare."

"So you're going to have another gunfight?" Lipscomb shook his head and lifted the scatter-gun. "I don't think so."

"You have a better idea?"

"Damn right I do. I'm going to go down there and put a stop to this." The sheriff glared at The Kid and added, "You stay right there. That's an order."

The Kid wasn't in the habit of taking orders, especially from overbearing tin stars. But maybe, just maybe, Lipscomb could put a stop to this incident without anybody else getting hurt. The Kid sort of doubted that, but the man was the law there. The Kid supposed he ought to give Lipscomb a chance.

But Annabelle's life might be at stake, The Kid reminded himself, so he said, "You'd better be careful, Sheriff. They've got a prisoner down there, and there's no telling what they might do."

"I can handle a bunch of cheap gunmen," Lipscomb said. He started toward the church, holding the shotgun slanted across his chest in front of him. He glanced around at the crowd and added, "Everybody clear the street. Now!"

People hurried to obey the order. The Kid and Father Jardine stayed where they were, beside the wagon. The priest said quietly, "I have a bad feeling about this."

"You and me both, padre," The Kid agreed. "You and me both."

Sheriff Lipscomb stalked the length of the street and stopped in front of the church. "You men in there!" he shouted. "Come out with your hands up!"

There was no response from inside the church.

"Let the woman go!" Lipscomb called. "Send Father Horatio out, too!"

Still nothing.

"All right, if that's the way you want it, by God! I'm coming in! You're all going to be under arrest!"

Back down the street, The Kid looked on and breathed, "Oh, Lord. He's dumber than I thought he was."

The lawman strode toward the heavy double doors of the church. One of the doors opened before he got there, and a hand holding a revolver thrust out.

"Hold it right there, Sheriff," a man said in a voice that sounded like a wagon traveling over a bad gravel road. The town was so quiet that The Kid could make out the words even from a distance. Everyone seemed to hold their breath to see what was going to happen. "We told that old priest to send Kid Morgan down here."

"Jackson!" Sheriff Lipscomb said. "Is that you, Lew Jackson? Who else is in there?"

"Never you mind about that," the gravelly voice of the man inside the church replied. "Just back away now, lawman, and you won't get hurt. Our fight's with that low-down bastard who killed Culhane and Mawson and Jericho."

"There aren't going to be any more gunfights," Lipscomb insisted. "Morgan's down the street, and I've given him orders to stay right where he is and let me handle this. That's what I'm going to do. Now release your prisoners and come on out, or you're going to find yourself in more trouble than you've ever been in before."

A laugh came from the man called Jackson. "Somehow I doubt that, Sheriff. You ain't gonna skedaddle, are you?"

"I told you, I'm not going anywhere until you release Father Horatio and the woman and come out with your hands up."

"You always were an arrogant son of a bitch, star packer."

The Kid saw Lipscomb lift the shotgun, heard him exclaim, "Why, you—"

Flame geysered from the muzzle of the handgun protruding from the doorway, and the sharp sound of a shot filled the tense silence in the settlement.

The bullet knocked Lipscomb back a couple of steps. He struggled to stay on his feet and lift the shotgun. The weapon slipped through his fingers, though, and thudded to the ground at his feet. The impact made one of the barrels discharge with a dull boom, sending the load of buckshot harmlessly into the air. As the echoes of that blast rolled through the street, Lipscomb turned, pawed at his chest for a second, and then pitched forward on his face.

A shocked Father Jardine stared at the lawman's body and then began praying in Latin.

"Morgan!" the gravelly voice yelled from inside the church. "You hear me, Morgan?"

The Kid stepped away from the wagon. "I hear you!"

"You saw what just happened, Morgan! I gunned down a lawman! That means we ain't got nothin' to lose now! You know what we'll do to this red-headed gal if you don't come down here and face us, man to man!"

"Three against one . . . again," The Kid muttered. "Folks in this town sure have a funny idea what man to man means."

Father Jardine gripped The Kid's arm. "What are you going to do, Mr. Morgan? If they killed the sheriff, they won't hesitate to hurt Dr. Dare!"

The Kid nodded. "I know." He pulled loose from the priest. "That's why I'm going down there."

"But they'll just shoot you, too!"

"Not if I shoot them first." The Kid turned to look at Father Jardine. "And that's where you come in, padre."

Chapter 13

A few minutes later, Father Jardine walked slowly toward the church. He had to detour around the body of Sheriff Lipscomb, which still lay face-down in the street. No one had yet dared to venture out and retrieve it.

Father Jardine swallowed as he came to a stop and looked at the door, which still stood open a few inches even though the hand holding the gun had been withdrawn. "Hello?" he called tentatively. "Hello in there? It's Father Jardine."

The gravelly voice came from the dim interior. "What do you want, padre? You were supposed to send Morgan down here, or we're gonna kill the girl."

Father Jardine sounded utterly miserable as he said, "I'm sorry, but Mr. Morgan is . . . gone."

"Gone! What the hell do you mean by that?"

"He . . . he got on his horse and rode away. He said he wasn't going to get himself killed over a woman he met only two days ago."

It was true that The Kid had swung up onto the buckskin's saddle and galloped out of Las Cruces, heading west toward the Rio Grande. The church didn't have any windows in the wall facing the street, only the double doors, but just in case the men inside had found some way to keep an eye on him, he wanted it to look like he was lighting a shuck out of there. He had explained all that to Father Jardine before he rode out, along with what he wanted the priest to do.

Someone inside the church pushed the door open even more. An ugly, beard-stubbled face glared out at Father Jardine over the barrel of a gun. The man stayed back far enough so that if anybody outside was trying to draw a bead on him, they wouldn't be able to, but Father Jardine could see him.

"Morgan left? Ran out just like that?"

"I'm afraid that's right. So you see, it won't do you any good to threaten Dr. Dare now. You can let her go, along with Father Horatio."

"Let her go?" the man repeated. "You see that dead lawdog layin' in the street, padre? My pards and me are gonna be on the run! The girl's goin' with us, just to make sure nobody hereabouts gets any ideas about puttin' together a posse to come after us."

"No one will molest you," Father Jardine said. He held out his hands imploringly. "You'll be allowed to leave Las Cruces, if you'll just release Dr. Dare and Father Horatio."

The man laughed. It was a rough, unpleasant sound. "Who's gonna stop us if we take 'em with us?" he demanded. "Who's gonna get in our way?"

Father Jardine had no answer for that. But he had to keep the man talking anyway. He glanced up . . . then quickly began praying in a loud voice, so that the killer inside the church would think that he had just been casting his eyes toward Heaven, instead of what he was actually doing.

Which was looking at the roof and waiting for Kid Morgan to show up.

The Kid had circled wide around the settlement, then approached the church directly from the rear. There were no windows back there, either, so he doubted that the three gunmen holed up in the church would see him coming. He was sort of counting on that, in fact. They had probably barred the back door after sneaking in that way.

The church had *vigas,* ceiling beams that protruded out from the adobe wall just below the red tile roof. The Kid uncoiled his lariat and shook out a loop. He wasn't much of a hand with a rope, but he had been practicing. If Father Jardine could keep the killers occupied, maybe it wouldn't take too many tosses of the lariat to snag something that would hold his weight, The Kid thought.

As a matter of fact, the loop caught on one of the vigas on the third throw. The Kid pulled the lariat tight, hauling down hard on it to check how sturdy the beam was. It didn't budge. He took off his hat and boots and dropped them on the ground next to the buckskin. Then he carefully pulled himself up so that he was standing on the saddle. Might as well not climb any farther than he had to, he told himself.

The adobe walls of the church looked smooth,

even close up, but there was just enough texture to them to give his feet some purchase through his socks. He hung on to the rope and planted a foot against the wall, then braced himself and stepped off the saddle with the other foot. The strain on the muscles in his arms and shoulders was painful, but he gritted his teeth and walked up the wall, pulling himself hand over hand up the rope at the same time.

It took him several minutes to reach the roof. He hoped Father Jardine had the gift of gab and could keep those killers distracted. He hoped as well that the men wouldn't shoot the priest. Surely they weren't loco enough to gun down a man of God.

But they had invaded a church and taken a woman and another priest prisoner, The Kid reminded himself, and had followed that outrage by murdering a lawman in cold blood. Given that evidence, he had to assume those hombres were capable of just about anything.

Father Jardine had known the risks, though, and had been willing to go along with The Kid's plan if it meant that they might be able to save Annabelle's life. The Kid didn't see any other way to do that.

He reached up, grabbed one of the roof tiles, and hauled himself up until he could get a foot onto the viga where the rope was attached. He pushed himself the rest of the way onto the roof and sprawled flat on the tiles, which were hot from the sun. It was uncomfortable, he was out of breath, and his muscles trembled from the effort he had just put them through. He rested for a minute or so then crawled toward the roof's peak.

The bell tower was at the front of the church. That was his destination. He crawled part of the way, then stood up and catfooted toward it, making as little noise as possible. He heard Father Jardine praying loudly in the street in front of the building. The priest was playing his part to the hilt, The Kid thought with a grim smile. The three gunmen would be less likely to hear him moving around up there with Father Jardine carrying on like that.

The tower stuck up about five feet from the roof, then was open on all four sides except for the wooden pillars that supported its red tiled roof over it. When The Kid reached the tower, he looked over the wall and saw the big, heavy bell hanging from a crossbeam. A thick rope was connected to a metal ring on top of the bell and then ran through a pulley arrangement and dangled toward the ground, so that the local priest or whoever he designated for the task could stand down there and ring the bell by pulling on the rope.

There was a narrow ledge inside the tower. A man could stand on it and clean the bell. A ladder led down from the ledge. That was The Kid's path into the church.

He pulled himself up and over the wall, then dropped carefully onto the ledge. He didn't want to fall, and he didn't want to lose his balance and have to grab the rope or the bell to steady himself. That would cause the bell to ring, and the clamor would warn the gunmen that somebody was up there. The Kid climbed down the ladder toward the little room at the base of the tower.

He paused as he heard the front door slam and then angry voices floated upward.

"Damn it, Lew, what're we gonna do now? You said Morgan'd come down here to save the girl!"

"I figured he would," replied the gravelly voice that belonged to the killer called Lew Jackson. "I didn't know he was such a gutless coward."

The Kid's jaw tightened. Jackson could think whatever he wanted; soon, he would know different.

The third man said, "Why the hell did you have to go and shoot Lipscomb? If they catch us, they'll hang us for killin' a lawman!"

"Like they weren't gonna hang you for killin' that woman back in Texas?" Jackson shot back. "And you, Chuck, you killed two guards when you busted out of jail in Kansas. Let's face it, we've all had the hangman waitin' for us for a long time, and he ain't got us yet. He won't this time, either."

"I still don't see why we had to try to even the score for Culhane and them other two, to start with," one of the men complained.

"Because they would've done it for us," Jackson insisted.

"You can believe that if you want to, Lew, but I ain't convinced of it."

126

The third man said, "It's too late to argue about that part of it now. What are we gonna do to get out of here?"

"Kill the girl and the priest," Jackson said. "Then we'll set the church on fire. That'll keep the townsfolk busy while we're makin' our getaway."

"The church is adobe. It ain't gonna burn."

"The insides of it will, especially if we throw some kerosene around. I saw a can of it they use for the lanterns. It's over there in that little room under the bell tower. Go get it, Chuck."

The Kid looked down. Sure enough, among several items being stored in the room below him was a large can of kerosene. He grimaced as he heard footsteps approaching the open door of the room.

"Bring the girl over here," Jackson ordered as Chuck stepped through the doorway underneath The Kid.

He didn't have time to climb the rest of the way down the ladder. All he could do was draw his gun and let go of the ladder, falling the rest of the way.

He landed on Chuck, who let out a startled yell as The Kid's weight unexpectedly crashed into him. The collision drove Chuck to the floor. The Kid chopped down at his head with the heavy revolver and felt it crunch satisfyingly against the gunman's skull.

Then he rolled into the doorway as Jackson and the other man shouted in alarm and opened fire on him. Bullets whipped through the air above him and knocked chunks from the adobe walls on both sides of the door.

Lying on his belly, The Kid triggered two shots and saw one of the men go stumbling backward as the slugs hammered into him. The Kid had no way of knowing if it was Jackson or the other man. The survivor stopped shooting and ducked away as The Kid snapped a shot at him. Crouching, the man ran between two pews toward the other side of the sanctuary.

The Kid scrambled to his feet and looked around for Annabelle and Father Horatio. He spotted them lying on the floor near the altar. Their captors had tied and gagged them, but other than that, they appeared to be unharmed.

A shot blasted and a bullet burned through the air next to The Kid's ear as he started toward the prisoners. He had to duck between two of the pews himself. Another slug chewed splinters from the top of one of the long benches.

"Morgan, you son of a bitch!" The voice had such a rough rasp to it that it almost made The Kid's ears hurt to listen to it. That would be Lew Jackson, he thought, remembering the way the unlucky Sheriff Lipscomb had addressed the man. "Why wouldn't you face us like a man?"

"Because you didn't deserve it!" The Kid called back. "Anybody who would threaten a woman and a priest is lower than a dog!"

"Yeah, well, I'll kill 'em both after I've blowed a hole in your mangy hide! What do you think about that?"

The Kid figured Jackson was on the move. That was why the man was yelling, to cover up the sounds of his movements. The Kid slid underneath the pews and started crawling toward the front of the church.

He heard frantic, muffled cries coming from Annabelle and Father Horatio and suddenly realized that Jackson might try to hurt them to lure him out into the open. He rolled into the aisle and surged to his feet just in time to see that Jackson had gotten that can of kerosene from the tower room and was splashing it on the floor around the altar, including the two prisoners.

"Jackson!" The Kid shouted as the sharp reek of the fuel bit into his nose.

Jackson whirled around and flung the half-empty can at him. The Kid ducked to keep it from braining him. That gave Jackson the chance to yank his gun out and blaze away. The Kid flung himself forward, diving to the floor as he triggered a round at the killer.

Annabelle screamed through her gag, and the next second The Kid heard a terrible *whoosh!* He scrambled to his feet and saw that Jackson had managed to light the kerosene. Blue and yellow flames raced across the floor. They had already reached Father Horatio, who writhed and shrieked as the fire ignited his kerosene-soaked robe and engulfed him.

The Kid dashed toward Annabelle catching only a glimpse of Jackson. He emptied his gun at the fleeing figure, then dropped it and reached down to grab Annabelle and snatch her up just before the flames reached her. Wrapping his arms around her, he ran clear of the kerosene.

Jackson was gone. The Kid didn't know what had happened to the killer and didn't care. All that mattered at the moment was getting Annabelle out of the church. Her clothes were covered with kerosene, and it would only take a spark to set them ablaze.

He burst out the front door of the church. Father Jardine was waiting there anxiously. "Dear God in Heaven!" the priest exclaimed. "Is she—"

"She's all right," The Kid said. He set the half-conscious Annabelle on her feet. "Hold her up." He pulled the Bowie knife from the sheath on his left hip and cut the cords that bound her feet together. "Now get her away from here!" he told Father Jardine. "The church is on fire, and she's soaked in kerosene! Get those clothes off of her!"

"But . . . but I can't . . . it wouldn't be . . ."

"No time for modesty, padre. Move!"

With an arm around Annabelle's waist, Father Jardine helped her stumble down the street, away from the church. Smoke came from inside the building. The Kid ran back in and grabbed his Colt from the floor. There was nothing he could do for

Father Horatio, who was now just a burned husk. The man he'd shot was dead, and so was Chuck, he saw when he checked on the man in the room at the base of the bell tower. That blow from the gun had crushed Chuck's skull.

That left Jackson, and there was no sign of the gravel-voiced man. He must have decided that it made more sense to cut his losses and get away from there.

Coughing from the smoke, The Kid hurried back outside and found the street thronged with people. "Get a bucket brigade going and wet down these other buildings!" he shouted at them. "Keep that fire from spreading!"

Father Jardine came up to him. "Where's Father Horatio?"

The Kid just shook his head. Father Jardine covered his face with his hands for a moment and groaned.

Before the priest could start praying again, The Kid asked, "Where's Annabelle?"

"I . . . I took her into the hotel. Some women there said that they would take care of her. I came back to see about Father Horatio, and to find out if there was anything I could do to help."

"Just do what you do best, Father . . . pray."

"And just what is it that you do best, Mr. Morgan?" the priest asked coldly.

The Kid glanced at the burning church and said, "Cause all hell to break loose, from the looks of it."

Chapter 14

The Kid retrieved his hat and boots from behind the church while the fire continued to burn inside. He knew that by the time it was finally out, the building would be gutted. The walls might remain standing, though, so the people of Las Cruces could rebuild it if they wanted to.

It had been a rough day. The settlement had lost its sheriff, its priest, and one of its churches.

All because those three hombres who'd confronted him in the store wanted to be known as the men who'd killed Kid Morgan, The Kid thought. What a tragic waste.

He didn't consider the death and devastation his fault. He hadn't forced Culhane and the other two to come after him in the first place, and it wasn't his idea that Jackson and his friends should want revenge. When a man picked up a gun with murder in his heart, bad things happened. Plain and simple as that.

The citizens of Las Cruces didn't have to form a bucket brigade from the public well. The town had a volunteer fire brigade with a wagon that had a water tank and a hand pump mounted on it. The members of the brigade swung into action, using the rig to spray water over the buildings closest to the blaze. It was too late for them to save the church; the structure was too far gone. The Kid watched long enough to see that their efforts were going to keep the fire from spreading to any of the other buildings.

Satisfied that the whole town wasn't in danger of burning down, he walked into the hotel to look for Annabelle. Father Jardine had gone back there earlier.

The Kid saw a couple of women in the lobby and approached them, frowning as he noticed how they recoiled slightly from him. He suppressed the irritation he felt and said, "I'm looking for Dr. Dare. Do you know where she is?"

"The wife of the man who owns the hotel took her up to their living quarters," one of the women replied. "Upstairs to the left, I believe."

The other woman said, "You're not going to shoot anyone in here, are you?"

He supposed he couldn't blame them for worrying about that. He had killed five men in the past half hour, after all. But understanding that didn't stop him from replying rather curtly, "Only if somebody shoots at me." He turned and went to the stairs, his long-legged strides taking them two at a time until he reached the second floor landing.

The door of one of the rooms to his left down the hallway stood open. The Kid walked over to it and looked into the sitting room of a suite. Annabelle sat in a ladderback chair while a middle-aged woman brushed out her hair, which was wet from being washed. The Kid supposed she'd wanted to get the kerosene out of it.

Annabelle wore a plain gray dress that didn't fit her. Her shoulders were too wide for it and her arms were too long. This was the first time he had seen her in a dress, The Kid realized. Until now she had always worn boots, trousers, and a man's shirt. He had to admit that she might look pretty nice if she was wearing a gown that actually fit her.

She looked up at him and scowled. "What happened to Father Horatio?"

"He didn't make it," The Kid replied with a shake of his head.

"How many dead men does that make?"

"You mean today?" The Kid shot back, angered by the tone of disapproval in her voice.

The hotel owner's wife said sternly, "Young man, this poor young lady has been through an ordeal. I won't have you coming in here and speaking to her like that."

He took off his hat and gave the woman a polite nod. "You're right, ma'am. I apologize. I reckon it's been an ordeal for all of us."

The woman sniffed. "From what I hear about you, Mr. Morgan, you should be used to trouble following you around by now."

The Kid reined in his temper. "Yes, ma'am, I should. Could I, uh, speak to Dr. Dare in private?"

"Are you going to try to browbeat her?"

The idea of anybody being able to browbeat

Annabelle Dare struck The Kid as pretty far-fetched. But he just said, "No, ma'am. I give you my word that I'll be polite."

The woman set the hair brush aside. "Very well. I'll go in the other room. But you call if you need me, Doctor."

"Of course," Annabelle said. "It'll be fine. Thank you so much for your help."

The woman left the room. Annabelle said, "I'm sorry, Mr. Morgan. I shouldn't have snapped at you like that. I know it wasn't your fault that those men attacked you in the store, nor were you to blame for what happened at the church."

"If I didn't have a reputation as a fast gun, they wouldn't have come after me," The Kid said with a shrug.

"Yes, but what else can you do except defend yourself when you're attacked?"

The Kid shrugged again. That was the same thing he had thought earlier, but he was glad that Annabelle realized it.

"And when those men took poor Father Horatio and me prisoner, you were just trying to rescue us," she went on.

"It's a shame I couldn't get the padre out, too."

"Yes, but you saved my life, and I appreciate that." She laughed softly, humorlessly. "One could say that all the violence is *my* fault for asking you to come with me and Father Jardine."

"Start thinking like that and you'll wind up going

around and around in circles until you drive your-self loco," The Kid told her.

"Do you speak from experience?"

The Kid didn't answer that question. Instead he asked one of his own. "Did those varmints hurt you?"

"Not to speak of," Annabelle replied. "They han-dled me rather roughly when they were tying me up, but I'm not injured."

A faint flush spread across her face, and The Kid was willing to bet that they'd pawed her pretty good. He wasn't going to make things worse for her by mentioning it again.

"Good," he said. "I'm glad you're all right. I reckon you want to continue the journey?"

"Of course! The Konigsberg Candlestick is still out there somewhere, along with the secret of the Twelve Pearls. We have to find them."

"Well, we won't be moving on tonight, after all." The Kid nodded toward the window. Even though gauzy curtains were closed over it, they could tell that the sun had set and night was settling down over Las Cruces. "It was Sheriff Lipscomb who wanted us to leave, and Jackson killed him."

"Yes. I heard the shot."

"Where are your clothes?"

"Mrs. Franklin sent them down to the laundry to be cleaned, if that's possible. She wasn't sure anyone would be able to get the smell of kerosene out of them, though."

The Kid nodded. "Well, if they can't, you can pick up some new duds at the store. We'll pull out first thing in the morning, if no one objects."

She gave that quiet, grim laugh again. "Do you really think anyone will object to us moving on, after what's happened today?"

"I doubt it," The Kid said.

He left Annabelle in the hotel and went back outside to lead the buckskin across the street to the livery stable. After arranging for the horse to be kept there for the night, The Kid struck a deal with the proprietor to park the wagon and turn the team into the corral.

"I'll probably sleep in the wagon," he mentioned.

"It don't matter to me where you sleep, mister," the wizened old man who ran the establishment told him. "Just don't shoot up the place."

That seemed to be a common worry in Las Cruces. "I'll try not to," The Kid said dryly.

After driving the wagon over and tending to the team, The Kid started toward the hotel again, intending to check on Annabelle before he got something to eat and then come back to the wagon to turn in and get some well-deserved sleep. Before he reached the hotel, though, a man came up to him in the street and said, "Mr. Morgan, I need to talk to you."

The hombre was young and nervous-looking, but

he had a badge pinned to his vest. The Kid stopped and said, "I reckon you'd be the deputy who's taking over for Sheriff Lipscomb."

"That's right. My name's Jake Nye. The town council's appointed me acting sheriff. I want to know if you and your friends are gonna leave town tonight, like Sheriff Lipscomb told you to."

"It's late," The Kid said. "Dr. Dare and Father Jardine have gone through a lot today. Besides, I've already put the team away, over at the livery stable, and it would be hard to find a good spot to camp in the dark. I'm hoping you'll say that under the circumstances, it's all right for us to spend the night, Deputy."

"Acting sheriff," the young man reminded him.

"Sure. I meant Sheriff Nye."

The youngster seemed to like the sound of that. It didn't ease his nervousness much, though. Clearly, he didn't want to have to try to run Kid Morgan out of the settlement.

To make the decision a little easier, The Kid went on, "It would sure be considerate of the lady not to make her leave town tonight."

Acting Sheriff Nye nodded. In the light that spilled through the big front windows of the hotel, The Kid could read his thoughts as they played across his face. Nobody could fault him for being considerate of a lady, Nye was thinking.

"All right," he said. "I reckon you don't have to leave tonight. But first thing in the morning . . ."

"As soon as we fill our water barrels," The Kid promised.

He continued on into the hotel and found Annabelle and Father Jardine sitting in the lobby. Annabelle still didn't have her regular clothes on, but she wore a bottle green dress that fit her a lot better. One of the ladies staying at the hotel had loaned it to her after seeing her in the ill-fitting gray dress, she explained.

"They're still serving in the dining room," she said with a nod toward the arched entrance that led off the lobby. "I thought we could all eat supper together."

"That sounds like a good idea to me," The Kid agreed. It seemed that Annabelle had gotten over being quite so upset with him, and it was simpler all around if things stayed that way.

Father Jardine wasn't as enthusiastic about the idea, but he didn't object. All he said was, "I'm afraid I may not have much of an appetite tonight."

The Kid didn't care how hungry the priest was. He was famished, himself.

But then, having to kill a bunch of murdering hardcases had never bothered *his* appetite all that much.

Chapter 15

After supper, The Kid said his goodnights to his two companions and left them with a warning to be careful and keep their eyes open.

"You mean because Fortunato could still have some agents working here," Annabelle said.

"I mean because trouble seems to be dogging our trail, no matter where it comes from," The Kid replied.

"I don't know what happened to my gun. Those men took it away, and I never saw it again."

The Kid figured Annabelle's .38 was somewhere in the smoldering rubble of the church's interior. Even if the fire hadn't damaged it beyond repair, it would be easier to buy her a new one than to dig the old one out.

"We'll take care of that in the morning," he said. He lifted a hand in farewell and left the hotel, walking across the street toward the livery stable and wagon yard.

He was in almost the exact middle of the street when a gun roared somewhere behind him.

At the same instant that he heard the shot, The Kid felt the hot breath of a slug as it passed his head, only inches from his ear. Instinct took over, sending him twisting and diving to the ground as his hand flashed to the gun on his hip. He had the revolver out as he rolled over. Another bullet kicked up dirt next to him, but that time he saw where it came from. He fired twice toward the spot where Colt flame had bloomed in the dark mouth of an alley.

As soon as those shots blasted from the muzzle of his gun, he was up and on his feet, weaving toward the alley in a zigzagging run. Thankfully, everybody had cleared off the street when the ruckus broke out, so The Kid didn't have to worry about an innocent bystander getting in the way of a stray slug.

The bushwhacker loosed another round at him. The Kid heard it whip past him. He ducked behind a wagon that was parked at the edge of the street. A bullet thudded into the vehicle's sideboards but couldn't penetrate them. The Kid edged along it to the tailgate, then crouched and snapped a shot around the end of the wagon. He heard lots of curious shouting going on, and then the slap of boots against the ground as someone hurried toward him. He spun around and leveled his Colt at a shadowy figure running across the street.

"Don't shoot!" the man called. "It's just me, Acting Sheriff—"

Muzzle flame lanced from the alley again, and Acting Sheriff Jake Nye said, *"Urk!"* and stepped backwards as if he had run into a wall and bounced off of it. The Kid bit back a curse as he triggered two more shots into the alley. He was really going to be disgusted if two of Las Cruces's lawmen had gotten themselves killed because they stuck their noses into his fights.

Nye wasn't dead, though. The young star packer rolled over and started crawling toward the wagon where The Kid had taken cover. "Mr. Morgan?" he called.

"Yeah," The Kid said. "How bad are you hit, Sheriff?"

"I . . . I'm not sure. I think he just got me in the arm."

Serious or not, the wound had to be painful. The Kid could hear the strain in Nye's voice. "Which arm?" he asked as the acting sheriff reached the wagon.

"The left one."

"Good," The Kid said as he reached down to grasp Nye's right arm and help him to his feet. "You can still use a gun, then."

"I guess. What happened? What's going on here?"

The Kid nodded toward the alley mouth, which was still dark and now quiet. "I was walking across the street to the livery stable when somebody started taking potshots at me."

"Did you see who it was?"

"Nope."

And there was really no way of telling who the would-be killer was, The Kid thought, since there were so many hombres around who wanted him dead.

Nye drew the revolver on his hip, then said, "I'll cover you while you run over there to the boardwalk in front of the hardware store. Whoever's in the alley can't get a shot at you from there. Then you can fire around the corner of the building at them."

Despite the pain he was in, the young lawman sounded fairly cool and calm. The Kid wouldn't have expected that, as nervous as Nye had seemed earlier, but some men were like that. It took actual danger to settle them down and make them the fighters they were capable of being.

The Kid finished thumbing fresh cartridges into the Colt's cylinder. He closed it and gave Nye a nod.

"Any time you're ready."

Nye thrust his revolver over the top of the wagon. "Go!"

Shots roared out from the lawman's gun as he poured lead into the alley. The Kid ran out from behind the wagon and reached the boardwalk in front of the hardware store in a handful of swift strides. He put his back against the wall of the building and slid along it until he was only a step away from the alley mouth.

As Nye's gun fell silent, The Kid thrust his around the corner and opened up with it. He had filled the wheel, six rounds, and he triggered off three of them as fast as he could, sweeping the barrel across the alley.

The shots didn't draw any response. The Kid wondered if the bushwhacker was dead or just playing possum. Of course, it was also possible that the man had fled once Nye joined the fight. Two to one odds might have been too much for him.

The Kid reached into his pocket and found a match. He snapped it into life with the thumbnail of his left hand and tossed it into the alley. No response to that, either. As the match hit the ground and flickered out, The Kid called over to Nye, "Do you see anything in there, Sheriff?"

"Nothing but a rain barrel and some old crates," Nye replied. "The bushwhacker could be hiding behind them."

The feeling that the gunman was gone was starting to grow stronger in The Kid. He said, "Cover this end of the alley. I'm going to circle around to the back."

"All right. Be careful, Mr. Morgan."

The Kid intended to be careful, all right . . . but a fella could only be so careful when he was about to go up a dark alley where a man with a gun might be hiding.

He loped along the boardwalk, then cut through the next passage between buildings. When he reached the rear corner of the hardware store, he took a careful look. The light was bad back there, but he could make out the deeper patch of darkness that marked the alley where the bushwhacker had hidden. He paused long enough to replace the three bullets he had fired a few moments earlier, then started toward the alley. He leveled the Colt in front of him, finger taut on the trigger and ready to fire instantly.

He had almost reached the alley when a growl stopped him. A frown creased his forehead. He saw movement and realized that a dog had been rooting around in the garbage behind the hotel. The Kid was a little surprised that the shots hadn't chased it off. Then he realized that the animal was terrified, too scared to move as it pressed itself to the rear wall of the hotel, but still defiant enough to growl at the strange human approaching him.

That growl was liable to give away his presence to anybody still lurking in the alley, The Kid thought. He had told Acting Sheriff Nye what his plan was, so if the bushwhacker was in there, he had heard what The Kid said. The dog's growl would alert the would-be killer that The Kid was in position at the rear mouth of the alley. He dropped to one knee and made reassuring motions at the dog . . . for all the good that would do.

The move backfired. The dog stopped growling and started across the mouth of the alley, coming toward The Kid to get his ears scratched and his belly rubbed.

A gun blasted again and again in the alley. The bushwhacker was crouched there in the darkness, aware that he was trapped between The Kid and

Jake Nye, and his nerves were drawn so tight that the slightest flicker of movement—in this case, the dog—had caused them to snap and he blazed away at it. Dirt flew in the air as the slugs chewed up the ground around the startled animal.

The Kid thrust his head and his right arm and shoulder around the corner and slammed two shots toward the muzzle flashes that lit up the alley. The glare from his own gun revealed the dark, bulky shape of a man lunging across the alley and crashing into the wall of the hotel.

Except the wall gave inward, because it wasn't a wall at all. It was a door of some sort, probably a service entrance. From the sound of wood rending and splintering, the door had been locked, but the impact of the bushwhacker's body had torn it open. The Kid snapped another shot at the fleeing figure as it disappeared into the building.

"Sheriff! He's in the hotel!" The Kid shouted as he ran toward the back door. Somewhere inside the building, a woman screamed.

Annabelle and Father Jardine were in there, The Kid thought. He hoped they were already in their rooms and had the good sense to stay put.

The hotel's rear door was locked, too. One kick from The Kid's boot sent it flying open. He ran into the building and found himself in the kitchen. Another door led into the dining room, which was empty. The Kid dashed through it as more shots blasted outside.

When he ran into the lobby, the scared clerk peeking over the top of the desk waved toward the front doors and said, "He ran out that way!"

Warily, The Kid ran out onto the porch. He heard hoofbeats drumming somewhere down the street. But he didn't see anybody, not even Acting Sheriff Nye.

"Morgan!"

The weak cry came from the young star packer. The Kid hurried over to the wagon where both he and Nye had taken cover earlier and found the lawman sitting in the street with his back propped against one of the wheels. Nye had a hand clamped to his right thigh.

"He hit me again and knocked me down when he came out of the hotel," Nye said. "I'm sorry I couldn't stop him, Mr. Morgan. He grabbed a horse that was tied at one of the hitch rails and rode away down the street."

The Kid nodded. "Yeah, I heard him taking off for the tall and uncut." He knelt beside the lawman. "How bad is this wound?"

"Bad enough I'm not going to be dancing a jig any time soon," Nye said. "It doesn't seem to be bleeding too much, though, so I reckon I'll live."

"Did you get a good look at the bastard who shot you?"

Nye nodded. "Yeah, I saw him when he ran out of the hotel. It was Lew Jackson, the son of a bitch who shot Sheriff Lipscomb. I've seen him around town enough in the past few months to recognize him. He was always causing some kind of trouble, him and the rest of that bunch of no-good hard-cases he ran with."

"Culhane and the others?"

"Yeah." Nye grimaced. "I reckon they're all dead now, except for Jackson . . . but so's the sheriff."

"You'll do fine," The Kid told him.

"How can I? I've got a couple of bullet holes in me! I'll be laid up for a while."

"Are there any more deputies?"

"Well, yeah. Three more. And they're good men."

The Kid nodded. "They can hold down the fort until you're on your feet again."

"I suppose so."

The Kid tried not to heave a sigh of relief. He'd been afraid for a second that Nye was going to ask *him* to pin on a badge and take over. And that just definitely wasn't going to happen.

"Speaking of being on my feet again . . ."

"Yeah, let me give you a hand." The Kid helped Nye upright. "Where's the nearest doctor's office?"

"Right down the street in the next block."

The doctor saw them coming and hurried out to help get Nye inside. Once The Kid was satisfied that the lawman was in good hands, he returned to the hotel. He went into the alley beside it and lit another match. The glare that came from the flame revealed a splash of crimson on the ground. Jackson was hit, but there was no telling how bad. From the looks of it, he hadn't lost enough blood to slow him down much.

A whining sound caught The Kid's attention as the match flickered out. He struck another one and strode toward the end of the alley. The mutt that had spooked Jackson into firing was standing there, looking up at The Kid expectantly.

The Kid dropped to a knee and ruffled the hair on top of the dog's head. The dog licked his hand eagerly. The Kid didn't see any blood on the animal. He ran his hands over its body, searching for wounds, and didn't find any.

"I didn't know dogs could have guardian angels, fella, but I reckon you do," The Kid said. "With all the lead flying around, I figured you were a goner for sure."

The dog, a scrawny yellow animal with floppy ears, reached up with its head and tried to lick The Kid's face. The Kid laughed and petted it some more. Then he gathered it up into his arms.

When he walked into the hotel lobby, quite a crowd had gathered, including Dr. Annabelle Dare and Father Jardine. Several people wanted to know how Acting Sheriff Nye was doing.

"The doctor's tending to him now," The Kid reported. "I think he's going to be fine."

Annabelle looked at him and said, "When I heard all that shooting, somehow I had a pretty good idea you were mixed up in it, Mr. Morgan. After all, it had been more than an hour since you shot at anybody."

The Kid didn't have to reply to that gibe, because Father Jardine asked, "Who was it this time, Mr. Morgan?"

"That fella Jackson, the one who made it out of the church this afternoon. He must have been lying low somewhere in town, waiting for a chance to bushwhack me and even the score."

"It would hardly be even, considering that you killed five of his friends."

"Well . . . as even as he could get it, anyway. He wound up just catching a bullet, though."

"He's dead?" Annabelle asked.

The Kid shook his head. "No, he got away."

"Then he could still come after you," Father Jardine pointed out.

"He could," The Kid admitted.

"Doesn't that worry you?"

"Not particularly."

Annabelle said, "Why should it, Father? Mr. Morgan already has plenty of people with a grudge against him. One more shouldn't really matter."

For somebody who wanted his help, she sure had a sharp tongue on her, The Kid thought. He supposed that was just her nature, though. She couldn't help it.

With a nod toward the dog, Annabelle went on, "What are you doing with that mangy beast?"

"I don't see any mange on him," The Kid replied, "and he and I have sort of become friends."

"You're not thinking of taking him along with us, are you?"

The Kid shook his head. The Jornada del Muerto was no place for a dog. It was no place for humans, either, but he and his companions didn't have much choice.

"No, he's not coming with us," The Kid said. "But I think I know somebody who might be interested in giving him a home."

Chapter 16

"You want me to keep him?" the little boy called Jamie asked the next morning as he hugged the dog to him and looked up at The Kid. "Really?"

"Really," The Kid said. "As long as your ma and pa say it's all right, that is."

"They told me a while back I could have a dog. We just ain't gotten around to findin' one yet."

"Well, there you go." The Kid grinned. "And I bet you'll be the only youngster in Las Cruces with a dog that helped somebody win a gunfight."

"Yeah!"

The Kid ruffled Jamie's hair, then scratched the dog's ears before he stood up. Jamie's folks stood on the porch of the neat little house behind the boy. The Kid had asked at the general store where he could find Jamie, figuring that the clerks there might know the youngster. Sure enough, they had been able to direct him to the right house on one of Las Cruces's side streets.

The Kid lifted a hand in a wave to the little boy's parents, then said, "So long, Jamie. Have a good time with your new friend there."

"I will!" The boy paused, and then as The Kid turned away, he went on, "Mr. Morgan?"

The Kid looked back at him. "Yeah?"

"Will you ever be comin' back this way again?"

"Well, Jamie, I don't rightly know." Given the sort of life he led, The Kid had no idea how long he would survive, nor any way of knowing where his trail might lead him next. "But if I do, you can be sure that I'll stop by to say howdy to you and that floppy-eared varmint."

Jamie smiled. "All right. Thanks!"

The Kid waved again and then strode back to the main street. The wagon was parked beside the public well, where he had used the windlass and bucket to fill up their water barrels earlier. The buckskin's reins were tied to the rear of the wagon.

Annabelle and Father Jardine sat on the driver's box. Annabelle wore the new trousers, shirt, and hat that The Kid had purchased at the general store that morning. The Chinese laundryman had insisted, loudly and at length, that nobody could get those kerosene-soaked clothes clean.

Annabelle also had a new gunbelt strapped around her waist, along with a new revolver in the holster. It wasn't a Smith & Wesson .38 like the one she had carried before. It was a .41 caliber Colt Lightning, the model sometimes also known as the Thunderer, with a four and a half inch barrel. Comparable in size and weight to the S&W .38, it fired a slightly heavier round, and The Kid thought Annabelle could handle it.

"Ready to go?" he asked her as he walked up.

"We've been ready for a good while," Annabelle said. "Did that little boy like his new pet?"

The Kid smiled. "He sure did. I think he'll take good care of the little fella."

He went to the back of the wagon and untied the buckskin. He swung into the saddle and moved the horse up alongside the driver's seat.

"Let's go," The Kid said.

Annabelle slapped the reins against the rumps of the team and got the horses moving. The Kid rode alongside. As they passed the building that housed the doctor's practice, one of the deputies stepped out onto the porch to watch them go. His eyes were narrowed and unfriendly.

The Kid had stopped by earlier to let Acting Sheriff Nye know that they were leaving. The young lawman's left arm and right leg were heavily bandaged, but he seemed alert and fairly strong as he sat propped up in the bed where he had spent the night.

"I don't know where you're going, Mr. Morgan," he had said, "but be careful along the way. No offense, but you seem to attract trouble."

The Kid had chuckled. "None taken. You're not the first person to point that out."

"I expect not."

The Kid and his companions were leaving, and with any luck, peace and quiet would descend on Las Cruces once more. The Kid wouldn't have bet a hat on that—there were always troublemakers around any town—but at least maybe the odds would be a little better for the settlement's tranquility with him gone.

They kept the valley of the Rio Grande on their left and some low, rugged mountains on their right as they headed north. They hadn't gone very far after leaving Las Cruces when they came to a row of empty adobe buildings. The structures had been abandoned and were slowly crumbling away. To The Kid's eye, the way they were arranged had the look of a military post, and when he asked Annabelle about them, she nodded.

"This used to be an army outpost called Fort Selden," she said. "The army withdrew its troops six or seven years ago, and since then it's just been sitting here."

"You must've studied the route you plan to take through the Jornada del Muerto," The Kid commented.

"Of course. We'd have been fools not to."

The Kid reserved comment on that. He couldn't very well tell Annabelle and Father Jardine that they were loco to attempt what they were doing, when he was going along with them of his own free will.

Annabelle hauled back on the reins and brought the team to a halt as they passed the last of the abandoned military buildings. The Kid stopped the buckskin beside the wagon. Annabelle pointed to the Rio Grande, which curved away to the west.

"We leave the river here and head almost due north for a while. The trail curves gradually to the northwest. At least, it did on the old maps I studied."

"You don't really know what we're going to find up there, do you?" The Kid asked.

Annabelle hesitated before answering. "Not firsthand, no. But I've read several accounts by Spanish missionaries and traders and conquistadors who traveled through the area in the past."

"How long ago?"

"A hundred years or more. But just how quickly do you think an empty, uninhabited desert changes, Mr. Morgan? I suspect the Jornada del Muerto will look almost exactly the same a hundred years from now as it does today." She smirked at him. "In fact, I'd bet a hat on it."

"Careful," The Kid said. "We didn't bring along a spare this time."

Father Jardine chuckled, then looked away innocently as Annabelle shot him a quick glare. She turned back to The Kid and went on, "There's supposed to be a waterhole at a place called Paraje Parillo about twenty miles north of here, but that's the last water we can count on for another eighty miles after that. There are some dry lake beds that sometimes have water in them if it's rained recently, but you can imagine how uncommon that is in country like this."

"Pretty rare, I expect," The Kid said. "We have

enough water in those barrels to last us ten or twelve days, depending on how careful we are. I'd suggest we be mighty careful."

"I agree. There's another waterhole at Paraje Fra Cristobal, at the northern end of the basin."

"Sometimes waterholes go dry in this part of the country," The Kid pointed out. "What if we get there and there's no water?"

"Then I suspect we may all die. If you don't want to run the risk, Mr. Morgan, you can always turn around and go back to Las Cruces . . . although I'm not sure the citizens there would welcome you with open arms."

The Kid said, "Once I take cards in a game, I play the hand out to the end."

"Sometimes that just means you're throwing good money after bad. Or in this case, risking your life."

"It's mine to risk," The Kid said.

Annabelle shrugged and nodded. She clucked at the horses and snapped the reins against them. The wagon lurched into motion again.

From the sound of what Annabelle had said, she had put in a lot of work before she and Father Jardine started north, studying everything she could find about the trail through this desolate landscape. Even so, the Jornada del Muerto was big and empty, and The Kid had to wonder how she expected to find something as small as the Konigsberg Candlestick and the secret of the

Twelve Pearls, whatever that turned out to be. That old German fleeing from the Inquisition could have hidden his so-called treasure anywhere. An hombre could search blindly through the desert for a year and never find it.

Which suggested to The Kid that Annabelle and the priest really knew more than they had told him so far. They had to have some sort of clue that pointed them to the location of what they were looking for. The Kid didn't particularly blame them for holding it back. Even though he had risked his life to help them on several occasions, they probably still didn't trust him one hundred percent. They were smart to feel that way. He wasn't going to double cross them, but they couldn't be sure of that.

The heat built rapidly as the sun rose higher in the sky. The Kid was glad for the broad-brimmed hat he wore to keep the sun off his head. When that fiery orb reached its zenith, it was capable of frying a man's brain in its own juices without something to shield it from the glare.

Because of the heat, they had to stop fairly often to rest the horses. During one of those halts, The Kid said, "You might want to consider traveling at night and laying up in the shade somewhere during the day."

"Just how much shade do you think we'll find out here, Mr. Morgan?" Annabelle asked with a nod toward their flat, almost barren surroundings.

The only vegetation to be seen were occasional clumps of coarse grass, some stunted mesquite trees, and beds of thorny cactus.

"How would we see where we were going?" Father Jardine added.

"You can always crawl under the wagon," The Kid said. "That doesn't help the horses, but they can stand the heat better than we can. As for seeing where we're going, padre, the stars give plenty of light. When there's a big moon, it's almost like day out here."

"I thought you hadn't been through the Jornada del Muerto before," Annabelle said.

The Kid shrugged. "I haven't. But I've been through other deserts. I know a few things about them. For example, we can get a little moisture from cactus if we have to. It's hard to live on that and nothing else, but it'll keep you alive for a while, anyway."

"Well, I'm glad we have an experienced companion, if not a guide."

"Guiding is your job, Doctor. I know north from south, but I don't know where anything is out here, as far as landmarks go."

He resisted the impulse to ask her where they were going to start looking for the Konigsberg Candlestick. Annabelle and Father Jardine would get around to revealing their secrets in their own good time, The Kid supposed.

The slow-paced journey through the almost featureless landscape grew mighty boring, mighty fast. The Kid's interest perked up when some low mountains came into view ahead of them and to the west.

"Those should be the Caballos," Annabelle said when he pointed them out to her.

"The Horse Mountains," The Kid said.

"Exactly. Don't ask me how they got the name, though. I have no idea."

They weren't going toward the mountains. Their route would take them east of the Caballos. They didn't draw even with the mountains as they traveled on. Those low, rounded peaks seemed to keep receding to the north.

The Kid knew that was an illusion. He and his companions actually were putting some miles behind them; it was just difficult to tell that out there in the wasteland.

The Kid estimated that they covered about ten miles. That wasn't bad, he thought. If they could maintain that pace, he was confident their water would hold out until they reached the other end of the hellish passage. Especially if the waterhole at Paraje Parillo hadn't dried up. With luck they would reach it the next day, and if there was water there, they could top off the barrels.

When they called a halt for the night and the horses had been taken care of, The Kid built a small fire to cook their supper and boil some coffee before darkness fell. Once they had eaten, he scooped sand on the flames to put them out.

The light vanished suddenly, almost as soon as the sun had set. That didn't surprise The Kid. It seemed to spook Annabelle a little, though. As she sat on the wagon's lowered tailgate and looked at the desolation all around them, she said quietly, "It's very lonely out here, isn't it?"

The Kid hunkered on his heels, his hat thumbed back on his head as he sipped the last of the coffee in his cup. "It is," he agreed. "Some places look empty, but they're really not. The life just hides during the heat of the day and comes out at night. You'd find birds and coyotes and all sorts of other varmints moving around once it cools off a mite." He shook his head. "Not out here, though. I've got a feeling that not even the coyotes venture very far out into this desert. They've got more sense than that. Might find a snake or a lizard, but that's about it."

"What about God's children?" Father Jardine asked.

"You mean people?"

"Who else would I mean?"

"I don't know, padre," The Kid said. "The way folks act sometimes, I'm not sure even the Good Lord would want to claim them." Before the priest could argue with him about his bleak outlook on life, he went on, "I wouldn't be surprised if we were the only human beings within ten miles, maybe more."

161

But as he glanced off to the south, the way they had come from, he thought that he wouldn't be surprised if they *weren't* the only people out there that night.

Somewhere back there, their enemies were still on their trail, The Kid's gut told him.

The only questions were who and how many.

Chapter 17

Manuelito lay on his belly, watching his quarry, separated from them by perhaps half a mile. The brilliant stars that had popped into view in the blackness above the desert cast enough of a silvery glow for the Apache to be able to make out the dark shape of the wagon with its lighter canvas cover. The two white men and the woman had no fire tonight.

They were learning.

But their caution would not save them, Manuelito vowed to himself. In the end, he would kill the men and have the woman. His need for that burned even stronger than the fiery pain in his side where the bullet had plowed a furrow in his flesh several nights earlier.

He had made a poultice from the flesh of the cactus and bound it in place over the wound with strips of cloth cut from his tunic. That should have drawn out the corruption and allowed him to heal, but Manuelito could tell that he had a sickness growing inside him. He was confident he could hold it at bay long enough for him to have his revenge, and once he had done that, he didn't really care what happened to him afterward. He could die happily, his lust for vengeance—and for the woman—satisfied.

"Manuelito!"

The whisper came from behind him. Manuelito looked over his shoulder and saw that Azza-hij had crawled up almost even with him. The young warrior sounded nervous—which came as no surprise considering the way he had turned and run when the whites put up a surprisingly strong fight. As the rest of the war party had died, Azza-hij had fled. For that reason, Manuelito had come very close to slitting the young man's throat himself.

But Azza-hij might help him achieve his desired goals, so Manuelito allowed him to live for the time being. How he conducted himself from then on would have a lot to do with whether he survived to return to the mountains across the border in Mexico.

Manuelito knew he would not survive that trek. Not with the burning in his side. But he could live with that . . . and die with it.

"What do you want?" he asked Azza-hij.

"They are up there, the white men and the woman? We have found them?"

Manuelito's lip curled in a sneer. "Look for yourself. Use your eyes, young fool! Do you not see them?"

"Yes. I see them."

"Is that all you wanted?"

"No, Manuelito. I came to tell you that someone is coming."

Manuelito turned. His hand shot out and gripped Azza-hij's arm so tightly that the young warrior made a small sound of pain.

"How many?"

"One man on horseback."

"A white man?"

"Or a Mexican." Even though he lay stretched out on his belly, Azza-hij managed to shrug. "Who can tell?" He was silent for a moment while Manuelito thought about the news. Then Azza-hij asked, "Are we going to kill him?"

"No," Manuelito decided. "He might manage to shoot his gun, and that would warn the ones we're after. We will let him go on his way."

"But what if he joins the men with the wagon?"

It was Manuelito's turn to shrug. "One more white man makes no difference. When the time comes, we will just kill him, too."

Azza-hij smiled and nodded. He was eager to atone for his cowardice, Manuelito knew. Or at least, Azza-hij claimed to be eager. The real test would be when the time for killing came again.

Manuelito heard the hoofbeats of the horse as it approached slowly. He jerked his hand in a commanding gesture and then faded off into the night with Azza-hij following him.

The rider stopped, though, instead of moving closer to the wagon. Manuelito watched as the man dismounted and tied his horse to a short, gnarled mesquite tree. Then the man stretched out on the ground, tipped his hat over his eyes, and appeared to go to sleep.

It would be easy to creep up on him and cut his throat, Manuelito thought. So easy . . .

But then the man shifted, and his hand drew a revolver from the holster at his waist. He settled down again with his fingers curled around the butt of the gun and his thumb looped over the hammer. Killing him without allowing him to get a shot off would be difficult, Manuelito told himself as he watched the man. Better not to risk it.

Again he motioned for Azza-hij to follow him, then crawled off into the shadows.

The pain made it hard for Lew Jackson to sleep, even though he was sick and exhausted. One of the shots that bastard Morgan had fired into the alley had caught him high on the left shoulder. Jackson was pretty sure the bullet had missed the bone and just torn through the flesh, but his shoulder hurt like hell, and that arm was damn near useless.

One more mark against the son of a bitch, Jackson thought. One more score to settle.

After the disastrous shootout in the church, it would have been easier just to ride away, to forget about everything that had happened. Forget about the men who had died. That's what most fellas would have done if they'd found themselves in his position.

Most men wouldn't have even tried to get revenge for Culhane, Jericho, and Mawson in the first place. They would have just told themselves, well, it was too bad Morgan had killed those three hombres, but there was nothing to be done about it.

The hell there wasn't. The problem with the world was that nobody had any loyalty anymore. Nobody stuck up for a friend and tried to do what was right. Jackson could see that, even if nobody else could.

So he and Chuck and McDermott had taken the redheaded girl hostage, along with that fat little Mex priest, and tried to avenge Culhane and the others. Chuck and McDermott weren't too keen on the idea to start with, but they had gone along with what Jackson wanted, just like they always did.

Then Morgan had to go and double cross them and sneak into the church through the bell tower. What a damned sorry thing to do.

Jackson muttered curses under his breath as a throbbing pain went through his shoulder. He had tied up the wound as best he could, but it really needed a sawbones. Maybe when Morgan was dead, he could go back to Las Cruces and have it tended to properly.

No, that was out, he told himself. They'd be on the lookout for him since he'd killed that damn popinjay of a sheriff and maybe killed the deputy. He'd have to find some other town with a doctor.

Something in the night made Jackson's skin crawl as he lay there trying to sleep. He felt almost like he was being watched, but he knew that was impossible. Morgan and the two with the wagon were at least half a mile ahead of him, maybe more. He had been about a mile behind them during the day, far enough back to stay out of sight as he followed the tracks left by the wagon and Morgan's horse. Once night had fallen he had ridden on for a little while longer, then stopped so that he wouldn't stumble right into their camp without warning. And there wasn't anything else out there in the barren wilderness to watch him.

He tightened his grip on the revolver anyway. It made him feel better.

There had been so much uproar going on after he escaped from that burning church that he'd been able to duck through some alleys and then hide in the crib of a half-breed whore he knew. She wouldn't betray him, because she knew he would kill her if she tried to. Come nightfall, he'd snuck out and waited in the alley beside the hotel, figuring that sooner or later he would see Morgan pass by in the street.

Sure enough, the bastard had walked out there big as life, and Jackson had lined up his shot just perfect . . . but somehow, the bullet had missed Morgan. Just barely, but that was enough to ruin everything. Jackson's eyes were still irritated from the smoke that had gotten in them that afternoon, and he figured that's what caused him to miss.

Regardless of the reason, he had missed, and then that damned deputy had come along and butted in, and then Morgan had winged him as he waited in the alley to try to get another shot. Jackson had made it out of Las Cruces by the skin of his teeth, as the old-timers said.

Again, the smart thing to do would be to ride away and forget about Kid Morgan.

Jackson knew he couldn't do it. He'd hidden out at the crumbling ruins of the old fort north of town, tended to his wounded shoulder as best he could, and then waited. He knew from what he'd overheard in town that Morgan and his two companions were heading north, through the Jornada del Muerto. That would be a perfect place to ambush them, Jackson told himself.

That morning, he'd still been hiding in the abandoned fort when they paused there. He had thought about throwing down on them then and there, but decided it was too close to town. People would hear the shots and come to investigate. Better to wait until they were miles from anywhere.

Tomorrow, he told himself as the chill of the desert night stole over him. Tomorrow, Kid Morgan and the old priest would die, and then he could take his own sweet time dealing with the woman.

It was such a pleasant thought that his lips curved in a faint smile as he finally drifted off to sleep.

"Over there, Arturo," Count Eduardo Fortunato snapped as he pointed to the hotel, which was built of adobe and had two stories with a balcony over the front porch. "That appears to be the only remotely suitable establishment in this godforsaken hellhole."

Arturo sent the wagon toward the hotel and brought it to a stop in front. He would have hopped to the ground and helped Fortunato climb down, but the count didn't wait. Fortunato swung down lithely from the wagon seat with the grace of the exceptional athlete he was.

"Stay with the wagon," he said as he went up the steps to the porch and strode into the hotel. Someone had tried to make the place look elegant, he saw as he glanced around the lobby, with Indian rugs on the floor, paintings on the walls, overstuffed furniture, and several potted plants. But, to eyes accustomed to the glories of Continental hostelries, the hotel just looked shabby and dusty. Sand gritted under Fortunato's feet as he approached the desk.

"I need your finest suite," he said to the narrow-shouldered, pale-faced clerk who stood there gaping at him.

"Sorry, sir," the man said. "We don't, uh, we don't have any suites, just single rooms."

"Do any of them adjoin?"

"Yes, sir."

"Then I shall require three rooms, two of them adjoining. Those two will serve as a suite while I'm staying here. You'll need to have the bed moved out of one room and some extra chairs and a table brought in. My servant will stay in the other room."

The clerk swallowed. "Well, I, uh, I really ought to talk to the owner about something like that before I—"

"Nonsense." Fortunato took an American fifty dollar bill from his coat pocket and slapped it on the desk. "That should cover the arrangements. If you need more later on, let me know."

The clerk's eyes widened at the sight of the bill. He probably didn't see very many that large. He said, "Yes, sir, I reckon I can do that!" and the money disappeared from the desk with a deft swipe of his hand. He turned his head and yelled, "Pablo! Get your sorry ass over here. We got a gentleman staying here, and he needs us to take care of him proper-like."

An elderly Mexican man hurried over and asked Fortunato, "Your bags, *señor?*"

"My servant will get them," Fortunato said.

"Pablo, this gentleman needs us to change Room Seven into a sitting room so that it'll form a suite with Room Eight," the clerk explained.

Pablo frowned. "Can such a thing be done?" He sounded doubtful.

"It can," the clerk insisted. "See to it!"

"*Si, si,*" the old-timer muttered. He started toward the stairs.

"And make sure the rooms are spotless!" the clerk called after him. Then he smiled at Fortunato

171

and went on, "Is there anything else we can do to accommodate you, sir?"

Fortunato grunted. "You could allow me to register."

"Oh! Yes, of course." The clerk slid the book in front of him, took the pen from its inkwell, and handed it to the count. Fortunato scrawled his name, and in the place for his home address, he wrote Venice, Italy. The clerk's already-impressed eyes widened even more when he saw that. He asked in an awed voice, "You're a real count?"

"Of course I am," Fortunato said coldly. "A nobleman would not lie about such a thing."

"No, sir, of course not! I didn't mean to imply—"

Fortunato shut him up with a casual wave. "Is there a bar in this hotel?"

"Yes, sir, right through there." The clerk pointed at an arched doorway on the opposite side of the lobby from the dining room.

"Send someone to inform me when my suite is ready."

"Yes, sir!"

Fortunato strolled through the door into the bar and took off the soft felt hat he wore. The place wasn't very busy. A handful of men in garish suits and derby hats who were probably traveling salesmen, a pair of better-dressed men who might be the local banker and the owner of a successful business, a frock-coated gambler who was dealing the cards at a baize-covered table occupied by a couple of townsmen and three American cowboys . . . and a woman. She stood at the bar talking to the bartender, a chunky, middle-aged man with several dark strands of hair plastered across the otherwise bald top of his head. When Fortunato came into the room, she turned and looked at him, her gaze cool and appraising.

Thick, honey-colored hair was piled high on her head in an elaborate arrangement of curls. She wore a high-necked blue dress that buttoned to the throat, but it wasn't as decorous as it might have been because the fabric hugged her body snugly enough so that her ample breasts were clearly outlined. She wasn't very tall, but Fortunato didn't mind that. He was attracted to her immediately, and judging by the bold look in her eyes, she returned the feeling.

Smiling, she said something to the bartender, then came forward to meet Fortunato. "Hello," she said in a throaty voice. "Are you staying here at the hotel?"

"That's right," he said. "And you?"

"Yes, of course. It's the only decent place to stay in this part of the territory. They even have a bottle of cognac here that's not too bad."

"I wouldn't mind sampling it . . . if, of course, you would do me the honor of joining me."

She held out her hand. "It would be my pleasure. You can call me Jess."

He could tell that she was going to be disappointed if he didn't kiss the back of her hand. He did so, bending over it and pressing his lips to the soft skin. "Eduardo," he murmured.

"Eduardo," she repeated. "I adore European names. And European men."

If she felt that way, she would probably be so excited she'd wet herself if he told her he was a count. Later, he thought. When they were alone.

He had no doubt that they would be. She was a prostitute, he made no mistake about that, but at least she had a certain amount of elegance and breeding about her, not to mention the fact that she was quite attractive. He missed his mistress back in Venice and the special ways she had of easing the melancholies that gripped him from time to time. He had even considered bringing her with him when he started to America but ultimately had decided against it. He had regretted that decision more than once since then.

But he might have found an acceptable substitute in this woman who called herself Jess. As they sat together at one of the tables and enjoyed the bottle of cognac the bartender brought to them, Fortunato told himself that she might be a pleasant way of passing the time until those new gunmen Braddock was sending to him arrived in Las Cruces. He had nothing else to do. The Yaquis were trailing Dr. Dare and the priest and the stranger. When the time came, they would find him and lead him right to his prey.

Until then, he looked forward to getting to know Jess better.

The clerk from the desk in the lobby came into the bar. He approached the table respectfully and said, "Excuse me, Mr. Fortunato—I mean, Count Fortunato—your suite is ready now. Your servant has already taken up all your bags."

Jess looked across the table at Fortunato and said, "Count?"

He inclined his head. So she learned the truth about him a little earlier than he had planned. It didn't matter.

"A family title."

"Count Fortunato," she repeated in a voice that was almost a purr. "And you have a suite? I didn't know they even had any suites in this hotel, except for the owner's living quarters."

"They didn't," Fortunato said, "until I arrived." He picked up the snifter on the table in front of him and downed the last of the cognac in it, enjoying the warmth that the fiery liquor kindled in his belly. "Would you like to see it?"

"Yes, I would," Jess said. "Very much."

Fortunato nodded. In his mind her answer had never been in doubt. He looked at the clerk and said, "Have some food sent up in an hour, along with another bottle of this cognac."

"The, uh, dining room is closed, Count . . ." The clerk's voice trailed away as Fortunato gave him a chilly stare. "But I'll see what I can do," he went on hurriedly. "Yes, sir, I'll take care of it. You can count on that." The clerk paused. "Say—"

Fortunato lifted a hand to forestall the inevitable feeble witticism. He got to his feet, reached across the table, and took Jess's hand. She stood and came to his side. He linked his arm with hers, and they left the bar walking through the lobby, trailed by the clerk, who stopped at the desk with a sigh of envy.

Fortunato knew what the young man was thinking. This stranger to Las Cruces had it all—wealth, breeding, the prettiest whore in town.

Soon he would have even more, thought Fortunato. He would have the Konigsberg Candlestick and the secret of the Twelve Pearls . . . and the lives of Dr. Dare and the priest and the young gunman, all in the palm of his hand, waiting for him to close it and crush them, whenever the whim struck him.

Chapter 18

No one bothered the camp that night. The Kid and Annabelle took turns standing guard, as usual. Father Jardine didn't even ask to take a turn, since The Kid had made it clear that he didn't think it was a good idea. The Father just crawled under the wagon and went to sleep instead.

The Kid never lost the uneasy feeling that nagged at him, despite the quiet, peaceful night. It remained with him the next morning as they continued northward.

From time to time he reined the buckskin to a halt and turned the horse around so that he could study the landscape behind them. He even pulled his field glasses from his saddlebags and raised them to his eyes. Looking through the lenses didn't tell him any more than his naked eyes did. If somebody was trailing them, they were damned good at it.

Of course, following them at a distance wouldn't be that difficult, he told himself. The wagon's wheels left distinct impressions in the sandy dirt. A fella would have to be half blind not to be able to trail them. He began keeping his eyes open for something they could do about that.

"What's the matter?" Annabelle asked him one of the times when he stopped to check their backtrail. "Do you see anyone following us?"

The Kid shook his head. "Nope. But that doesn't

mean they're not back there. I never met the man, but from what you told me about Count Fortunato, he doesn't sound like the sort of hombre who would give up easily."

Annabelle hauled back on the reins and brought the team to a stop as well. Their plan was to continue resting the horses frequently.

"He's not going to give up," she stated flatly. "Not until he's dead. And if I were the superstitious sort, I wouldn't even be too sure of that."

"What do you think, padre?" The Kid asked with a grin. "If I kill Fortunato, is his ghost going to haunt us?"

Father Jardine frowned in disapproval. "Don't make jokes like that, my son."

"Yes, let's not tempt fate," Annabelle added. She slapped the reins against the horses' rumps and started them plodding forward again.

The landscape was as barren and boring as it had been the day before. The Caballo Mountains still seemed to be receding ever northward. Around the middle of the day The Kid spotted something else up ahead, to the right of the trail. It was just a dark hump on the horizon, some sort of knob that stuck up from the flat land all around it.

He pointed the shape out to Annabelle and asked, "Was that on the old maps you studied?"

She frowned in thought for a moment, then said, "I believe it's a landmark called Point of Rocks. A group of Spanish soldiers led by a conquistador named Oñate camped there on an early expedition through the Jornada. The waterhole at Paraje Perillo is near there."

The Kid nodded. "So that's the last water for, what did you say, eighty miles?"

"That's right." Annabelle glanced at him. "Thinking about turning back?"

"Not hardly," The Kid said.

They pushed on, and Point of Rocks, if that's what it was, exhibited the same sort of behavior as the Caballo Mountains—it didn't seem to ever get any closer.

The Kid knew that that was just an illusion. If what Annabelle said about the old maps she'd studied was correct, Point of Rocks and Paraje Perillo were about ten miles north of where they had camped the night before, which meant they ought to reach those landmarks by nightfall.

As the afternoon wore on, he began to be able to discern that they were closer to the knob. It even took on a greenish tinge, telling him that there was vegetation growing on it, maybe even trees. If that proved to be the case, it would be a good idea to stock up on firewood while they were stopped there. There wasn't much fuel in the desert, only the scrubby, gnarled mesquites.

The Kid continued checking their backtrail. Late in the afternoon, when he could tell that Point of Rocks was only about a mile away, he said, "I'm going to ride ahead and climb up there. From the top, I ought to be able to see for miles around."

"So you can see if there's anyone following us," Annabelle said.

The Kid nodded. "That's the idea."

He heeled the buckskin into a trot. The long days and the heat and arid conditions were wearing down the horse a little, but the buckskin had always had plenty of grit and stamina to spare. He even seemed to enjoy stretching his legs and moving a little faster.

As The Kid drew closer, he saw that the sides of the knob were dotted with pine trees, some of them pretty good size. He could definitely chop some firewood. The coarse grass was thicker around the knob, too. That fact, along with the presence of the trees, combined to tell him that any underground water in the area must be closer to the surface there than in the surrounding desert. That boded well for the spring at Paraje Perillo not being dry.

When he reached the base of the slope, he paused to let the buckskin rest for a couple of minutes before starting up the hill. Point of Rocks rose to a considerable height above him, at least for that mostly flat country, and it took another ten minutes or so for him to ride to the top.

The landmark got its name from its rocky nature and the fact that it narrowed to a rather small point as it ascended. It gave that appearance, anyway. When The Kid reached its flat top, he found that there was actually considerable area up there. He dismounted, took the field glasses from his saddlebags, and used them to scan the countryside to the south, behind the slowly moving wagon.

He stiffened less than a minute later when he spotted a black dot against the rust and tan of the desert about a mile behind the wagon, maybe a little more. It was moving slowly northward and as The Kid squinted through the lenses, the shape gradually resolved itself into that of a man on horseback.

The hombre was alone, and he wasn't in any hurry, just moseying along. The Kid couldn't make out enough details to recognize him. One of Fortunato's men, he wondered, trailing them so that he could report back to the count?

That was the most likely explanation, but it wasn't the only one. It was even possible that the rider didn't have anything to do with Annabelle and Father Jardine at all, that he was just some stranger heading north through the Jornada del Muerto.

Would anybody be foolish enough to start out alone across this hellish land? The Kid supposed it was possible. No matter how foolish a thing was, there would always be somebody, somewhere, who would attempt it. One thing was certain, though, he thought as he lowered the field glasses. He had to find out who that hombre was, or he wouldn't sleep well that night. Not well at all.

• • •

It bothered The Kid to see the rider following the wagon, but he didn't waste the opportunity to take a good look everywhere else around Point of Rocks. He saw another area where the vegetation was thicker and greener, about five hundred yards to the west. As he focused the glasses on it, he even caught a glimpse of sunlight glinting on water. That would be Paraje Perillo, he thought, and the waterhole wasn't dry. That was good news.

By the time he rode back down to the base of the knob, the wagon was less than a quarter mile away. They could refill the water barrels in the morning before they started, he decided. For the night, he wanted them to camp there at Point of Rocks.

He dismounted and stood holding the buckskin's reins while Annabelle drove the wagon closer. The Kid's eyes narrowed as he looked past the vehicle, but from there he couldn't see the rider who was behind them. The fella was too far back. Whether that was deliberate or an accident, The Kid couldn't say, but he intended to find out.

"This is it," Annabelle said as she brought the team to a halt. "Point of Rocks. I recognize it from Oñate's account. Paraje Perillo is over there." She pointed toward the green spot to the west.

The Kid explained his plan about topping off the water barrels in the morning, then said, "We'll make camp here tonight. We can unhitch the team and lead them to the top of the hill. You'll sleep up there, too."

"Why would we want to do that?" Annabelle asked.

"This may be the last high ground we see for quite a while," The Kid said. "I reckon we ought to take advantage of it. If anybody tries to sneak up on us during the night, they'll have a tougher time of it if we're on top of that knob."

Annabelle shrugged, set the brake, and climbed down from the box. "That'll leave the wagon undefended, you know," she pointed out.

"Yeah, but nobody's after the wagon. It's you and the padre they want."

She couldn't argue with that logic. For the next half hour, Annabelle carried the things they would need for the night to the top of the hill while The Kid unhitched the team and led the horses up the slope. When he got to the top with them, he picketed them where they would have some decent graze.

He was a little surprised that Annabelle was able to get a small, almost smokeless fire going. She had been paying attention after all, he decided. The sun was nearing the western horizon as she hunkered next to the fire to fry bacon and heat up some beans and biscuits.

"The conquistadors thought they were going to die of thirst when they got here," she said. "They were coming from the north, and it had been a long, thirsty trip. They had a little dog with them, and after they made camp, it wandered off. When it came back, its paws were muddy. They back-tracked along the trail the dog had left and found the waterhole. It didn't have much water in it, but there was enough to keep them alive and let them make it out of the Jornada. They named the water-hole after the little dog that found it."

The Kid enjoyed listening to her talk. He said, "Did you read that story in those old documents in Mexico City?"

"That's right. There are several accounts of the Oñate expedition. All of them mention Point of Rocks and Paraje Perillo."

"*Paraje* means spot, doesn't it?"

"That's right."

The Kid grinned. "Maybe it was a little spotted dog."

Annabelle shook her head at him, then chuckled in spite of herself.

Father Jardine was sitting on a rock, listening to the conversation. Without warning, he said, "You saw something from up here earlier, didn't you, Mr. Morgan?"

The Kid glanced up at him in surprise. "What do you mean, Father?"

"You saw something through those field glasses of yours," the priest said. "Something that worried you enough you decided we needed to camp up here where it would be more difficult for our enemies to get to us."

The old-timer was sharp, The Kid thought. Annabelle hadn't put that together, but Father Jardine had. Quietly, he said, "There was a rider about a mile back."

With a note of alarm in her voice, Annabelle said, "Following us?"

The Kid shrugged. "*Quien sabe?* He might be just another pilgrim."

"Out here in the middle of nowhere?"

"People have been using this desert as a shortcut for a long time," The Kid pointed out. "Like that old German, Albrecht Konigsberg. It's risky, but if people didn't travel through here, it wouldn't have gotten the reputation it has."

Annabelle gave him a level stare and said, "But you don't believe it, do you?"

"That the hombre just happens to be back there?" The Kid shook his head. "Nope. I don't."

"It was just one man, you said?"

"That's right."

Father Jardine said, "A scout for Count Fortunato, perhaps."

Annabelle nodded. "I don't know who else it could be. If he knows that we're camping here, he's liable to go back to the count with the news, and then Fortunato will attack us."

"We don't know that he's close enough to do that," The Kid said. "Besides, this hill would be pretty easily defended. I reckon it's more likely that he's just keeping an eye on us. I intend to find out for sure."

"How are you going to do that?" Annabelle demanded.

The coffee was ready. The Kid picked up the pot using a thick piece of leather to protect his hand and poured some of the strong, black brew into his tin cup. He blew on it to cool it, then said, "When it gets good and dark, I'm gonna go do a little visiting."

Chapter 19

Lew Jackson was beginning to realize what a bad mistake he had made by following Morgan into the Jornada del Muerto. The place had gotten that name for a good reason. It was hellishly hot and dry. Not only that, but his wounded shoulder hurt like a son of a bitch, and the canteen that had been strapped to the saddle of the horse he had stolen had only a few drops of water left in it. On top of that, for the past two days, the only thing he'd had to eat was a handful of stale biscuits he'd found in the saddlebags.

He guessed maybe he hadn't been thinking too straight when he set off into the desert to seek revenge on the man who'd killed his friends.

But it was too late to turn back. Stubbornly, Jackson had followed the wagon all day, being careful not to push his mount too hard. He didn't really know this horse, what with it being stolen and all, so he wasn't sure how much the animal could stand. If he rode the horse into the ground, he really would be in a bad fix.

During the afternoon, he had seen the hill up ahead. Vaguely, he remembered hearing some talk about there being a waterhole somewhere up there, near a big hill that jutted up out of the desert. That had to be the hill, and if he could find the water-hole, he could refill the canteen.

It would be a lot better, he told himself, if he could just take that wagon with its full water barrels. Then he could ride in comfort and style, with plenty to drink and probably plenty of food as well. That would get him out of the Jornada del Muerto. He could find the Rio Grande again and follow it all the way to Albuquerque. There would be a sawbones there to look at his wounded shoulder, and saloons and whores and everything else he needed.

All he had to do was get his hands on that wagon, and all he had to do to accomplish that goal was to kill Morgan and the girl and the old priest. That's what he'd set out to do in the first place.

Simple as hell.

They'd be camped at either the hill or the waterhole. He could sneak up on both places and find out which, as soon as it got good and dark. Meanwhile, as twilight settled down over the desert, he reined in and dismounted to wait for nightfall. That wouldn't take long. It never did once the sun went down.

Jackson took the canteen and shook it back and forth next to his ear, listening to the faint sloshing sound of the tiny bit of tepid water left in it. He unscrewed the cap and carefully lifted the canteen to his mouth. It was the last of the water, so he couldn't afford to spill even a drop. The life-giving liquid flowed into his mouth and trickled down his throat, but it barely did anything to cut the coating of dust that covered the inside of his mouth. He was so dry he could spit cotton.

In the fading light, he took his knife and hacked a chunk off a cactus. He shaved the needles off it, then sucked on the inner flesh. It was bitter, but he was able to draw some moisture from it. He should have done that first, he told himself, then finished off the water in the canteen. Too late to do anything about that.

His stomach cramped from hunger. The biscuits were all gone. He had to kill his quarry and take the wagon tonight, he realized. He had no choice. He couldn't make it another day without food.

The horse nudged his wounded shoulder. Pain shot through him. Jackson stumbled away from the animal, knowing that the horse was just thirsty. That knowledge didn't do anything to help the throbbing agony coursing through him. He fought down the impulse to grab his gun and vent his fury by putting a bullet in the damn jughead's brain.

Might as well put the next one in his own brain if he did that, he told himself. He had actually reached down and grasped the butt of his revolver. He released it now and let it slide back down into the holster.

Something brushed against his neck. He started to look down, but then what felt like an iron bar clamped with brutal pressure across his throat. It jerked Jackson backward. As his good arm rose and he used that hand to paw instinctively at whatever had hold of him, he realized it was an arm. He felt a hard-muscled chest against his back. A surprised, scared gurgle escaped from his mouth. That was the only sound that could get past the arm pressing inexorably on his throat.

Blackness dropped over his eyes, but it wasn't the sudden fall of night in the desert. There were no stars winking into existence where Lew Jackson was. There was nothing, just an empty void.

During the next hour, as he prayed for death, Jackson wished fervently that it had stayed that way.

The Kid waited until an hour after nightfall before leaving the camp atop Point of Rocks. He figured that would give the man who'd been following them time to get good and asleep.

"How do you intend to find him?" Annabelle had asked before he started down the slope. "There's a lot of empty country out there."

"He won't be camped too far off our trail," The Kid said, "and a horse is big enough I should be able to spot it, even if I don't see the man."

"But if you *can* see him, won't he see you, too, or at least hear you coming?"

"The moon won't be up for another hour yet. The stars give off enough light so a fella can get around all right, but he won't be able to see very far. Also, he was staying far enough behind us that he probably thinks we don't even know he's there, so he won't be expecting anybody to come looking for him. As for hearing me . . . I can move pretty quiet-like when I want to."

Stealth was another thing he had learned from observing Frank Morgan.

"Be careful," Father Jardine said. "I'd hate to see anything happen to you because you involved yourself in our troubles, Mr. Morgan."

"I'll be fine," The Kid assured them.

Father Jardine stopped him with another question before he departed. "Are you going to . . . kill this man?"

"Only if he doesn't give me any other choice," The Kid replied, suppressing the impatience he was starting to feel. "I want to find out who he is, that's all. Once I know, I'll take his horse and his gun."

"Isn't putting him afoot in this wasteland the same thing as killing him?"

"Not really. There's water over there at Paraje Perillo, and he can walk to it easily enough. If he can convince me that he doesn't mean us any harm, I'll just tie him up so that it'll take him a while to get loose. We can leave his horse and gun at the waterhole for him to retrieve once we've gotten a head start."

That answer had seemed to satisfy the priest.

The Kid left his hat at the camp and traded his boots for a pair of tough-soled moccasins he took from his saddlebags. The moccasins allowed him

191

to move quietly across the desert while still protecting his feet. He relied mostly on instinct to guide him as he backtracked along the trail they had followed earlier.

Despite what he had told Annabelle and Father Jardine, he thought there was a good chance the hombre he was stalking wouldn't surrender peacefully, especially if he was one of Count Fortunato's men. But The Kid would deal with that when the time came, and if he wound up having to tell his companions something slightly less than the truth . . . well, he could handle that, too. He had dealt with a lot worse in his life.

His eyes moved constantly over the star-lit landscape as he walked quietly along the trail. When he estimated that he had come at least a mile from the camp, he stopped and frowned. He thought he should have seen some sign of the man by then. He listened intently, hoping to hear the horse moving around or blowing air through its nose.

Nothing. The night was as quiet as could be.

Then The Kid heard something that at first he took to be the blowing of the wind. It took a minute before he realized that it was actual moaning.

The sound came from his left. He listened until he was sure, then started in that direction, moving even more quietly than he had before. After a moment, he spotted a dark shape splayed out on the ground. The Colt whispered from the holster on his hip as he drew it.

The dark figure didn't move, and after a few more seconds went by, The Kid was certain that was where the moans were coming from. He approached carefully with the gun in his hand. A faint, coppery smell drifted to his nostrils. The Kid stiffened as he recognized it.

Freshly spilled blood—and quite a bit of it, too.

"Son of a . . ." he breathed. He moved closer, saw that the shape was that of a man with his arms and legs stretched out as far as they would go to his sides. They didn't move, and that fact, along with the position they were in, suggested to The Kid that someone had tied the man's hands and feet to stakes driven into the ground.

His first impulse was to go to the man's side, drop to a knee, and try to find out who he was and how badly he was hurt. A warning voice in the back of his head that sounded something like his father's told him he had better make sure there weren't any other surprises waiting for him first. When he was still about twenty yards away from the staked-out man, The Kid circled completely around him, searching the night for any signs of danger.

As soon as he was satisfied that no one was lurking nearby, The Kid approached the man on the ground. The man still let out a soft moan from time to time. The agonized sounds were muffled by something. The Kid knelt beside him, reached toward the man's mouth with his free hand, then jerked his fingers back when something painfully jabbed one of them. He looked closer and saw that someone had jammed a large piece of cactus, needles and all, into the man's mouth.

That wasn't the worst thing that had happened to him, though. The large black pool of liquid soaking into the sand under his hips told The Kid that the man had been mutilated. His pants were down around his ankles. It appeared that his genitals had been hacked off.

His torso was covered with deep slashes, as was his face. The Kid had never actually seen a victim of Apache torture before, but he had no doubt that was what he was looking at.

Incredibly, given the terrible things that had been done to the man and the amount of blood he had lost, he was still alive. That was another common characteristic of how the Apache treated their prisoners, The Kid recalled from listening to Frank recount some of his experiences. The Apaches were experts at keeping a man alive for hours or even days while they put him through the worst sort of hell on earth.

The kindest thing The Kid could do for this hombre would be to either cut his throat or put a bullet in his brain. The Kid holstered the Colt, unwilling to fire a shot unless he had to. The sound might carry for miles in this thin, clear desert air. He still wanted to know who the man was, so instead of reaching for the knife on his left hip, he fished a match from his pocket. He cupped his other hand around it to shield the glow as much as possible from any watching eyes and snapped the match to life.

The faint light showed The Kid an ugly, beard-stubbled face made even uglier by the slashes and the blood that had welled from them. The cuts had been made long enough ago that the blood smeared on the man's face was starting to dry.

Even though The Kid had gotten only a glimpse of this man's face back in the church in Las Cruces, he recognized Lew Jackson. That was something of a surprise, but not too much of one. Jackson had already made one try for revenge after the shootout in the church. Obviously, he had followed them into the Jornada del Muerto, still bent on settling the score for the men The Kid had killed.

Bloody bandages swathed Jackson's left shoulder. That was where one of the bullets fired by The Kid or Acting Sheriff Jake Nye had hit him during the ruckus that followed Jackson's attempt to bushwhack The Kid. That wound was the least of Jackson's worries now.

The Kid had a pretty big worry of his own. Who had done this to Jackson? An Apache, from the looks of it. One or both of the survivors from the attack on the wagon a few nights earlier? That was the most obvious answer. But The Kid supposed it was possible that a white man had carved up Jackson like this to make it *look* like an Indian was responsible. Would one of Fortunato's men do that?

The Kid didn't have any answers. Maybe Jackson would, if The Kid could get him to talk. He drew his knife, leaned forward, and used the tip of the blade to spear the chunk of cactus in Jackson's mouth. Jackson jerked and heaved against the rawhide thongs binding his wrists and ankles to stakes made from mesquite limbs. He screamed as best he could while The Kid pried the cactus free.

Then Jackson slumped back flat, a wet, bubbling noise coming from his ravaged mouth. At first, The Kid couldn't hear anything comprehensible in the sound.

Then he realized that Jackson was pleading, "Kill me . . . kill me . . ."

The Kid leaned closer. "Who did this to you, Jackson?" he asked. "Did you get a look at them?"

Jackson was so far gone in his world of pain that he didn't understand The Kid, might not have even heard him. The Kid tried again, asking, "Who tortured you?", but Jackson just repeated his slurred, blood-choked entreaty.

The Kid grimaced and shook his head. Jackson would never be able to talk coherently again. He was already too close to death. It was all he had left. The Kid took a deep breath through his mouth so he wouldn't have to smell the spilled blood quite so strongly and tightened his grip on the knife. One quick slash across the throat would finish Jackson off and give him the peace he probably didn't deserve, The Kid thought, remembering how Father Horatio had burned to death back there in Las Cruces. He wasn't sure his conscience would let him stand up and walk away, though, leaving Jackson to die in his own not-so-sweet time.

The sudden rush of feet behind him took the decision out of The Kid's hands. He dropped the knife and twisted around, reaching for the gun on his hip, but he was too late. Something came out of the night and crashed into him, knocking him over backwards onto Lew Jackson's bloody, mutilated body.

Chapter 20

His attacker let out a blood-curdling screech that assaulted The Kid's ears like a physical blow. A hand closed around his throat, cutting off his air. As he looked up, he saw a dark shape blotting out some of the stars above him. The light from those stars winked faintly on the blade of a knife the Apache held over his head with his other hand, poised to drive it down into The Kid's chest.

Before the knife could fall, The Kid swung a fist and crashed it into the side of the Apache's head. The blow landed solidly enough to knock the Indian off him. The Kid rolled the other way, off the tortured, still-living body of the mutilated Jackson. As he came up on his knees, he palmed out his gun, but before he could trigger a shot, the Apache came sailing over Jackson and tackled him again. The Colt slipped out of The Kid's grasp as his hand struck hard against the ground.

The Apache had dropped his knife when The Kid punched him so they were on equal terms. The man clawed at The Kid's face with one hand while trying to get his other hand on the white man's throat once again. The Kid hammered a punch home to the Indian's midsection. He rammed the heel of his other hand under the Apache's chin, forcing his head up and back. The Kid arched his body, heaving it up from the ground, threw his opponent off to the side.

He went after his enemy. When the Apache surged back up from the ground, The Kid grabbed his shoulders and flung him down again. He leaped and landed with both knees in the warrior's belly. The Apache grunted in pain and tried to twist away, but The Kid's weight pinned him to the ground. The Kid swung his fists, smashing a left and a right into the Apache's face. The punches landed with enough force to stun the man, who went limp under The Kid.

Quickly, The Kid scrambled to his feet and looked around for the gun he had dropped a moment earlier. Spotting it lying on the ground, he hurried toward it, but the Apache jumped him from behind before he reached it. The son of a bitch had faked being knocked out, The Kid thought as he was driven to the ground with the Apache on top of him. The warrior looped an arm around his neck and pulled back. At the same time, the Apache dug a knee into the small of The Kid's back. The Kid felt his spine bending and creaking under the tremendous pressure. His head spun from the lack of air. The arm across his throat was cutting off his breath.

He knew that if the Apache kept him pinned in the chokehold for another minute or two, he'd pass out. Then the chokehold would become a death-grip, either because the Apache would continue to strangle him or make him a prisoner and do to him what he'd done to Lew Jackson.

The Kid didn't like either of those alternatives.

So he found another one. His left hand wrapped around the handle of the Bowie knife on his hip and drew it from its sheath. He brought it up and back as hard as he could and felt the knife strike something. The razor-sharp blade penetrated with ease, and the Apache howled in sudden pain. The grip on The Kid's neck disappeared. He jerked the knife free and struck a second time with it. Again the blade sliced into flesh. Fists began to hammer the back of The Kid's head in a rage.

He bucked up from the ground. The wounded Apache toppled off him. Gasping for air, The Kid pushed up on his hands and knees, just before a savage kick landed on his shoulder, rolling him over. The Apache came after him, kicking and stomping. The Bowie flew out of The Kid's hand as one of the kicks connected with his wrist leaving him unarmed.

The Apache landed on top of him and locked both hands around The Kid's throat. He'd been able to gulp down a little air, but was still dizzy from lack of oxygen and on the verge of passing out. His strength was deserting him. He threw an arm out to the side and fumbled around on the ground, thinking that he might find a rock or something else he could use as a weapon.

Instead, his fingers landed on an arm. Jackson's

arm, The Kid realized. He was lying next to the tortured man. His hand followed that arm to the wrist, where he felt the rawhide thongs binding Jackson to the stake at the end of that arm.

Desperate hope flared to life inside The Kid. His fingers scrabbled around until he found the stake that jutted up six inches or so from the ground. His hand closed around it, and he began to work it back and forth in the dirt, trying to loosen it. Did he have the strength to do that? Would he remain conscious long enough?

He didn't know, but he was damned if he was going to give up without fighting to the last breath. His father had taught him better than that. And so had his wife.

The stake came free from the ground. The Kid didn't know how sharp it was. All he could do was slam it into the side of the man who was choking him to death—and hope.

The stake penetrated flesh. The Kid felt it grind and scrape against bone. He pushed harder, driving the stake deeper. The Apache let out a thin little cry and jerked back, releasing The Kid's throat. The Kid's other hand shot up in a punch that landed on the warrior's jaw. The blow didn't have much power behind it, but it was enough to make the Apache fall to the side.

The Kid rolled onto his belly and gulped air into his starved lungs. A few feet away, the Apache writhed on the ground as he pawed at the stake protruding from his side. A great spasm suddenly shook him and caused him to stretch out his legs. He kicked once, twice, then sagged onto his back and sighed.

After that, he didn't move.

The Kid lay there propped on his elbows, still breathing heavily, as he watched the Indian for signs of life and didn't see any. The point of that stake must have gone between a couple of ribs and found his heart. That could have just as easily been him lying there dead, The Kid knew. Only luck and his dogged determination had carried him through that fight.

But there had been *two* survivors from that Apache war party, he suddenly recalled.

One of the Indians had been wounded. He might have died since then.

Or he might not have. He could be lurking somewhere nearby, about to attack The Kid, too. The Kid's gun still lay where he had dropped it. He climbed shakily to his feet and hurried over to the Colt. He felt a little better once his hand closed around its walnut grips. Holding the gun in front of him, he turned slowly, searching the night with his eyes and ears for any sign of that second Apache.

He didn't see or hear anything. That was no guarantee the Indian wasn't out there, he told himself, but at least he wasn't already under attack again.

The Kid's pulse still pounded in his head. His heart slugged in his chest. But he could feel himself recovering. The hardships he had endured in recent months had strengthened his already sturdy constitution that much more. He'd rather not have to deal with any more trouble, but if it came his way, he would give it a warm welcome. Maybe even a hot lead one.

The night was quiet.

The stillness of death, The Kid thought. He went over to Jackson and hunkered next to the man. With his Colt still in his right hand, he rested his left on Jackson's chest and felt for any signs of life. Jackson's chest didn't move. While The Kid was engaged in his own life and death struggle, the Grim Reaper had claimed Jackson.

He'd be dead, too, The Kid told himself, if the Apache hadn't tortured Jackson. Staking him out like that had provided The Kid with the weapon that had saved his life. He didn't feel any gratitude toward Jackson. The murdering hardcase hadn't had anything to do with it. The Kid didn't intend to bury him.

There might not be many animals in the Jornada del Muerto, but he had a hunch the buzzards cruised over it pretty regular-like.

He turned away from the mutilated corpse and studied the Apache's body. The Indian still hadn't moved. The Kid was reasonably certain the warrior was dead, but he had to make sure beyond any doubt. He thought about shooting the Apache in the head, then decided against that. There was no telling who else was out there in the darkness. The Kid didn't want to fire a shot unless he absolutely had to.

He looked around until he found his Bowie knife. Then a single slash across the Indian's throat settled the matter. The blood just welled out slowly, instead of spurting, so The Kid knew that the Apache's heart had stopped pumping minutes earlier.

Feeling a little disgusted with himself for doing such a thing, no matter how necessary it had been, The Kid wiped the blood off on the sand and sheathed the knife. His Colt was still in his other hand as he trotted back toward Point of Rocks.

He didn't pouch the iron until he was almost there. The darkness at his back seemed like a living thing, still fraught with menace as it followed him.

Fifty yards from the spot where Azza-hij had died, Manuelito lay motionless as he watched the white man head back toward the knob where he and his companions had camped. There had been several times during the battle between the white man and Azza-hij that Manuelito could have taken a hand and slain the enemy.

He had chosen not to do so because he wanted to see whether or not Azza-hij could redeem himself for the cowardice he had shown in the earlier fight. Manuelito hoped sincerely that the young warrior would emerge victorious from the struggle, but it was one battle Azza-hij had to win on his own. Manuelito's code in matters of honor such as this was stern and unyielding.

So Azza-hij had died, and the white man still lived. That wasn't the outcome Manuelito wanted, but he would accept it and move on. Azza-hij's death was one more grievance to be avenged when the time finally came for Manuelito to deal with the white man.

At least he had had the pleasure of torturing the other white man. Manuelito had captured him, then Azza-hij had staked him out and they had both worked on him with their knives, taking great joy in the terrified, agonized squealing and moaning that emerged past the cactus they had stuffed into his mouth. It would have been good to take all night at such sport, but Manuelito had had a hunch that the young white man accompanying the wagon might show up. The one they had captured had been a fool, venturing too close to his quarry, never realizing that they might be able to see him from the top of that knob. Manuelito had thought of that, however, and he suspected that the young white man would come looking for the one who followed them. He and Azza-hij had staked out their victim, tortured him, then left him there to serve as bait. The plan had worked.

Then Manuelito had whispered to Azza-hij, telling him to go stealthily and kill the young white man. That *hadn't* worked.

Manuelito sat up, wincing at the pain in his side. The sickness from the wound had grown. He could feel it spreading through his body. But he knew how much he could stand. His time to die was not yet.

Not until the other three whites were dead, too.

Chapter 21

The Kid heard the sound of Annabelle working the Winchester's lever and called softly to her, "It's just me, Doctor."

"Oh!" she exclaimed, relief filling her voice. "Thank God. You've been gone a long time, Mr. Morgan."

He padded into the camp in his moccasins. The moon had risen, so he could see Annabelle and Father Jardine as they emerged from the shadows underneath the pine trees.

With a smile, he asked, "Does that mean you were getting worried about me?"

Annabelle sniffed. "Worried that you had gotten yourself into some trouble from which we'd have to rescue you, perhaps. That's all."

"What did you find, Mr. Morgan?" Father Jardine asked. "Were you able to identify the man who was following us?"

"I know who he was, all right," The Kid said. "Lew Jackson, the only one of those hardcases who made it out of that burning church in Las Cruces alive. I reckon he was following us in hopes of having a chance to get even with me for what happened."

"Was?" the priest repeated.

"He's dead." Before Father Jardine could respond to that, The Kid went on, "I didn't kill him.

He was dying when I found him. One of those Apaches who jumped us the other night had got hold of him and tortured him. Then he jumped me while I was checking on Jackson."

"And I suppose *you* killed *him,*" Annabelle said. It wasn't a question.

"He was doing his best to kill me."

"Why in the world would those Indians be following us?" she asked.

The Kid sat down on a log to take the moccasins off and pull his boots back on. "The same reason Jackson was . . . revenge," he said. "We wiped out most of their war party, remember? I'm not surprised that they want to avenge the warriors we killed."

"But what would be the point? Killing us wouldn't bring the other Indians back to life."

The Kid looked up at her and said, "You know, Doctor, if I didn't already know that you're from back east, that comment right there would have told me."

Anger flared in Annabelle's voice as she shot back, "What do you mean by that?"

"Just that people who live too long in civilization either forget or never really knew what the real world is like. It's not a pretty place, and if you're weak, sooner or later it'll crush you."

"You don't believe there's any beauty, any goodness in the world?"

"That's not what I said. Sure, there's plenty of

beauty and goodness both. If you're lucky, you might have some of those things for yourself. But then, if you're not careful, the world snatches them away."

Father Jardine said, "What does this have to do with those savages wanting vengeance on us?"

"Any time anybody loses something they care about, it makes them mad," The Kid said. "Somebody who has a clearer view of what the world is really like knows he has to strike back. If you just accept it, you're showing weakness, and then there'll be even more folks who want to take advantage of you and hurt you."

Annabelle sounded disgusted as she said, "So you're saying that the whole world is against you, and if you don't go around seeking bloody-handed vengeance on everyone who does you the least little wrong, the world will sense your weakness and crush you."

The Kid smiled at her, but the expression held no warmth. "Now you're starting to understand," he said. "You have to pick your battles, of course, but if somebody hurts you bad enough, you'd damned well better make them hurt worse, if you want to have any chance in life."

"You're insane," Annabelle said, her voice as cold as his smile had been. "You're as much a savage as those Apaches."

The Kid shrugged. "Been called worse."

She shook her head and turned away. Father

Jardine came closer, though, and said quietly, "You've been hurt very badly in life, haven't you, my son?"

"No offense, padre, but my life is my business." The Kid paused. "For what it's worth, there was a time when I was a lot like Dr. Dare. But then I learned better."

"And I'm sorry you had to learn that, Mr. Morgan. It must have been a very painful lesson."

Painful? The Kid thought about what had happened to Rebel.

It had ripped his heart right out of his body, that's all.

Nothing else was said the next morning about what had taken place the night before, except for one moment when Father Jardine asked The Kid, "I don't suppose you buried those two men who died last night?"

"Sorry, padre, I didn't. After what Jackson did back in Las Cruces, I didn't figure he deserved anything better than being left for the buzzards."

"And I don't suppose you can understand how I—and the Lord—can forgive a man for his sins."

"You and your boss are in the forgiving business, padre," The Kid said. "I'm not."

No one had bothered the wagon during the night. The Kid took the horses back down the slope and hitched them up while Annabelle and Father Jardine loaded the rest of their supplies that had been unloaded the night before. Then Annabelle drove the wagon over to the waterhole known as Paraje Perillo, named after the little dog that had found it for those conquistadors a couple of hundred years earlier.

It didn't amount to much, just a little pond with some grass growing around it and down into its muddy edges. The Kid took the lids off the water barrels and used a bucket to fill them after checking the water and determining that it was suitable to drink. He didn't toss the bucket into the back of the wagon until the barrels were full to the brim.

"There may be water at Laguna del Muerto," Annabelle said. "That's three or four days north of here. If it's dry, the next water will be at Fra Cristobal, three or four days north of that, where the trail goes between the mountains and the lava fields to the east. That's the northern end of the Jornada."

"So we're looking at maybe a week's travel without coming to any water," The Kid mused.

"That's right."

He slapped one of the barrels. "These will get us through, if nothing happens to them."

"Bite your tongue!" Annabelle said.

"No thanks." The Kid rubbed his jaw for a moment, then went on, "So somewhere between here and this Fra Cristobal, you expect to find the Konigsberg Candlestick and the secret of the Twelve Pearls."

Annabelle and Father Jardine glanced at each other. The Kid didn't miss the look that went between them.

"That's right," Annabelle said. "That's why we're here, after all."

The Kid waved a hand toward the north. "Mighty big stretch of nothing up there. How do you intend to find what you're looking for? Look under every rock when you drive past it? Poke your hand into every little hole you see? What about what the ones you *don't* see?"

Father Jardine sighed. "We might as well go ahead and tell him, Doctor. We knew we had to, sooner or later."

"Yeah, considering the fact that you asked me to come along and help you, I reckon you *ought* to start trusting me, sooner or later," The Kid said with a flash of anger he didn't bother to suppress.

Annabelle glared back at him stubbornly, but after a moment, she shrugged her shoulders and said, "All right. We know a little more about the location of the candlestick than we told you. One of the journals I read in Mexico City was written by the officer in command of an outpost at Fra Cristobal. It's generally thought that Albrecht Konigsberg, or El Aleman, as he called himself by that time, died at a spot about halfway between here and Laguna del Muerto. Some human bones were found scattered near there, years later, and they were assumed to be his. But according to the journal I read, Konigsberg actually made it as far north as the southern end of the lava field. It was there he realized that he probably wasn't going to survive, so he hid his treasure and sent his servant for help."

"Have you got a map?" The Kid guessed.

Annabelle shook her head. "No map. Just directions, and sketchy ones, at that. But if we can find the right landmarks, not far from the southern edge of those lava fields, we should be able to find the hiding place."

The Kid nodded slowly. "So you're going into the malpais."

"I think that's what they call it, yes. It's still considered part of the Jornada del Muerto, because there's certainly no water out there."

"What about that so-called secret of the Twelve Pearls? Do you know what that is, too?"

Father Jardine gave a solemn shake of his head and said, "No, Mr. Morgan, we don't, and I give you my word on that. No one has ever been able to discover what the German meant by those references. Our hope is that when we find it, we'll know."

"This place where we're going, from what you've said, it's still a good ways north."

"That's right," Annabelle said. "And we'll have to leave the regular trail and cut off to the east into the lava field as well. It's not going to be an easy journey." She paused. "You're not thinking of leaving us, are you, Mr. Morgan? If you are, it's only two days' ride back to Las Cruces. You can fill up your canteens here and make it without too much trouble."

"I already plan to fill up my canteens," The Kid said. "You can't take too much water with you out here. But if I turn around and head back, I'm liable to run right into Count Fortunato."

"There's a chance he doesn't know who you are. He might not bother you."

The Kid shook his head. "He had to be using a telescopic sight when he winged you that day his men were chasing the wagon across the flats and I butted in. I'm betting he took a pretty good look at me through that sight."

"He may have had agents watching us at other times, as well," Father Jardine added. "The man is a devil. He always seems to know more than he should."

"I'll stay with you two," The Kid said as he knocked the lids down on the water barrels. "I'll admit, by now I'm pretty curious about that fancy candlestick. I'd like to take a look at it. I wouldn't mind knowing what that business about the Twelve Pearls is all about, either."

"All right, if that's what you want," Annabelle said. Although she made a show of being casual about it, The Kid thought she really was relieved that he wasn't running out on them.

That wasn't going to happen. Like he had told

her before, once he took cards in a game, he stayed in it until the end.

The bitter, bloody end.

"Ready to go?" Annabelle asked as she took the reins of the team.

The Kid swung into the buckskin's saddle. "Ready to go," he said.

Chapter 22

The soft knocking on the hotel room door gradually penetrated Count Eduardo Fortunato's brain. He swam up out of the deep slumber he'd been in and shifted in the bed. The woman beside him responded to that movement even though she was still asleep. She snuggled her nude, lush body closer against him.

Fortunato forced his eyes open. He blew a strand of Jess's hair away from his nose, where it had been tickling him. She murmured, "Mmmmm?" but didn't actually wake up. Fortunato had an arm around her. He pulled it back and sat up, throwing the covers aside so that he could swing his legs out of bed.

He knew who was knocking on the door. It had to be Arturo. The pattern was familiar—three soft raps, followed by "Excellency?" Then the knocking was repeated, and the servant called out quietly again. That would go on until Fortunato opened the door, no matter how long it took.

Growling a curse, he stood up, grabbed his robe from the foot of the bed, and wrapped it around him as he went to the door. He knotted the belt around his waist, then jerked the door open and asked harshly, "What is it?"

Arturo blinked and sniffed, offended by Fortunato's tone but pretending he wasn't going to show it. "There are men downstairs looking for you," he said. "Six of them."

"The men Braddock sent from El Paso? It's damned well about time."

"I wouldn't know about that, Excellency. All *I* know is that there are six men downstairs in the lobby who wish to speak to you."

"All right. What the hell time is it, anyway?"

"Eleven o'clock in the morning."

Fortunato grunted. It was easy to slip into a life of ease when all he had to fill his time were liquor, cards, and a beautiful, willing woman.

But it was time to focus on his goal again. His backbone stiffened. "Tell them I'll be down shortly," he instructed Arturo.

"Of course, Excellency. Will there be anything else?"

He started to tell Arturo to see to it that the whore was dressed and out of his room as soon as possible after he went downstairs. But he decided to wait on that. It was possible, though unlikely, that the men looking for him *weren't* the ones Braddock had sent from El Paso. In that case, he would still need Jess around to help him pass the idle hours.

"No, that's all," he said. He stepped back and closed the door.

From the bed, Jess asked in a voice heavy with sleep, "What's going on? I thought I heard voices . . ."

"Nothing you need to concern yourself with, my

dear," Fortunato replied. "Just some business I must attend to. Why don't you just go back to sleep?"

"Is it noon yet?"

"No."

She snuggled down deeper in the pillows. "All right, then."

She really was a decadent animal, Fortunato thought as he dressed in a dark suit and a white shirt. He buttoned the shirt collar but didn't put on a tie. He glanced at the shape of her under the sheet and thought that he would miss her . . . a little. She had met all of his desires with enthusiasm, no matter how unusual they might be, and she had come up with some intriguing variations of her own.

Fortunato pushed those thoughts out of his mind as he left the room and went downstairs. When he reached the lobby, he saw the six men waiting near the front doors. They turned, and one of them walked toward him.

The man was several inches taller than Fortunato, with hair as black as a raven's wing and a rugged, lantern-jawed face. He carried a black Stetson in his left hand. He wore a red shirt, a black leather vest, and black whipcord trousers. The gun-belt strapped around his lean hips was black, as well, as was the butt of the gun that stuck up from the holster. The clothes gave the man the look of a dandy, but one glance at the cold, agate-like eyes told Fortunato that the man was no harmless fop.

"Mr. Fortunato?" he said.

"Count Fortunato," the Italian corrected.

A faint smile tugged at the man's mouth, as if to say that he'd go along with whatever Fortunato wanted, but he didn't really give a damn either way.

"My name is Thomas Novak. An hombre called Braddock said you were looking for six good men." Novak used the hat in his hand to gesture toward his companions. "There are five of them, right there."

"And the sixth?" Fortunato asked.

"The best of the bunch. You're looking at him."

The man didn't lack for confidence, even arrogance. That was often a good thing, as Fortunato knew very well since he possessed the same sort of confidence. But it could lead to trouble when two such men met and one had to take orders from the other.

"Twenty thousand dollars," Fortunato said sharply. "Five to you, the remaining fifteen divided among the others. And you do what I say."

Best to get everything out in the open right away, so there would be no misunderstandings later on.

"The price sounds fair," Novak said. "As for the rest of it . . . Braddock said you're going into the Jornada del Muerto."

"That is correct."

"You know much about it?"

Fortunato shrugged. "Some. I have never been there."

"Well, I have. Been across it a couple of times, in fact. So here's my counteroffer. We'll follow your orders without hesitation . . . unless you tell us to do something that's going to get us killed. Then there's gonna have to be some discussion."

Fortunato fought down the impulse to slap the gunman across his smirking face. The man obviously had no concept of the way the world worked. Those who were superior made the rules. Novak would learn that before this was over, Fortunato vowed.

But only after he had outlived his usefulness.

"Before we reach an agreement, don't you want to know why I'm hiring you?"

Novak shrugged. "Braddock just said you needed men who are good with their guns and willing to use them. All of us fit that description."

"And you don't care how you have to use those guns?"

"For that kind of money, I don't care, and I don't reckon those other fellas do, either."

Fortunato thought it over, but only for a few seconds. He prided himself on being a shrewd judge of character, and he didn't like Thomas Novak. Not one damned bit.

But he believed that the man could be trusted, at least to the extent that any hired gunman could be. He didn't think that Novak would shrink from killing a woman or a priest, either, if it came to that.

"A thousand apiece now, the rest when the job is done."

Novak's eyes narrowed. "I was thinking half."

"You were thinking incorrectly." With the bulk of the payoff postponed, they would be less likely to betray him, Fortunato knew.

After a moment, Novak shrugged. "Done."

"You can speak for the others?"

"That's right. I'm ramrodding the bunch. You can ask them if you don't believe me."

"No, I'll take your word for it. If we're going to be working together, we should trust each other."

"Sure," Novak said with a smile. His eyes remained as reptilian as ever, though.

No, he didn't like this gunman, Fortunato mused. But he knew a kindred spirit when he met one.

Novak introduced him to the rest of the men. Wesley was the youngest, barely twenty but with a wild light in his eyes. Green was the oldest, white-haired and stolid. The other three—Hobart, Bayne, and Donaldson—were typical hardcases, men in their thirties who had seen and done enough to have grown calluses on their souls. After meeting them, Fortunato nodded in satisfaction and turned to Novak.

"I assume you all have horses?"

"Sure. How do you think we got here?"

Fortunato ignored the question and went on, "Go to every livery stable in Las Cruces if you have to. Buy the twelve best horses you can find, the absolute best this primitive settlement has to offer."

Novak frowned and asked, "Why do we need a dozen more horses? Our mounts are good ones, and Braddock said you have a wagon you travel in."

"I'm leaving the wagon here. Our quarry has had several days to gain on us. We have to eliminate that lead. Therefore, we'll be switching horses on a regular basis, so our mounts will stay fresher and faster."

Novak thought it over and then nodded. "Makes sense, I reckon. Can you stand up to a long, hard ride like that, Count?"

"Of course. I'm an excellent horseman."

"It's a little different, traveling through the desert instead of cantering around some park in Europe."

"I said I can do it," Fortunato snapped.

Novak shrugged. "You're the boss."

"That's right."

Arturo was going to complain about the decision to abandon the wagon, Fortunato thought, although he would do it subtly. Fortunato knew that the servant could ride a little, but Arturo's experiences hadn't prepared him for what was to come. Fortunato wasn't going to set out into the Jornada del Muerto without him, though.

Something else occurred to him. He turned back

to Novak and added, "We'll need pack animals, too. Three or perhaps four."

"All right. We'll get mules for that. They can handle the job better than horses."

"I'll leave that to your discretion."

"Anything else?"

"There are some supplies in my wagon, but we'll need to replenish them. We should take enough to last all of us at least a week. Ten days would be even better. Then there's the matter of water."

"I'll take care of it," Novak said. "Like I told you, I've been through the Jornada a couple of times. I know what we'll need."

Fortunato nodded. "Very well, then. I'll rely upon your experience and judgment."

"You won't be disappointed," Novak said with a grin.

"We'll see," Fortunato replied curtly.

He went upstairs, through the sitting room and into the bedroom. Jess still slept soundly. Fortunato went over to the bed and reached down to rest a hand on her hip where it curved up under the sheet. He gave it a good shake.

She let out a groan of protest as she began to stir. Fortunato shook her again and said, "Wake up, Jess."

She rolled onto her back, pushed the disarrayed, honey-colored hair out of her face, and muttered, "Why?" Then a smile curved her lips, and she said, "Oh. You want to—"

"Unfortunately, no. You must get up and dress."

"Why?" She reached out and caught hold of his hand. "It's a lot more fun when we're undressed."

As if to illustrate the point, she used her other hand to throw back the sheet and reveal her nude beauty. Normally, Fortunato would have taken great pleasure in the sight—Jess really was a stunning woman—but his attention was once more focused on the prize that had brought him to America in the first place.

"I'm leaving," he said. "You'll have to go."

"Leaving?" she repeated. She frowned prettily. "Where are you going?"

"That's none of your business. Now, I believe we should conclude our arrangement. I'll speak to Arturo and have him see to it that you're compensated fairly—"

Jess sat up in bed. "Now wait just a damn minute," she said. "You think you're gonna just pay me off like I'm some common saloon girl—"

"But that *is* what you are," Fortunato said. Experience had taught him that the truth, no matter how blunt and painful it might be for people to hear at times, often cut through otherwise complicated situations. "I thought that was clear between us from the outset. You are a prostitute, and I am your customer. Was your customer."

"You think I'm nothing but a soiled dove! Why . . . why, you son of a bitch! I thought you understood I'm more than that. I've got culture, I've got breeding, I've got—"

Fortunato's voice sliced into her angry words. He told her in no uncertain terms exactly what she had that had interested him, then added, "And that's all, my dear." He pointed toward the door that opened into the hall. "Once you're dressed, you can leave that way. Go downstairs and wait in the bar. I'll have Arturo find you and settle up, as you Americans say."

"You . . . you—"

His hand shot out and seized her chin. His fingers dug cruelly under her jawline on both sides of her mouth as he wrenched her head back.

"I suggest that you don't call me any more vile names," he whispered. "I don't like it. Now, I'm going in the other room, and when I come back in here, you'll be gone. Do you understand?" When she just glared up at him, his fingers pressed even harder into her flesh and she gave a muffled cry of pain. "I said, do you understand?"

She managed to nod slightly, despite his brutal grip on her chin and jaw.

"All right," he said as he let go of her and stepped back. "Please don't think that just because this is ending badly that I didn't enjoy our time together, my dear. I assure you I did."

As he turned and went to the door of the sitting room, she whispered something behind him. He couldn't make it out, and while his first impulse was to turn back and force her to repeat it, he decided that wouldn't be worth the time and effort. He went into the other room and closed the door behind him.

He found Arturo waiting there, sitting quietly in one of the armchairs. Fortunato took a cigar from his pocket and said, "The lady will be waiting downstairs in the bar for you shortly."

Arturo nodded. "The usual arrangement, Excellency?"

"That's right. I trust you to know what's fair."

"Of course." Arturo paused. "Was she upset?"

Fortunato stuck the cigar between his lips and grinned around it. "Somewhat."

"Splendid," Arturo said sarcastically as he got to his feet. "There's nothing I like better than dealing with an enraged prostitute."

"Arturo!" Fortunato said as the servant started toward the hallway door. "We'll be leaving Las Cruces shortly. Those men I spoke to earlier will accompany us."

"I assume you'll want me to continue driving the wagon?"

Fortunato shook his head. "We're not taking the wagon."

That news actually penetrated Arturo's normally unflappable demeanor. He frowned and said, "We're not?"

"No. We'll be traveling by horseback, with pack animals. We'll be moving fast. Dr. Dare and the priest and that meddlesome stranger are probably thirty or forty miles ahead of us by now. That won't be the case for long."

The frown still creased Arturo's forehead. "But I've never ridden any great distance on horseback."

"You'll get used to it," Fortunato said around the cigar. He struck a match and held the flame to the end of the tightly packed cylinder of tobacco. "Besides, it can't be any worse than dealing with an enraged prostitute, now can it?"

Chapter 23

As far as the terrain went, the next two days were more of the same for The Kid, Dr. Annabelle Dare, and Father Jardine. The land was flat, sandy, and hot. Vegetation was sparse, although the stubborn mesquite trees still dotted the scenery. Those trees were no taller than shrubs and their branches were gnarled like the arms and legs of little old men. The dried bean pods that hung from their branches made a clicking sound whenever one of the blistering, vagrant breezes blew them together. Clumps of grass still grew here and there, enough to provide some graze for the horses. Occasionally, dry washes twisted across the landscape, with no sign of any water having run through them in months, if not years.

"It must have been a dry spring and summer," Annabelle commented when they passed one of the parched arroyos. "That doesn't bode well for the possibility of Laguna del Muerto having any water in it."

"We have enough water in the barrels," The Kid told her. They had been very careful so far, rationing out the precious, life-giving liquid. "We can make it to this Fra Cristobal place you told me about."

"Even with the side trip into the lava field?"

The Kid nodded. "We'll be all right . . . as long as nothing happens to those barrels."

The main difference during this stretch of the journey was that no one attacked them. The Kid didn't know if that last Apache was still trailing them, or even if the warrior was still alive, but it was possible. It seemed likely that Fortunato was still back there somewhere, too. Annabelle and Father Jardine were convinced that the Italian wouldn't give up. By now he'd had time to recruit more hired gun-wolves. The Kid and his two companions had a good lead, but the wagon could only go so fast. If Fortunato's men came after them on horseback, as they probably would, they could cut into that lead fairly rapidly.

For that reason, he checked behind them frequently, scanning the endless desert with the field glasses. He was surprised to find that the longer he went without seeing any signs of pursuit, the more worried he became.

Annabelle noticed the frown on his face after one such occasion. As he turned the buckskin and started riding alongside the wagon once more, she asked, "What's wrong? Did you see something back there?"

The Kid shook his head. "Nope."

"But you look like something's bothering you," Annabelle said, sounding puzzled.

"It is."

"I don't understand. The fact that no one's chasing us is a good thing, right?"

The Kid thought about it for a moment, then said,

"You know how it feels before a storm, when the air's so heavy you can't get your breath and you know it's going to start pouring down rain any minute . . . but it doesn't do it?"

"I suppose so."

"You want it to just go ahead and storm and get it over with," The Kid said. "That's how this feels to me. I get tired of just waiting for something to happen."

"So you'd rather we were attacked?" Annabelle shook her head. "I'm sorry, Mr. Morgan, but I don't agree. It would be fine with me if I never saw Count Eduardo Fortunato again, and the same goes for that other Apache you've been worrying about."

The Kid knew she was right. More violence still seemed inevitable to him, however.

The waiting's always the hardest part, Frank had said to him once. *I learned that back during the war. Standing in some trees and looking out at a field, knowing there were Yankees in the trees on the other side and that they were waiting, too, and that when the orders came down the line we'd all walk out there into the open and try to kill each other . . . Those are the times that gnaw holes in a man's soul, son.*

Like a lot of other things, Frank was right about that. But The Kid knew there was nothing he and Annabelle and Father Jardine could do except keep going.

They had finally drawn even with the Caballo

Mountains, so when they looked due west, the rugged gray peaks loomed there. On the other side of those mountains lay the valley of the Rio Grande, a green, fertile strip in an otherwise dry and dusty land. Over here in the Jornada del Muerto, it might as well have been on the moon. That was how far away the river seemed from this wasteland. They wouldn't see the river again until they were north of the malpais.

Mid-afternoon of the second day after leaving Paraje Perillo, Annabelle said, "We ought to reach Aleman soon. Definitely by nightfall."

"The place where folks believed the old German died?"

She nodded as she wearily flicked the reins against the backs of the team. "That's right. From what I was able to discover about the place, several people have tried to establish a homestead there. There are some trees, and that fooled them into thinking that there might be water. One man even dug a well, thinking that he'd start a ranch. He didn't have any luck."

"Dry hole?"

"Actually, no. A little water seeped in when he dug deep enough. But it was too alkaline to drink. He had even started to build a house there. He abandoned it before it was finished."

"Too bad. He should have figured, though, that there's a good reason this part of the country is so empty. It's not fit for humans to live here."

Father Jardine said, "God made this land, the same as He did all the other. There must have been a reason for it."

"Well, when you figure it out, padre, you tell me," The Kid said with a smile.

A short time after that, when The Kid reined in and turned the buckskin so that he could study their backtrail, he noticed an odd haze in the air on the southern horizon. He pulled the field glasses from his saddlebags and lifted them to his eyes. His jaw tightened as he peered through the lenses and saw a dust cloud rising from the desert.

The trouble that had been looming over them for the past two days? Well, it was back there, sure enough, The Kid thought.

And it was on its way.

Fast.

Annabelle had kept the wagon moving while he stopped to check behind them, as usual. The Kid studied the dust through the field glasses for a few seconds longer, then shoved the glasses back in the saddlebags and turned his mount hurriedly to the north once again. The wagon was about fifty yards ahead of him. It took only a moment to catch up.

Annabelle heard the buckskin's hoofs drumming on the ground and sensed that something was wrong. She was hauling back on the reins and bringing the team to a halt when The Kid reached the wagon.

"Keep going!" he called to her, waving her ahead. "Don't slow down!"

"What is it?" Annabelle cried as she did as he said and slashed at the horses' rumps with the reins.

"Riders coming up from the south! Looks like quite a few of them!"

Father Jardine closed his eyes, and since he made the sign of the cross a moment later, The Kid figured he had just muttered a prayer.

"Could you tell who they are?" the priest asked.

The Kid shook his head. "No, they're too far back for that. I can see their dust, that's all."

"Perhaps they're not pursuing us," Father Jardine suggested. Annabelle had the team moving even faster than usual and the rougher pace made the priest sway back and forth on the seat. "Perhaps they're just fellow travelers—"

"You know better, Father!" she said. "It's Fortunato's men. It has to be! He may even be with them!"

"Dear Lord, let us hope not. From everything I know of him, the man's a veritable devil!"

The Kid figured that was a pretty good description. During the journey, Father Jardine had spoken of other holy artifacts the Church had tried to recover, only to have Fortunato get his hands on them first. The man's palazzo in Venice must be full of art, sculpture, and other objets d'art, both secular and religious, from all over the world.

And The Kid had seen firsthand that Fortunato

wouldn't stop at murder to get what he wanted. The bullet that had grazed Annabelle's arm would have taken her head off if its trajectory had been a few degrees different.

Of course, the same was true where he was concerned, he realized, and for the first time, it occurred to him that Fortunato might have been aiming at *him* that day, rather than Annabelle.

It didn't matter, The Kid told himself. Either way, the Italian was a dangerous son of a bitch.

He twisted in the saddle to look back. The haze in the air had sharpened until even with the naked eye it appeared to be a dust cloud. That meant the pursuers were closer, cutting into the wagon's lead.

Veering the buckskin nearer to the wagon, The Kid called to Annabelle, "You said there's an abandoned homestead at this Aleman place?"

"That's what I've read. I don't know it for a fact."

"We'd better hope that there is," The Kid said.

"Why?"

"Because I reckon we're going to need a place to fort up."

"Oh, my dear!" Arturo cried as he clutched at the saddle horn and bounced wildly on the horse's back. "Oh, my dear Lord! Can't we slow down, Excellency?"

"We're already behind all the others," Fortunato said. "I don't like breathing their dust, either!"

As soon as they had spotted the wagon, he had

ordered Novak and the other gunmen to go ahead. All of them except Green were a couple hundred yards ahead of Fortunato and Arturo, closing on the wagon. The oldest of the gunmen had held back, leading the pack horses and keeping track of the spare saddle mounts, all of which were tethered together. And even *they* were ahead of Fortunato and Arturo.

If Novak and the others had captured the three people with the vehicle by the time Fortunato and his servant caught up, that would be all right with the count. He had no particular desire to engage in battle personally. He paid others to run those risks.

Over the past day and a half, as the group traveled north through the Jornada del Muerto, Fortunato had discussed the job with Novak, making it clear to the leader of the gunmen that Dr. Dare and Father Jardine were not to be killed when they overhauled the wagon. Fortunato didn't want those two even harmed, if at all possible.

As for the young stranger who had interfered with the count's previous attempt to close his hand around his quarry, Fortunato felt a certain amount of curiosity about him; that was undeniable. He would like to know who the stranger was and why he had involved himself in affairs that were none of his concern, as far as Fortunato could see.

For that reason, he preferred that the young man be taken alive, but as he had told Novak, that wasn't absolutely necessary. If the stranger was killed in the fighting, Fortunato could always persuade Dr. Dare or Father Jardine to reveal who he'd been.

But only *after* they had been persuaded to tell him how to find the Konigsberg Candlestick and the secret of the Twelve Pearls, of course. It was a matter of priorities, and Fortunato was a man who always had his own priorities in their proper order.

"Oh, my!" Arturo yelped again. "Oh, my!"

The servant had complained almost unceasingly since they'd left Las Cruces. Count Fortunato was a man who craved his creature comforts, but the same was true of Arturo. He didn't like the dust, he didn't like the heat, and he didn't like the hat with the huge brim that he wore to keep the sun off his head. The hat had a ribbon that tied under Arturo's chin to keep it on. It looked ridiculous, Arturo said, but he liked the sun blistering his head even less.

The only reason he hadn't complained too much about the food was that he had taken over preparing it himself, not trusting any of the hired gunmen to do an acceptable job. He claimed that dust got into the supplies, so that everything he cooked tasted like sand, no matter hard he tried to keep it out.

The worst thing was the result of the seemingly endless hours in the saddle. That didn't bother Fortunato—well, not much, anyway—but by the end of the first day, Arturo's nether regions had been so sore that he could barely hobble around.

They were even worse the next morning, when the muscles had had time to stiffen up.

But for all the complaining, Arturo had never fallen behind. He was still right there beside his master, doing his best to keep up and perform his duties. That was one reason Fortunato tolerated Arturo's sarcasm and arrogance. For all his bad qualities, Arturo was still an excellent servant.

Fortunato looked at him as they galloped over the desert and asked, "Do you have your gun?"

"My gun? Surely you don't expect me to *shoot* anyone, Excellency?"

"You won't have to, if Novak and his men do their job. But just in case . . ."

"Yes, I have it," Arturo said. "It's even loaded, as you ordered. But, Excellency, really, I . . . I don't think I'd be a very good shot."

"Let's hope it doesn't come to that," Fortunato said.

They would know soon, because he had just heard the rapid popping of gunfire coming from up ahead.

Chapter 24

Over the past week, The Kid had been careful to make sure they stopped the wagon often and allowed the team to rest. Annabelle had assured him that she had followed the same policy before he joined forces with them.

So the horses were in good shape, or at least as good a shape as they could be in, considering the heat and the poor graze and the distance they had covered.

But the best wagon team in the world couldn't outrun men on horseback for very long.

The Kid knew that. That was why he hoped they could reach the old homestead at Aleman before their pursuers caught up with them. If they were caught out in the open, they wouldn't have much chance of fighting off the attack.

He angled the buckskin closer to the galloping horses and took off his hat. He used the Stetson to swat the nearest member of the team on the rump and yelled, "Hyaaah! Hyaaah!" All the horses surged ahead a little faster.

The Kid twisted in the saddle to look back again. The dust cloud was visibly closer. He could make out dark specks at the base of it that were the riders whose mounts were kicking up all that dust.

But when he glanced ahead again, he saw a green blur on the horizon in the distance. Annabelle had mentioned that there were trees growing at Aleman. That might be it, he thought. He hoped so, and hoped as well that some of the walls of that old homestead were still standing.

Leaning forward in the saddle, he urged the buckskin on. His eyes were fixed on the clump of green, which grew steadily nearer. The Kid tried to keep his attention focused on that goal, but every minute or so, he couldn't resist the impulse to glance back.

Every time he did, the pursuit was closer.

The wagon swayed wildly as Annabelle kept the team moving at top speed. The effect of every little bump or rut was magnified. A new worry began to gnaw at The Kid's brain. If the wagon turned over, it was highly likely those water barrels lashed to its sides would burst open. That would be a catastrophe and would almost certainly doom them to a slow, lingering death by thirst.

But allowing their pursuers to catch up to them might be just as dangerous, he thought. Fortunato might keep them alive for a while, but The Kid had a feeling that if the Italian count got his hands on what he wanted, he wouldn't leave any witnesses behind to tell the story.

It was a calculated risk either way. The Kid didn't tell Annabelle to slow down. If Father Jardine knew any special prayers, he needed to be saying them. The horses pulling the wagon had about five minutes, maybe less, left in them at that speed.

Within a minute, The Kid began to make out individual trees. They were cottonwoods, which usually indicated the presence of water. He could understand why that would-be rancher had thought this might be a good place for a homestead. If it had worked out, the hombre would have had hundreds of square miles to himself. Nobody else wanted the range out there—and, as it turned out, for good reason.

He spotted some ruins among the trees and called to Annabelle, "There! Head for those walls! Find the best cover you can!"

"What are you going to do?" she shouted back at them.

The Kid pulled his Winchester from the saddle boot. "Try to discourage those varmints!"

"You can't just start shooting at them!" Father Jardine cried. "You don't know that they mean us any harm!"

The Kid was about to reply that he thought chasing them was indication enough that the riders weren't their friends, but he didn't have to say even that much. He heard the faint popping of gunfire over the pounding of the horses' hooves.

"They're shooting at us, padre!" he shouted. "That's plenty reason for me!"

He hauled on the reins and wheeled the buckskin around in a wide circle as the wagon raced toward the ruins at Aleman. As the horse came to a stop under him, The Kid lifted the rifle to his shoulder and began cranking off rounds toward the onrushing horsebackers as fast as he could work the weapon's lever. He wasn't trying for accuracy, since the riders were still several hundred yards away, and he didn't even care if he hit any of them—although a lucky shot or two that knocked a couple of them out of the saddle would be welcome. He was just trying to get their attention and maybe slow them down a mite.

More shots came from the pursuers, but they fell short, kicking up dust about fifty yards in front of The Kid. He supposed his bullets were landing short of the attackers, too. He raised the barrel of his rifle several inches and fired again.

The adjustment was rewarded by the sight of one of the riders suddenly leaning far back in his saddle, then toppling off. The Kid knew his shot had scored a hit. It was ninety-nine percent luck, of course, but he would take it.

The puffs of dust from the pursuers' slugs hitting the ground were getting closer. The Kid whirled the buckskin and dug his boot heels into the horse's flanks. The buckskin leaped into a gallop again as The Kid pounded after the wagon. Bullets fired by the riders continued to seek him, but he outran all of them.

Dust swirled up from the wagon wheels as Annabelle sent the vehicle racing behind the walls of the old homestead. Those walls had crumbled in places, although they were largely intact. There was no roof on the building, nor any doors or windows in the openings. The Kid supposed the rancher hadn't gotten that far in his construction project. The walls were made of adobe and appeared to be pretty thick. The Kid was glad to see that. A thick adobe wall would stop a bullet every time.

By the time he rode around the old house, Annabelle and Father Jardine had climbed down from the wagon seat. The Kid swung out of the saddle while the buckskin was still skidding to a halt. He waved toward the ruins and called, "Get inside! Stay low!"

Father Jardine hurried into the building, but Annabelle ran to the back of the wagon and reached over the tailgate. The Kid was about to yell at her again to get behind some cover, but then she brought her hand out of the wagon with a rifle in it. She obviously intended to do her part in mounting a defense, and considering the way she had fought when those Apaches attacked them, The Kid wasn't surprised.

"Find a window," he told her as they both ducked through an empty door into the ruins. "We can hold them off from in here."

Father Jardine stood with his back against a wall between two windows. His eyes were closed and his lips were moving. The Kid hoped the priest could do enough praying for all three of them, because he figured he and Annabelle would be a mite busy shooting for a while.

He knelt at one of the windows and poked the Winchester's barrel over the sill. The riders were still charging toward the ruins.

"Let 'em have it!" he told Annabelle.

The whipcrack reports of rifle shots echoed from the old walls as The Kid and Annabelle both opened fire. The Kid's Winchester clicked on an empty chamber after four rounds. He reached in his pocket, dug out a handful of fresh cartridges, and began thumbing them through the loading gate. He filled the magazine, then began firing again.

The riders spread out and began to turn back. The Kid couldn't tell if he and Annabelle had downed any more of them. It was hard to tell because of the dust, but he thought there were about half a dozen men out there. Those weren't terrible odds, considering that he and his companions had a fairly strong defensive position.

Then a potentially fatal weakness occurred to him, and he bit back a curse as he turned away from the window.

"Kid, what is it?" Annabelle called.

"I have to do something with the wagon and the team," he said. "We can't let those bastards get at them."

"The water!" Annabelle said in a voice choked with horror. "If they shot the water barrels—"

The Kid didn't hear the rest of it. He ran out the

door on the other side of the ruins, where they had left the wagon and the team.

There was another old building about fifty yards away that had crumbled even more. It must have been intended to be the barn, he thought, because the opening in the front of it was wide enough for two big doors. More importantly, it was wide enough for the wagon to fit through it.

The Kid turned and called over his shoulder to Annabelle, "There's an old barn over there! I'm going to put the wagon in it. Come on while we've got the chance!"

The riders had pulled back to regroup and figure out what they were going to do next, but The Kid knew it wouldn't be long before they attacked again. He grabbed the harness of one of the lead horses and tugged the animal toward the old, abandoned barn. The rest of the team followed.

The Kid heard a couple of shots behind him as he led the horses toward the barn. Then Annabelle and Father Jardine ran out of the house and hurried after the wagon.

"I gave them a couple shots to keep them thinking," Annabelle said. "That might delay them a few more seconds."

"We can use all the seconds we can get," The Kid agreed.

They were about halfway to the barn when Father Jardine cried, "Here they come again!"

The Kid heard the shots but kept his attention

focused on the job at hand, which was getting the wagon—and those precious water barrels—safely behind some thick walls.

"Go ahead!" he called to his companions. "Get inside the barn!"

"You go, Father," Annabelle said. "I'll hold them off."

She turned, lifted the rifle to her shoulder, and began firing again. The Kid didn't hold the curse back this time as he looked over his shoulder and saw what she was doing. Standing out there in the open like that, she was a perfect target.

For some reason, no shots came anywhere near her. The Kid expected slugs to kick up dust around her feet, but it didn't happen. It was almost like the pursuers were deliberately trying not to shoot her.

As soon as that thought went through his head, The Kid knew it was true. He knew, as well, that those gunmen worked for Count Eduardo Fortunato. The count wanted Annabelle alive, because she knew where to look for the Konigsberg Candlestick and the secret of the Twelve Pearls. The same probably held true for Father Jardine.

He was the only one who was truly expendable, The Kid thought with a grim smile as he led the horses through the opening where the barn's double doors should have been. He whistled for the buckskin to follow them into the barn.

One wall was still mostly intact. The Kid led the

team over to it. That would give the wagon the most protection possible in those ruins. He left it there and ran back to the entrance, where Father Jardine waited.

"Go get under the wagon and stay there, Father," The Kid said. "Unless you want to grab a gun and join the fight."

"You know I can't do that, Mr. Morgan."

"Then stay out of the way," The Kid said. He didn't mean to be rude about it, but he wasn't going to waste any time trying to spare the priest's feelings.

He looked out and saw Annabelle backing toward the barn, still firing the rifle as she retreated. The riders dashed toward the old house where The Kid and his companions had first taken shelter. Annabelle tried to keep them from reaching the cover, but they galloped behind the ruins too fast for her to stop them.

"Come on!" The Kid called. "Get in here, Doctor!"

Annabelle turned and ran toward the barn entrance. At the same time, shots blasted from the corner of the house as some of the enemy threw lead at The Kid as he stood there. He ducked back as dust and chips of adobe flew into the air where the slugs smacked into the wall beside his head.

Then Annabelle let out a sharp cry and fell, sprawling facedown on the ground ten yards short of the barn.

Chapter 25

"Son of a *bitch!*" Thomas Novak grated between clenched teeth. "You weren't supposed to shoot the girl, Wesley!"

The snake-eyed youngster turned his head and glanced at Novak. "I didn't," he said. "I was aiming at the hombre in the barn. Didn't come anywhere close to the girl."

"Maybe one of the others winged her. I hope she's not hurt too bad. That fella Fortunato won't like it if she is."

"Wait a minute," Wesley said as he and Novak crouched at one corner of the ruins. "She's on her feet again."

Novak was glad to see that. He watched as Dr. Dare limped into the barn. He hated to let her get under cover like that, but there was no way they could stop her without shooting her, and Fortunato had made it clear that the redheaded young woman had to survive, along with the priest. That made the job a lot harder . . . but they would be getting well paid for it, Novak supposed.

Bayne and Hobart had gone to the other end of the old building. Green was still coming up with the pack animals and the extra horses, and Donaldson was with him, nursing the wounded arm that had gotten ventilated while they were chasing their quarry.

And somewhere back there were Count Fortunato and that prissy, smart-ass servant of his. Novak figured they would stay well out of the line of fire and show up after the fighting was over.

The next couple of minutes proved him wrong. He heard hoofbeats and looked over his shoulder to see Fortunato approaching the ruins at a gallop, trailed by a wildly bouncing Arturo. The two men hauled back on their reins and brought their horses to a stop, Arturo shouting frantically, "Whoa! Whoa!" as he did so.

Fortunato dismounted and came over to the corner where Novak and Wesley waited. Arturo remained in the saddle, slumped forward over the horn as he clutched it and tried to catch his breath.

"Where are they?" Fortunato demanded.

"In that old barn over yonder," Novak replied as he inclined his head in that direction. "They were able to get the wagon in there before we could stop them."

"So they have plenty of water and supplies."

Novak shrugged.

"This is a standoff, then," Fortunato said, anger edging into his tone. "I had hoped that you could prevent them from reaching shelter."

"I hoped so, too," Novak said. He kept a tight rein on his temper and told himself not to let the count's arrogant attitude get under his skin. "But they saw us coming up behind them too soon. We just didn't have time to catch them before they got here."

"What about Dr. Dare and the priest? Are they both all right?"

Novak hesitated. If he told Fortunato that the woman might be wounded, the Italian would probably fly off the handle. Anyway, Dr. Dare had gotten up and hustled on into the old barn under her own power. She'd been limping, but other than that she'd appeared to be all right. If she was injured, chances were that it wasn't too bad.

"They're fine as far as I know," he said, then glanced at Wesley to make sure the young killer wouldn't contradict him. Wesley was watching the barn, though, and didn't seem to be paying any attention to the conversation between Novak and Fortunato.

The count grunted. "Good. It's possible they may have written down what I need to know, but we can't depend on that. I need them alive."

"What about the other hombre?" Novak asked. "I know you said before that you were curious about him, but he wounded one of my men at long range. He may be too good with a gun. We may have to kill him to take him down."

"Do what must be done," Fortunato said. "My ultimate goal is much more important than any curiosity I may have about that stranger."

Novak nodded. "All right. We'll have to figure

out a way to smoke them out of there. Right now, it's a standoff, like you said, Count."

From horseback, Arturo said, "If I might . . . make a suggestion?" He was still a little breathless from the hard ride.

Fortunato and Novak both turned to look at the servant in surprise.

Arturo went on, "It appears that only Dr. Dare and the young man were firing at you and your men, Mr. Novak. I doubt if the priest's moral code will allow him to use firearms."

"So?" Novak said.

"That means they can only defend two sides of their shelter at once. It has four sides, does it not?"

Novak frowned. "You mean we should split up and come at them from all four directions at once?"

"It strikes me as a strategem that would have considerable chances for success. All you need to do is get one man into the barn so that he can kill the stranger, and then Dr. Dare and the priest will have no choice but to surrender."

Fortunato said, "You underestimate Dr. Dare, Arturo. As you said, she was using a gun, too."

"But surely she would be disheartened by her ally's demise. If she has an advanced university degree in history, she must be intelligent enough to know that she stands no chance of defending herself and Father Jardine successfully without the help of their unknown friend."

Novak rubbed his lantern jaw in thought. "I don't much like the idea of splitting up . . ."

"A general dividing his forces to attack from more than one direction is a time-honored military tactic," Arturo insisted. "I've read a number of books on military strategy."

Novak looked at Fortunato. "What do you think, Count?"

"We have them outnumbered by four to one," Fortunato said. "It seems foolish not to take advantage of that superiority."

"Four to one? I make it three to one, once Green and Donaldson get here."

Fortunato shook his head. "No, there will be eight of us if Arturo and I join in the attack."

"Wait just a moment, Excellency!" Arturo exclaimed. "I never said that *I* should take part, let alone yourself—"

A wolfish grin spread across Fortunato's face as he said, "No, you're right, Arturo. Splitting our forces is indeed a good tactic. Now get that gun of yours out, because you're going to get to see first-hand how it works."

The Kid's heart had leaped into his throat when he saw Annabelle go down. Despite knowing that it was the wrong thing to do, his instincts were about to send him dashing into the open to help her, when she looked up and called to him, "I'm all right."

Then she scrambled to her feet and ran into the barn, although she was limping rather heavily and wincing as she hurried inside.

The Kid reached out, caught hold of her arm, and pulled her into the shelter of the wall beside him. "What happened?" he asked her. "Are you hit?"

Annabelle shook her head as she leaned against the adobe wall. "I just tripped, damn it!" She glanced over at the priest. "Sorry, Father."

"It's all right," Father Jardine said. "I understand how upset you are, Doctor, and I'm quite certain the Lord does, too."

"I twisted my ankle when I fell," Annabelle went on. "I feel so stupid."

"No harm done . . . except to your ankle," The Kid told her. "When I saw you go down, I figured you'd been shot. That came as quite a surprise, the way they've been trying so hard to keep that from happening."

She frowned at him. "What do you mean?"

"Fortunato's men were shooting at me, not you," The Kid said. "They were being careful not to get any lead anywhere close to you, even though you were shooting at them. The count doesn't want anything happening to you."

Annabelle thought it over, then nodded. "No, I suppose not. He doesn't know exactly where to look for the candlestick, like Father Jardine and I do. That means we're safe, for the time being." Her eyes widened as something occurred to her. "I'll bet he was shooting at *you* that day. He wasn't trying to shoot me at all!"

The Kid nodded. "Yeah, I reckon you can bet your hat on that one. I thought about that, too."

"So you nearly got me killed!"

"After saving you from those other varmints who were trying to capture you," The Kid pointed out.

"Well . . . there is that," Annabelle admitted.

"And how long do you think you and the padre would live if Fortunato got his hands on what he's after?"

"Not long. Our usefulness would be at an end then, wouldn't it?"

"It sure would," The Kid said.

"Then the thing to do is stay out of his hands. The best way to accomplish that is by killing him."

"Doctor!" Father Jardine said.

"I'm sorry, Father, but it's true. Anyway, how many deaths has the Church been responsible for over the centuries, in order to accomplish what was thought to be a greater good? How many died in the Inquisition?"

"I'm not going to have this argument with you," Father Jardine said stiffly. "The things that were done in the past were done for good reasons."

The Kid couldn't think of a reason good enough for tearing somebody apart on the rack or burning anybody at the stake. He fully believed that some hombres were flat-out evil enough they deserved to die, but a hangrope, or better yet, a bullet in the brain would do the job just fine.

But like the priest said, those were arguments for another time. Right now, they had to concentrate on staying alive.

"It's fine to talk about killing Fortunato," he said, "but how are we going to do that? They have us pinned down here, and outnumbered, to boot."

"Yes, but I know enough about Fortunato to know that he's not a patient man," Annabelle said. "They could try to wait us out, but they're bound to know that we have plenty of supplies and water. We may have more than they do. So a siege isn't going to work. They have to try to take advantage of their superior numbers."

The Kid agreed with her. Those thoughts had started to form in his mind, too.

"So you think they'll attack?" he said.

"That's right. I realize you know more about this sort of thing than I do, Mr. Morgan, but that makes sense to me."

The Kid nodded. "To me, too. That means we're going to have to move fast."

"What are we going to do?"

The Kid looked around at the crumbling old barn. With no roof, and with three of the four walls having partially collapsed, they didn't have much cover except for the mostly intact wall right in front of them. He knew what he would do if he were ramrodding the bunch of gun-wolves Fortunato had hired.

"They'll split up and come at us from all four directions at once," he said. "We won't be able to stop them when they do."

Annabelle paled, making the band of freckles across her nose stand out more. "You're saying it's hopeless?"

The Kid shook his head. "No, I'm saying we're going to have to do something they don't expect, and we need to do it fast." He looked over at Father Jardine. "Father, if I give you my rifle, will you—"

He stopped short as the priest began shaking his head.

"Blast it, let me finish!" The Kid said. "Will you use it to fire over their heads, to make them think that I'm still here?"

Father Jardine frowned. "I don't like the idea of using a firearm at all, but I suppose I could do that."

"Where are you going to be?" Annabelle asked The Kid. "You're not going to abandon us, are you?"

"You know better than that," The Kid snapped. "But I'm not going to be where those hombres think I am."

Chapter 26

He left the Winchester with Father Jardine, who handled the rifle gingerly. Nobody was going to mistake the way he used it for the way The Kid would handle the weapon, at least not for very long.

But they didn't need the ruse to succeed for very long, he thought as he slid over the crumbling rear wall of the barn and ran in a low crouch toward a clump of mesquite and cottonwood about fifty yards away.

The Kid had been keeping an eye on the old homestead and knew that all of Fortunato's men were still hidden behind it. The gunfire had stopped as each side tensely watched the other.

But that meant Fortunato's men couldn't see what was happening directly behind the barn. They couldn't see him going over the wall and making his way into the concealment of the trees and brush. When he reached the cottonwoods, he turned and dropped to the ground so that he was looking back toward the barn.

If the boss gunman split his force, as The Kid fully expected him to do, the killers would circle wide around the old barn and then attack from all four directions at once. Would they launch their attack on horseback or on foot?

The Kid didn't know. Either way, he would have

to deal with it. One thing was for sure—they wouldn't be expecting him to be out there.

As that thought went through his head, Annabelle and Father Jardine opened fire again from inside the barn. The Kid had told them to position themselves on either side of the door and just take potshots at the house so the gunmen would know there were still two defenders in there. Chances were, they wouldn't suspect that Father Jardine was one of them.

The priest was worried that he might accidentally hit one of their enemies with his shots. The Kid figured that was highly unlikely, but he would consider it a stroke of good luck if it happened. Father Jardine wouldn't, but that was his problem.

The Kid's problem was keeping all three of them alive until they found what Annabelle and the padre were after . . . and beyond that, too.

As he watched, he saw dust rising on the other side of the old homestead. He wasn't sure what caused that, unless Fortunato's men had brought some extra horses with them and one of the hired guns was bringing them up now. The Kid heard hoofbeats and took that as an indication that his guess was correct.

But the dust continued to rise, and he still heard horses running. What in blazes was going on over there? he wondered with a puzzled frown.

There was a hot wind out of the south, as there nearly always was at that time of year in the hellish wasteland, and as The Kid watched, the dust cloud continued to grow and began to drift toward the barn.

The tricky sons of bitches! he thought. They were running their horses around and around to raise that cloud of dust, knowing that the wind would carry it over the barn and obscure the vision of the defenders. That would allow Fortunato's men to split up and come at the ruins from different directions without being seen. Somebody in that bunch knew how to use his brain.

The Kid could only hope that having the element of surprise on his side would be enough to keep the odds from being overpowering.

Annabelle and Father Jardine continued to fire their rifles inside the barn as the dust drifted over it, making it hard for The Kid to see them anymore. He knew they would be able to see even less. A moment later, two men darted into view from his right, carrying guns and angling toward the back of the barn.

Colt in hand, he stood up and called, "Hey!"

The men skidded to a halt and turned toward him, alarm etched on their hardbitten, beardstubbled faces. They swung their guns around.

That was as much chance as The Kid gave them. More chance than hired killers deserved. He fired, putting a slug in the chest of the nearest gunman, then switched his aim and triggered twice more at the second man, whose well-honed reflexes allowed him to get a shot of his own off before The Kid's bullets ripped into his body. The slug whipped past The Kid's head and thudded into the trunk of a cottonwood behind him.

Both gunmen were down, writhing in pain as blood welled from their wounds and life fled from their bodies. The Kid ran forward. He scooped up one of the fallen guns and kicked the other well out of reach of the man who had dropped it. Then he cut to his left to meet the attack that had to be coming from that direction. Annabelle and Father Jardine would have to hold the others off for a few minutes.

The rest of the hired gunmen had waited for a shot to serve as a signal for the attack to begin, as a volley of shots thundered through the air, the reports coming from several directions at once. The Kid reached the rear corner of one of the collapsed walls, dropped to a knee beside it, and leveled the guns in his hands. Two shapes loomed out of the dust cloud, flame gouting from the muzzles of their guns. The Kid pressed the triggers. The irons bucked and roared as he fired.

One of the men spun off his feet as The Kid's bullets pounded into him. The other stumbled but stayed on his feet. He snapped a shot at The Kid that struck the adobe wall and sprayed chips of it into The Kid's face. That made him duck and hold his fire for a second, and that was long enough for the man to turn and retreat. His figure, blurred by the dust in the air, disappeared.

The Kid didn't like it that one of the enemy had gotten away, but there was nothing he could do about it. At that moment, from inside the old barn, Annabelle cried desperately, "Kid!"

He vaulted over the crumbling wall and ran toward the sound of that frantic cry. Dust still blew over the ruins, making it hard to see. He made out a couple of struggling figures and realized that Annabelle was fighting with someone. The man wrenched the rifle out of her hands and shoved her to the ground, then spun toward The Kid.

For a split-second, the air cleared enough for The Kid to get a glimpse of a young, cruel face with dark, flint-like eyes. Then three shots roared out, all of them coming at the same instant so that they sounded like one.

The young killer staggered to the side, the crimson flower of a bloodstain spreading on his shirt front. He tried to lift his gun, but before he could pull the trigger, The Kid and Annabelle both fired again. The bullets drove into the gunman's chest and knocked him backward off his feet.

The man had taken the rifle away from Annabelle, but she still had the Colt Lightning, and the revolver was in her hand. She had used it to help gun down the young killer. The Kid reached her side and dropped the empty gun in his left hand so he could take hold of her arm and help her to her feet. She leaned against him, panting from fear and exertion.

The Kid's eyes darted around, searching for his next target. He didn't see anything except the swirling dust.

"Are you hit?" he asked Annabelle.

"No, I'm all right. What about you?"

"I'm fine. Where's the padre?"

"The last time I saw him, he was still over by the entrance."

The Kid turned in that direction. The dust was beginning to clear slightly, so he could make out the opening where double doors would have hung if the barn had ever been completed. He didn't see Father Jardine anywhere around it. Alarm leaped through him.

"He's not there," he told Annabelle.

"What?" she gasped.

The Kid pushed her against the adobe wall and said, "Stay here, and keep the wall at your back. I'll find him."

Knowing her personality, he halfway expected her to argue, but she just called, "Be careful, Kid," as he ran toward the entrance.

He was pretty sure they had accounted for four of their enemies. He didn't know how many that left, but from what he had seen of the group earlier, he thought there couldn't be more than another four or five of them, and at least one of them was wounded. He and Annabelle had cut the enemy in half—but they were still outnumbered.

"Padre!" The Kid called as he came up to the entrance. "Father Jardine!"

No answer came back.

The Kid leaned against the wall and checked his gun. He thumbed fresh cartridges into the cylinder to replace the expended ones. Then, moving fast, he went out of the barn in a low crouch and swept the Colt from side to side.

He didn't see anything, but he heard something. Hoofbeats.

It sounded like Fortunato's men were leaving.

There was only one explanation that made any sense, and The Kid didn't like it one damned bit. He ran toward the homestead where he and his companions had first taken shelter. No gunshots met him, but he still wasn't completely convinced this wasn't a trap.

He reached the building and pressed his back against the wall, holding the gun up beside his ear. He listened but didn't hear anything except the faint sigh of the wind and the fading sound of hoofbeats to the west. He edged along the wall until he came to the doorway, then stopped to listen again. Still nothing anywhere close. Silence hung over the abandoned homestead. The Kid turned and started to step through the doorway.

But then some instinct warned him, and even as alarm bells sounded in his mind, he knew he had inherited that trait from Frank Morgan. No man could live such a dangerous life as The Drifter for so long and not have an uncanny, almost supernatural ability to sense danger. Without really thinking about what he was doing, The Kid reached up with his free hand, snatched his hat off his head, and sent it sailing through the opening in front of him.

A gun blasted to his left as the taut nerves of the man waiting there to bushwhack him snapped and caused him to fire at the hat. The Kid had followed the Stetson in a rolling dive that brought him to a stop on his belly, facing the man who'd tried to ambush him. Tilting the barrel of the Colt upward, he slammed two swift shots into the bushwhacker, driving him back against the adobe wall behind him. The man hung there for a moment, eyes wide with shock and pain, as the gun in his hand slipped out of his nerveless fingers and thudded to the sandy ground.

Then the man slid down the wall, leaving a bloody smear on the adobe, and came to rest in a sitting position against it. His head drooped forward, but his eyes were still open. The Kid came quickly to his feet and hurried over to the dying man. The bloody froth on the man's lips told The Kid that his bullets had punctured the man's lungs, and the hombre would soon drown in his own blood.

But he wasn't dead yet. The Kid kicked the fallen gun out of reach, then knelt beside the man, took hold of his shock of white hair, and pulled his head up. The man had the weathered face of an old-timer. There was a fresh bloodstain on his side, and The Kid figured this was the man he had wounded a few minutes earlier. The others had left him there to try an ambush while they rode off.

Leaning close, The Kid said, "Fortunato's got the priest, doesn't he?"

The man blinked watery blue eyes and looked surprised. "You know about . . . Fortunato?"

"Damn right I do," The Kid said.

"Who . . . who are you?"

"Never mind that. Just answer my question. Does Fortunato have Father Jardine?"

"Why should I . . . tell you anything?"

"Because I'll give you some water and make you comfortable while you're waiting to die," The Kid said. "That's all anybody can do for you now, mister."

"You can . . . go to hell." A harsh laugh bubbled from the man's bloody lips. "I'll be . . . waitin' there . . . for you."

The Kid's mouth tightened in a grim line. "Shot the way you are, it's going to take you a long time to die, mister," he said. He put the muzzle of the Colt against the man's right knee. "You can spend it in a lot more pain than you have to, if that's the way you want it."

The man's eyes widened even more. "You . . . you wouldn't . . ."

"You've got two knees," The Kid pointed out. "And two elbows and ankles and wrists—"

"You son of a bitch! You snake-blooded bastard!" The man leaned forward and coughed, spewing more blood over his shirt front. "Yeah, Novak grabbed . . . the priest . . . Fortunato said . . . he could tell 'em where to go . . . Said . . . they'll get there . . . first . . ."

The Kid had already figured that out, but hearing it put into words just made the situation seem even worse. He took the gun away from the man's knee and slid it back into leather.

The man blinked up at him. "How about that water . . . you promised m—"

His head fell forward again. The Kid didn't bother raising it. The man was dead.

Annabelle said, "You told him he would take a long time to die."

The Kid jerked his head around and saw her standing behind him, the Lightning in her hand. "What are you doing here?" he asked her. "I told you to stay in the barn."

"I heard shots, and you didn't come back. I had to see if you were all right."

He straightened to his feet. "Yeah, I'm fine."

"You threatened to shoot that man in the knee."

"Yeah, well, I wanted to get him to talk, and I knew he didn't have much time left. He was hurt too bad to realize that."

"So you lied to him. About how long he had to

live, and about threatening to shoot him again."

"Yeah, whatever you say." The Kid stepped away from the body and picked up the hat he had tossed through the opening to draw the bushwhacker's fire. As he settled it on his head, he went on, "You heard what he said, about Fortunato and the others capturing Father Jardine?"

She nodded. "What are we going to do, Mr. Morgan?"

"Only one thing we can do," The Kid said as he walked out of the homestead and started looking around. He hoped that Fortunato's men had left a horse here for the old-timer. If they hadn't, then Annabelle would have to ride one of the horses from the wagon team.

She limped after him and demanded, "Well, are you going to tell me what you're talking about?"

"Does the padre know how to find the stuff that old German hid?"

"We've discussed it. He knows what landmarks to look for. I still have all the notes I took when I was reading through those old documents in Mexico City, though."

The Kid nodded. "Maybe that'll give us a little bit of an edge. We'll need it . . . because the only way to save Father Jardine and keep Fortunato from getting those artifacts is to find them first."

Chapter 27

Over the years, Count Eduardo Fortunato had learned that a man's luck was seldom all good or all bad. It was a mixture, and that had held true today.

The bad luck was that he had lost four out of the six men he had hired to help him in this quest. Novak and the gunman called Green were the only ones still alive, and Green was wounded. Donaldson, Wesley, Hobart, and Bayne were dead. At least, that was what Novak had told the count. Green was wounded badly enough that he might not live. That was why Novak had left him behind with orders to ambush and kill that deadly young stranger.

"Then you can catch up to us," Novak had told Green. Later, though, as they were riding away, Novak had shaken his head and said to Fortunato, "I don't reckon we'll ever see him again, even if he does get lucky and kill that bastard. He's not going to pull through."

The good luck was that during the confusion of the attack, Novak had managed to capture the priest. Once they had Father Jardine in their power, Fortunato had called off the attack and ordered them to fall back. The priest would lead them to Albrecht Konigsberg's hidden treasure, and they would reach it long before Dr. Dare and her ally could get there with the wagon.

Fortunato, Arturo, Novak, and Father Jardine rode west for half a mile or so after leaving the old homestead at Aleman, then turned north again. That took them around any remaining threat from Dr. Dare and her companion . . . not that Fortunato considered them any real danger anymore. He was confident that he had won. Now all he had to do was finish the job.

Novak led two extra horses, and Fortunato led two more. Arturo held the reins of the pack animals. They would continue to switch mounts frequently, so that they could move fast. He would have brought more of the horses, but Novak thought that having to keep up with the animals would just slow them down.

Father Jardine slumped forward in the saddle, a picture of despair and dejection. Fortunato urged his horse alongside the priest's and said, "Don't worry, Father. You'll be fine."

"I'm not worried about myself," Father Jardine said without looking up. "I'm concerned for Dr. Dare and Mr. Morgan."

"Morgan?" Novak repeated. "Not *Frank* Morgan?"

The surprise in the gunman's voice was enough to finally make Father Jardine raise his head. "I don't know the man's given name," he said. "He told us he was called Kid Morgan."

Novak pursed his lips in thought. He didn't look happy.

"Who's this Frank Morgan?" Fortunato asked.

"He's a gunfighter," Novak replied. "Some say the last of the old-time gunfighters. He's mighty fast on the draw. Not only that, he's smart and plenty tough, despite the fact that he's getting up there in years."

Father Jardine shook his head. "That's not the Morgan I know. Kid Morgan is a young man, still in his twenties."

"Yeah, but I've heard of him, too. Nobody knows where he came from, but he's made a rep for himself in a short time. A few months ago, he gunned down Clay Lasswell, and Lasswell was fast, mighty fast. Same thing goes for Jack Trace, and Morgan got him."

"Is he connected somehow to this other Morgan?" Fortunato asked.

"*Quien sabe?* Who knows? Morgan's not an unusual name. But it doesn't matter, because Kid Morgan's bad enough news all by himself. Green won't stand much of a chance against him."

Fortunato's face hardened. "Then it's possible he and Dr. Dare will be coming after us."

"Yeah, I reckon it is. But there's no way they can catch us in that wagon."

Arturo spoke up, saying, "What if they don't take the wagon?"

The others turned to look at him.

The servant went on, "I assume this Mr. Kid Morgan has a horse of his own, and we left a number of other saddle mounts back there. They might decide to abandon the wagon, take as much food and water as they can carry, and pursue us to our destination."

"He's right," Novak said. "We'd better not waste any time getting where we're going."

Fortunato thought about that and nodded. He had intended to put some more miles behind them before they stopped again, since there was still an hour or so of daylight left, but it might be better to go ahead and do what needed to be done now. Besides, he had just spotted something that would make the task simpler.

He reined in and motioned for the others to stop as well. As they did, the count said, "Father Jardine, the time has come for you to tell us what you know."

The old priest just smiled at him. "I'll never tell you anything, Count. The Lord will give me the strength to withstand whatever you do to me."

Fortunato shook his head. "You misunderstand, Father. I'm not going to do anything to you."

"Oh, my word!" Arturo exclaimed. "You're not going to order *me* to torture him, are you, Excellency?"

"Of course not," Fortunato said. He lifted a hand and pointed. "They're going to do it."

The others turned and saw the two half-breed Yaqui trackers riding toward them. Fortunato had noticed the Indians a moment earlier. They had come and gone like phantoms during the pursuit of the wagon, appearing to tell Fortunato that they were still on the right trail, then vanishing again. And they had refused to take part in the attack on the homestead. Fortunato had been angry about that, but he understood. The Yaquis had been hired for their tracking abilities, not as fighters. Novak and his men were supposed to handle that part of it.

But they were Yaquis. They would torture a priest for free, and judging by the pallor that had appeared on Father Jardine's face, he seemed to know that.

"Well, Father, it's up to you," Fortunato said with a cruel smile. "Shall we find out just how much strength the Lord can actually give you . . . or will you tell me what I want to know?"

Fortunato's men should have scattered the horses they left behind, but luckily for The Kid and Annabelle, they hadn't taken the time to do that. The extra horses had wandered off a ways, probably spooked by all the shooting, but once The Kid was mounted on the buckskin again, it took him only a few minutes to round up four of the animals.

"That'll give us each two saddle mounts, and we'll take one along for a pack horse," he explained to Annabelle as they went through the supplies in the wagon, deciding what to take with them. "That means we'll be on short rations, because we want to load as many full canteens as we can on that pack animal. The water's more important than food. We're both healthy enough we won't starve to death in a week."

"It'll just feel like we're going to if we run out of food," Annabelle said.

"When you set out after the Konigsberg Candlestick, nobody told you it was going to be easy, Doctor."

Annabelle took a side of salt pork wrapped in oil-cloth from a crate and slipped it into one of the saddlebags they were using for supplies. "I think we've been traveling together long enough that you could call me by my name, Kid. I'm Annabelle, and you are . . . ?"

"I told you my name."

"Oh, come now. Surely your parents didn't call you 'Kid'. You must have an actual name."

"Kid will do fine."

He knew his tone was curt. He couldn't help it. His *parents* hadn't named him, because Frank Morgan hadn't even known that Vivian was pregnant when her father ended the marriage and Frank was forced to leave Texas to keep from causing more trouble for her. His mother had dubbed him Conrad, and he had taken the last name of the man who married her and raised him, the man he'd believed was his real father until he was almost grown.

He had given himself the name Kid Morgan, when he needed a new identity to help him avenge the great wrong that had been done to him, and it was as good as any, he supposed.

That vengeance quest was in the past now, and while it was something he'd had to do, it hadn't really changed anything. The losses he had suffered were as painful as ever, but he was learning to live with that pain. There were moments when he could smile and laugh again, despite the hurt.

But he was damned if he would let anyone into his heart again, and he meant that thought literally. He *would* be damned. He was willing to help people who needed his help, and he might even come to care for them, but he couldn't allow *them* to care for *him*. He had to keep them at arm's length, so that when they went away, as they inevitably would, it wouldn't hurt as bad. Even when he was traveling with someone, as he was now, inside he still rode alone.

And he always would.

"Let's get these canteens filled, Doctor," he went on. "We need to get moving as quickly as we can."

"Of course," Annabelle said, her voice stiff with hurt and resentment.

They draped a dozen full canteens over the back of the pack horse, then Annabelle opened a trunk in the wagon and took out several leather notebooks. "All the information we need to find Konigsberg's cache is in here," she said as she put them in the saddlebags with the food and ammunition they had loaded earlier. "I've studied it enough that I know all of it by heart, but if something were to happen to me, you'll need it to find the candlestick and whatever else Konigsberg hid."

The Kid frowned. "You expect me to go on and find those things even if something happens to you?"

"Of course. What did you intend to do in a case like that?"

"Well . . . I hadn't really thought about it. I suppose I'd just kill Fortunato and whoever's left that's working for him."

"And that would accomplish exactly what?"

"I don't know, but I'm not a priest or a professor. What do I need with some dusty old artifacts?"

"You can take them to Santa Fe and turn them over to church authorities there. I'm sure you'd be amply rewarded for their safe return."

The Kid grunted. More money was one thing he didn't need, but Annabelle didn't know that. For all she knew, he was just a penniless drifter.

"Let's just keep you alive," he said. "Then we won't have to worry about that."

He had unhitched the wagon team, and when he and Annabelle were ready to leave the old homestead, she asked, "What about those horses? What's going to happen to them?"

"They'll drift back south to Paraje Perillo," The Kid told her. "There's enough graze along the way to keep them going, and they can make it that long without water as long as they're not pulling the wagon. I reckon the other horses from Fortunato's bunch that we're not taking will go with them. We can pick them up on our way back through here, assuming nobody else finds them first."

"And assuming we come back this way."

"I can," The Kid said. "Just to make sure they're all right."

After a moment, Annabelle smiled and nodded. "That's good. I'd hate to think that anything happened to them because of us."

"They'll be all right," The Kid assured her. He didn't know that for a fact, but he didn't want her spending her time worrying about the horses, when it was entirely possible that the two of them, as well as Father Jardine, might not survive the next few days.

As they mounted up, he asked, "How long will it take us to get where we're going?"

"I had planned on four days by wagon."

"We'll do it in two," The Kid said.

"It's almost dark," Annabelle pointed out.

"We'll ride by night, at least part of the time. I can steer by the stars well enough to keep us heading north, and we're bound to run into that lava field if we keep going in that direction."

"That's right. Do you really think we can get there before Fortunato?"

"It'll be a good race," The Kid said, "but it's one that I intend to win."

Chapter 28

The Kid kept them moving far into the night, until Annabelle was so exhausted that she was swaying in the saddle and in danger of toppling off her horse. When he finally called a halt, he had to help her down to make sure she didn't fall when she tried to dismount.

She leaned against him wearily and said, "This isn't really proper anymore. I mean, for the two of us to be traveling together without Father Jardine as a chaperone."

"Your virtue is safe with me, Doctor," The Kid said. "Anyway, it's almost a modern new century. People aren't going to worry about such things anymore."

She laughed. "Believe me, Kid, people are always going to worry about whether some things are proper. I encountered that when I set out to earn my doctorate."

"You got it, didn't you?"

"Yes, with a lot of sheer stubbornness."

"I'd say you've still got that in spades. Not many women would set out into the Jornada del Muerto, whether they were professors or not."

She looked up at him for a long moment, but the night was too dark for him to be able to really read her expression. Then, with a sigh, she stepped back.

"I suppose we'll need to stand guard until morning."

"That's right. I'll take the first turn. You go ahead and get some sleep."

"I'd argue with you . . . but I'm too blasted tired."

A few minutes later, Annabelle was curled up in her blankets, and the soft, regular sound of her breathing told The Kid that she was asleep.

He woke her after a couple of hours, told her everything was quiet, and said, "It'll be dawn in about an hour. Wake me then."

"You're only going to sleep for an hour?" She stifled a yawn. "I got twice that much, and I'm still exhausted."

"I'll be fine," The Kid assured her. "We'll travel until midday, then take a break and sleep some more during the hottest part of the day. We can move on later in the afternoon."

"All right."

When she shook him awake, it seemed like he had barely closed his eyes. His eyeballs felt like they had been plucked from their sockets, rolled around in the sand, and then shoved back into his head. Several cups of hot coffee helped a little with that sensation.

At midday, The Kid found a clump of mesquite that didn't have any rattlesnakes in it and told Annabelle to crawl under the scrubby trees and get some sleep. The mesquites didn't provide a lot of shade, but out there, at that time of day, any shade was better than none.

He let her sleep until he was nodding off, then woke her. "Any sign of Fortunato?" she asked as she came out from under the mesquites.

The Kid shook his head. "I haven't seen anybody or anything moving around here."

"Is that because we're ahead of them, or because they're ahead of us?"

"There's no way of knowing. I haven't spotted their tracks, but it's a big desert. They could still be west of us somewhere."

"That would mean they'd have farther to go to reach the spot in the lava field that was described in that old journal." Annabelle paused. "Do you think Father Jardine might be leading them astray on purpose?"

"It's possible," The Kid said. "If he is, though, and if Fortunato realizes that . . ." He shook his head. "Well, I wouldn't want to be the padre."

"He's a brave man, to set out on a mission like that at his age."

"He had his orders, didn't he?"

"Yes, but that doesn't mean he's any less coura-geous for carrying them out."

"Yeah, you're right about that," The Kid admitted. "He's got the courage of his convictions, that's for sure. I never saw a man so stubborn about doing what he thinks is the right thing." He paused and thought about Frank. "Well, maybe one."

He slept for several hours under the mesquites and felt better when he woke up. The sun had begun to dip toward the western horizon, and the air wasn't quite as blisteringly hot as it had been earlier, when he went to sleep.

"Everything still peaceful?" he asked Annabelle.

She nodded. "Yes, I haven't seen or heard anything. Are we going to ride all night again?"

"Most of it, I expect."

"Then if we push on all day, we might be able to reach the lava field by nightfall tomorrow."

The Kid nodded. "That's the plan. If they beat us there . . . we'll know that we did the best that we and the horses could do, anyway."

"That's not going to be enough."

"No," The Kid agreed. "It's not."

That night, under the light of a three-quarter moon, they came to a vast stretch of utterly flat, barren land. Nothing grew there, and cracks zigzagged crazily across the ground.

"Laguna del Muerto," Annabelle said. "It's an ancient dry lake bed. There's water here only when it rains, which it obviously hasn't for quite some time."

The Kid knew she was right. The ground was hard under the hooves of the horses, almost like stone. It took them about half an hour to cross it, and after that emptiness, The Kid was glad to see even the gnarled mesquites and the clumps of dry grass.

Switching horses regularly, they pushed on through the night, pausing to sleep for a short time, give the horses some water, and make a skimpy breakfast. The Caballo Mountains had fallen behind them, but as the sun climbed into the sky and they continued riding north, another mountain range rose to their left. Those were the Fra Cristobal Mountains, Annabelle explained, named after the same old Spanish missionary who had given his name to the waterhole somewhere ahead of them.

"The Jornada narrows down between the mountains and the lava flow," Annabelle said. "Fortunato and his men have to be either ahead of us or behind us now. They can't be paralleling us anymore."

"I'm going to vote for behind us," The Kid said.

She laughed. "I'm not sure you get a vote. That's not how it works."

"You don't think that we determine our own fate?"

"Well, that's not exactly the same thing, is it? Certainly, people have a degree of control over their lives, but not completely. Things can still come out of nowhere and change everything without any warning."

The Kid had reason to know the truth of that more so than most men, but he didn't say anything about his past. That was going to remain locked up inside him.

After spending so much time traveling through the gray and brown and tan landscape, the large area of black that appeared to the northeast that afternoon was a stark contrast. As The Kid reined in and studied it, Annabelle did likewise, saying, "That's the lava field. The malpais, as you called it. Scientists believe it's been there for hundreds of thousands of years, ever since a huge volcano north of here erupted."

"Not much chance of that happening again, is there?"

"Oh, no," she replied with a shake of her head. "All the volcanoes in this region are extinct now. The closest ones that might still erupt on occasion are down in Mexico, and even they're dormant."

"One less thing we have to worry about, then."

Annabelle smiled. "We should be thankful for small favors, is that it?"

The Kid just grinned back at her and hitched his horse into motion.

They angled toward the lava flow. During one of the stops to rest the horses, Annabelle knelt on the ground and used her finger to draw a crude map in the dirt, showing how the malpais curved down from the north to form a sort of peninsula in the desert.

"We're supposed to enter the lava field at its southernmost point, where there are two spires of rock that form a sort of gate, and proceed several miles into it until we reach a U-shaped ridge with its open end facing east. In the eastern slope of that ridge, in the very middle of it, there's a cave, and that's supposed to be where Albrecht Konigsberg hid the candlestick and whatever else he had with him that was valuable."

The Kid thumbed his hat back as he looked down at the lines Annabelle had drawn in the dirt, studying them until he had committed them to memory.

"The secret of the Twelve Pearls," he said.

Annabelle nodded. "I want to find out what that means, probably even more than I want to recover the Konigsberg Candlestick."

"You want to solve a historical mystery that no one's ever been able to solve."

"That's right," she said without hesitation.

"Because you think it would have impressed your father."

Her head snapped up. She glared at him. "Have you ever heard of Sigmund Freud?"

"Can't say as I have," The Kid said.

"He's a doctor in Austria working with patients who have mental problems. He claims that when people do something, their actions are really about something else, something that they may not even be aware of."

The Kid's eyes narrowed. "Maybe sometimes. But it doesn't seem too likely to me."

"Nor to me." She stood up and brushed her hands off. "So don't start thinking you know everything about me and why I do the things I do, Mr. Morgan."

"I thought you were calling me Kid now."

"Perhaps I really meant something else," she said in a chilly tone, then turned and walked away.

The Kid watched her go, then chuckled, making sure she didn't hear him.

Soon they were on the move again. They drew closer to the lava field and finally entered it when there were still a couple hours left until sundown, passing between the twin spires of rock that towered about a hundred feet in the air. The ride had been incredibly tiring, but The Kid felt an exhiliration that lifted his spirits as they rode into the malpais. They weren't far from their goal, and so far, he hadn't seen any horse droppings or tracks that indicated Fortunato was ahead of them.

He wouldn't see any tracks on the lava, either, except maybe an occasional place where a horseshoe had nicked it. The red, molten rock that had flowed from the erupting volcano had cooled and turned into black stone that still held a dull sheen, even after all those centuries. They had to proceed carefully, because in places, bubbles within the lava had left air pockets where the rock was thin and brittle. It could break when too much weight was put on it, leaving sharp edges that would slash a horse's legs to ribbons. They had to stay on the part that was solid, so The Kid went first, telling Annabelle to stay behind him and to ride where he rode.

"How do you know where you're going?" she asked.

"My father told me about places like this and how to find my way through them. Mostly, you just have to take it slow and easy and let your horse pick its way along. Their instincts are just as good or better than ours. They won't put their weight down on a place they don't trust."

Surprisingly, the malpais wasn't totally devoid of vegetation, like Laguna del Muerto had been. An occasional clump of hardy grass poked its way through the black rock, and there were puny bushes that made the gnarled mesquite of the desert look healthy. For the most part, though, the terrain was bare and eerie-looking. Once they were out of sight of the desert, so that they couldn't see anything except the ripples and ridges of the lava field, a shiver went through Annabelle.

"It's unearthly," she said in a hollow voice. "Like something on another planet."

"I figured out that's what unearthly meant," The Kid said.

"Don't try to tell me it doesn't make you nervous, too."

He shrugged. "I'm not overfond of it, that's for sure."

Their pace was slow, and it was almost an hour before they spotted a ridge that might be the one described in the old journal Annabelle had read.

"It's so hard to be sure," she said. "We almost need to be able to look at it from above."

"That's not going to happen unless you figure on sprouting wings. We'll circle around the end of it there—" The Kid pointed "—and follow it on around, see if it's shaped like a U and if there's a cave in it."

"And if there's not?"

"We keep looking, I reckon."

That wasn't going to be necessary he saw a short time later as they rounded the end of the ridge. He could see all the way to where it curved, and in the middle of that curve was an even deeper patch of blackness that marked the mouth of a cave.

Annabelle saw it, too. "That's it!" she said, unable to keep the excitement from creeping into her voice. "Oh, my God, that's it, Kid!"

He reined in and rested his hands on the saddle-horn. "Yeah, I reckon it is," he said.

"Do we have time to get there and get back out before it's dark?"

"We'll get there. We can spend the night in the cave if we have to."

"That might be a good idea. It'll give us more time to search if we need it."

Annabelle was so eager, she would have ridden ahead, but The Kid motioned her back and took the lead again. He was mounted on the buckskin and he trusted the horse's instincts. They made their way slowly and carefully along the ridge. He felt his nerves drawing tighter as they neared the cave mouth.

Would they find the Konigsberg Candlestick and the secret of the Twelve Pearls inside? Or would they discover that Count Eduardo Fortunato had beaten them to the prize?

Finally they were just below the cave mouth, which was about forty feet up the side of the ridge. The Kid swung down from the saddle and told Annabelle, "Wait here. I'll have a look inside."

"Are you insane? After coming all this way and going through all I've gone through, you think I'm going to let you go first?"

"Yeah, I do, because it might be a trap." The Kid slipped the Colt from its holster. "Stay here. I won't explore the place. I'll just make sure there aren't any nasty surprises waiting for us inside."

"Well . . . all right. But I don't have to like it."

"Nobody said you did."

The Kid started up the slope, being careful where he stepped. Just before he reached the opening, he bent down and picked up a loose piece of broken lava. He tossed it inside and waited to see if there would be any reaction. When there wasn't, he came closer and approached the opening from the side. When he went through it, he moved fast, crouching and twisting as he swept the gun from side to side.

Nothing. Just the sound of his boots scraping

against the rock echoing back from the close confines of the cave.

Once he was inside and no longer silhouetted against the opening, he dug a match from his pocket and struck it on the wall next to him. As the flame flared up, it revealed a chamber about twelve feet wide and twenty feet deep that was tall enough for him to stand up in. Although the pockmarked black lava was visible around the edges of the cave mouth, the interior walls were the sort of smooth gray stone that had been there before the eruption covered the area with molten rock. A layer of dust and dirt coated the floor, along with a few dried-out animal droppings. Not many animals ventured in here, just like the rest of the Jornada del Muerto.

Other than that, the place was empty. The Kid didn't see anywhere that the fugitive German could have hidden the treasures he had brought with him all the way from Europe.

The Kid breathed a curse. Annabelle was going to be mighty disappointed if this turned out not to be the place they were looking for. It matched the description. That U-shaped ridge was a hard landmark to miss.

Of course, it was still possible that Fortunato had gotten there first and already had the candlestick in his possession.

The match was about to flicker out when The Kid spotted a flash of something white from the rear wall. He dropped the match and lit another, then held it up higher as he approached whatever it was he had seen. He knelt to take a closer look.

The rear wall of the cave wasn't smooth, he saw. It sloped slightly and was made up of a large pile of smaller rocks, like the tailings from a mine shaft. The Kid glanced up at the ceiling. At one time the chamber had been deeper than it was now. There had been a cave-in, sealing off the rear wall.

And in that jumble of rocks, he saw as he leaned closer, was something white and smooth, although slightly porous . . .

That was a piece of bone he was looking at, he realized.

The Kid stiffened. He stood up from his crouch and holstered his gun. He could dig out the bone, but he would need help. He went back to the entrance and looked down at Annabelle waiting anxiously below.

"Come on up," he said. "I want you to meet Albrecht Konigsberg."

Chapter 29

One of the things they had brought along from the wagon was a small, collapsible lantern. Annabelle stood behind The Kid, holding the lantern so that he could see what he was doing as he moved chunks of rock left behind by the cave-in. He could sense her excitement growing as he uncovered several pieces of bone. They were badly broken, but Annabelle insisted that she could tell they were human.

The Kid thought so, too. He said, "I figure Konigsberg was nothing but a skeleton by the time the roof fell in. He'd made it this far and then died while that servant of his went to look for help."

"Then the candlestick and anything else he had might still be buried under those rocks," Annabelle said.

The Kid nodded as he shifted another chunk of stone. "They might not be in very good shape, though. That's a lot of weight that came down."

"Even if the candlestick is crushed, we may be able to tell what it is. The Church wants it back, either way."

The Kid continued digging. After a few more minutes, he uncovered something that wasn't rock or bone. He ran his fingers over its smooth surface and announced, "Looks like some sort of leather pouch. The air's dry enough in here that it hasn't rotted away."

Annabelle leaned forward. "Can you get it loose?"

"Hang on." With a grunt of effort, The Kid heaved a large piece of rock aside, then another and another. He could see that the thing he was digging out was definitely an old pouch of some sort.

When he lifted it out of its nesting place in the rubble, it was heavy in his hands. It was a good-sized bag, more than a foot and a half square. A flap on the top of it was held closed by a piece of rope that practically fell apart in The Kid's hands when he tugged on it. He pulled the flap back and slid his hand inside the pouch, thinking after he had already done so that he hoped the old German hadn't rigged some sort of trap in there.

His fingers brushed metal. He closed his hand around the thing and pulled it out. The light from the lantern gleamed dully on the golden surface of a heavy candlestick and struck scintillating reflections from the gems embedded in it.

"Oh," Annabelle said. That was clearly all she could manage.

The candlestick was dented and misshapen, but it was still easy enough to recognize for what it was. After more than two centuries, the Konigsberg Candlestick had emerged from its hiding place.

The Kid turned and held it out to Annabelle. She set the lantern on a rock and then gingerly took the artifact out of The Kid's hands. She looked at him with wide eyes and whispered, "This is it. This is really it. I've read all the descriptions. This is it."

"Yeah, I reckon it is," The Kid said. "But what else is in here?"

He stuck his hand back in the pouch. Annabelle was still gazing down in awe at the candlestick, but she lifted her eyes when The Kid went on, "I've got something."

He pulled out a bundle wrapped in some sort of cloth. It was thick and rectangular. He began unwrapping it, and within moments the cloth lay in a heap on the floor of the cave and The Kid held a book in his hands.

"A book?" Annabelle said. "That's the secret of the Twelve Pearls?"

"Must be." The Kid held the book in one hand and hefted the pouch with the other. "There's nothing else in here."

Annabelle set the candlestick aside. "Let me see it."

The book was bound in faded brown leather. There was no writing on the outside of it. The edges of the binding overlapped the pages, which The Kid riffled through with his thumb before he handed the volume over to Annabelle. As far as he could tell, the book hadn't been printed on a printing press. Its pages were filled with hand-written notations, along with columns of figures and carefully drawn figures and diagrams. He got a good enough look at the writing to tell that it was in German, no doubt Albrecht Konigsberg's work.

"Can you read German?" he asked Annabelle.

"Quite well, actually," she said. "A good working knowledge of various languages is an invaluable tool for a historian."

"What does it say?"

Annabelle flipped rapidly through the pages. "It seems to be . . . an astronomical journal of some sort. Konigsberg was a scientist, remember? He studied astronomy, and this appears to be a record of star sightings, of movements among the heavenly bodies . . . and predictions of things that Konigsberg believed were going to happen in the future, based on the stars."

"Like a fortune-teller?" The Kid asked with a frown.

Annabelle glanced up at him. "People have believed for thousands of years that there are portents in the stars that allow them to foretell the future. In those days, the science of where the stars were located and how they moved in the cosmos was all mixed together with the mystical and predictive aspects of the stars, what people call astrology. Konigsberg made a study of all of it, and . . ." She sank down on a rock. "It's going to take me some time to work this out."

"Go ahead," The Kid told her. "I'll go check on the horses and bring them up here so we can tie them close to the cave. We'll be spending the night here." In fact, it was already dark outside.

"Go ahead," Annabelle said, totally absorbed in what she was reading. "I'm going to be busy with this for a while."

The horses hadn't wandered off. There was nowhere to go in that wasteland. The Kid found a fairly level spot with a little grass and some of the scrawny bushes growing on it and tied the horses' reins to the bushes. Now that they had found what they were looking for, he was anxious to get out of there, but they couldn't retrace their path until morning. It wouldn't be safe to cross the malpais in the dark.

They would have to figure out what to do about Father Jardine. The Kid hoped he could find a place suitable for an ambush. If he could get the drop on Fortunato, the count might release Father Jardine to save his own life. Since The Kid and Annabelle already had the old German's treasure, the priest wasn't valuable to Fortunato anymore.

He took his time tending to the horses so that Annabelle could work undisturbed. When he finally went back into the cave, he saw that she was still bent over the book, looking back and forth from it to a piece of paper she had spread out on the rock beside her. That paper was covered with numbers. Annabelle added to them, scrawling more with the stub of a pencil she held in her hand. As The Kid watched, she scribbled away for a few more minutes, then looked up suddenly and said, "Of course! That's it!"

"You've figured it out?" The Kid asked.

She looked at him. "Yes. It's worthless, Kid. The secret of the Twelve Pearls doesn't mean a thing."

"Wait a minute. I thought you said Konigsberg hinted that it was worth a fortune."

Annabelle shook her head. "He may have believed that, but he was wrong." She snatched up the paper she'd been writing on. "Look, I'll show you the figures—"

The Kid held up a hand to stop her. "Just tell me what it's about, in plain English."

She shrugged and nodded. "All right. Like I told you, in Konigsberg's time, astronomy and astrology were all mixed up together. He seems to have been a halfway competent astronomer, but he also believed firmly in the ability of the stars to predict the future. The Twelve Pearls was his name for a group of a dozen different stars that he believed were going to line up in a certain order at some point in the future, something that would happen only once every few thousand years."

"And he thought when they did, something important was going to happen," The Kid guessed.

Annabelle nodded again. "That's right. According to Konigsberg, when the Twelve Pearls were in conjunction, they would unleash a power on the earth like nothing ever seen before, and that the man who could harness this power would be able to rule the world."

"Sounds a little loco to me."

"Yes, of course, because you're a modern man who doesn't believe in such things. But Konigsberg did, and he was desperate to remain alive until 1685 so that *he* would be that man." Annabelle started flipping through the pages. "But here's the interesting thing. Some of these calculations were done *after* he escaped from the Inquisition and fled to America. He realized, once he got to Mexico, that the perfect spot to view the conjunction of the Twelve Pearls was right here in what was then Nuevo Mexico."

"Wait a minute . . . You're saying that when he ran again from the agents of the Inquisition, he didn't come up here just to get away from them. He wanted to find a particular spot."

"Exactly. He didn't make it, though. According to his calculations, the place he was looking for was a couple of miles east of here." Annabelle snapped the book closed and tossed it aside. "Anyway, none of it matters, because while Konigsberg might have been an adequate astronomer, he was a terrible mathemetician. His calculations of the time when the Twelve Pearls are supposed to be in conjunction were incorrect. He worked out the date to be July 16, 1685, but he was off by two hundred and sixty years."

"You mean . . ."

Annabelle laughed. "That's right. Even if he was correct about the Twelve Pearls lining up like he thought, it's not going to happen for almost fifty years yet! He believed he had the key to immense power, but the only thing of value he really had was the candlestick he had stolen."

The Kid had to laugh, too, as he picked up the candlestick. "Well, we've got this, anyway. If we have to, we'll use it to bargain with Fortunato for the padre's life."

Annabelle looked surprised. "You can't mean to turn it over to that . . . that . . ."

"If we have to do that, we'll just steal it right back."

She shook her head. "No, you can't. You don't understand, Kid. Father Jardine would gladly give up his life to restore the candlestick to the Church. You can't give it to Fortunato, even to save him."

"Now, hold on. I know a hunk of gold this heavy is bound to be worth quite a bit, especially with those jewels stuck on it, but it's not worth a man's life."

"You don't know Father Jardine like I do." She stooped and picked up the worthless book she had thrown aside a few moments earlier. "This! This is what we'll use to bargain with."

The Kid thought about it and knew she might be on to something there. Fortunato wanted the secret of the Twelve Pearls. He might be willing to trade Father Jardine for it, and if The Kid and Annabelle and the padre could get away before Fortunato realized that the book wasn't worth anything . . .

They were going to have a chance to find out, because at that moment, a voice called from outside the cave, "Doctor! Dr. Dare! I know you're in there! Come out and bring the German's treasures with you, or I'll kill Father Jardine!"

Chapter 30

Fortunato had been furious when the Yaquis had come back from one of their scouting forays and told him that Dr. Dare and that so-called Kid Morgan were ahead of them. Arturo's prediction had proven to be correct; the woman and the gunfighter had abandoned the wagon and were racing toward the northern end of the Jornada del Muerto on horseback.

But after a moment's thought, Fortunato wasn't sure but that was a good thing after all. So far, Father Jardine had surprised him by holding up under the Yaquis' torture. The priest still refused to reveal what he knew about the hiding place of the Konigsberg Candlestick. It was inconvenient that Fortunato couldn't really turn the half-breeds loose on Father Jardine, but that would have meant risking his death and Fortunato couldn't afford that. So the Yaquis had not yet brought the full force of their inventive cruelty to bear on the old cleric.

Now they wouldn't need to. Fortunato could simply follow Dr. Dare to her destination and let the good doctor do the hard work for him. Then he would swoop in and take the spoils for himself.

That was where the situation stood now, with Fortunato, Novak, and the two Yaquis arranged in a rough half-circle below the mouth of the cave. That had to be it, Fortunato thought as he called out his ultimatum to Dr. Dare. The place where the Konigsberg Candlestick and the secret of the Twelve Pearls had rested for the past two centuries.

Father Jardine stood in the center of the half-circle, his hands tied in front of him and his head drooping from exhaustion and pain. Farther back, Arturo was waiting with the horses. That was the only job he could really be trusted with.

"Dr. Dare, did you hear me?" Fortunato called again. "If you want to save Father Jardine's life, you have no choice but to cooperate with me! I promise you, give me what I want, and no harm will come to any of you!"

That was a lie, of course, and Fortunato suspected that Dr. Dare knew it. Novak wanted to kill Kid Morgan for what he had done to his friends, and Fortunato wanted Dr. Dare and the priest dead because he never left any witnesses behind when he acquired a new treasure.

But despite knowing that Dr. Dare and Morgan wouldn't trust him, Fortunato felt certain that they wouldn't stand by and let Father Jardine be killed. They would try to negotiate with him, and those negotiations would probably involve some sort of trickery . . .

"Fortunato!"

That was a man's voice coming from the cave. Not Dr. Dare, then. Fortunato's hands tightened on the rifle he held as he shouted back, "Morgan! Kid Morgan! Is that you?"

For a moment, Morgan didn't answer. Then he said, "I reckon the padre told you my name."

"That's right. Come out, and you won't be harmed. You have my word on that. All I want are the things Albrecht Konigsberg concealed in that cave." Fortunato paused. "That *is* Konigsberg's hiding place, isn't it?"

"He was here, all right," Morgan said from deep in the cave, still not showing himself. "In fact, he's still here. His bones, anyway. But there was a cave-in, Fortunato. If the candlestick is here, it's buried under tons of rock."

The count felt a chill go through him. Morgan was probably lying, but it was possible he was telling the truth. The Konigsberg Candlestick might be crushed, ruined, lost forever. Fortunato wouldn't believe that until he saw the evidence with his own eyes. There was still the matter of the other precious thing Konigsberg had brought with him to America.

"But we have the secret of the Twelve Pearls!" Morgan called, as if he had just read Fortunato's mind. "We're willing to trade it for Father Jardine's life and safe passage out of this hellhole!"

From a few yards away, Novak called softly, "It's a trick!"

"Of course it is," Fortunato said. "Don't worry, I don't believe him." He raised his voice. "What is it,

Morgan? What is the secret of the Twelve Pearls?"

"It's a book," Morgan replied. "A book filled with writing in German. I can't read it, but Dr. Dare says that it's the instructions for how to acquire more power than anyone in the world has ever dreamed of. A new weapon, Fortunato, the likes of which nobody has ever seen!"

Fortunato's breath hissed between his teeth. Even though he was still distrustful, Morgan's words suddenly had the ring of truth. He gave in to his curiosity and asked, "What sort of weapon?"

"You'll have to figure that out for yourself. But you can do it if you have Konigsberg's book."

Novak said, "This is loco. No book could be worth that much."

"The book itself, perhaps not. But what's written in it . . ." Fortunato raised his voice again. "Throw the book out here. We'll take it and go, leaving Father Jardine."

"No deal," Morgan replied without hesitation. "Ride off and leave Father Jardine here with us. Once we're gone, you can come back and have everything that's in the cave, including Konigsberg's bones."

"That's unacceptable. I'm afraid we're at an impasse, Morgan. Do you know what that means?"

"A standoff," Morgan said. "In this case, I reckon you'd call it a New Mexican standoff."

Fortunato laughed. He couldn't help it. This Kid

301

Morgan had the sort of audacity he admired. It was a shame Morgan would have to die.

Novak said, "You really think some old book is really worth something?"

"I'd like to find out," Fortunato replied without hesitation. The promise of power was intriguing. He had wealth, more money than he could ever spend, in fact. And he had the treasures he had acquired over the years, the things that were his and his alone. If Konigsberg had really stumbled over something so powerful that it would make other weapons obsolete, then *that* should belong to him as well, Fortunato decided.

"I'm coming up there," he called toward the cave.

"What!" Novak exclaimed.

"You and the others stay here," Fortunato said as he stood up from where he had been crouched behind a boulder formed from the same lava that covered the ground. He strode forward and grasped Father Jardine's arm, then started up the slope toward the cave.

"Morgan!" he said. "I'm bringing the priest! I want that book!"

Manuelito understood enough of the white man's tongue to know that they were yelling about a book, and a candlestick, and a German, whatever that was. None of those things seemed important to him, but clearly they were to the white men. All that mattered to Manuelito was the need to kill them. He no longer cared about the redhaired woman. He wanted to kill her, too. He was too sick to do anything else.

The hate he felt toward all white men had kept him going the past two days, despite the fever that raged within him. And, although it was only a small consideration, he was curious, too. Where were all these insane white men going, and what was so important that they seemed to be racing with each other to get there? A book? A candlestick? A German? Madness!

Like most Apaches, Manuelito preferred horses for eating, rather than riding, but in this case, he never would have been able to keep up if he had not caught two of the horses left behind by the whites. He had trailed them at a distance, seldom pausing except to switch horses and take a small sip from one of the canteens. The fever made him thirsty, but he didn't give in to that. He just wanted to live long enough to kill them, and now they were all in one place, even the two Yaqui half-breeds who were polluted with white blood.

He would start with the easiest, he thought as he crept through the lava field. One of the men stood by himself, well back from the rest, holding the horses. Manuelito would kill him first, then the others.

He was outnumbered, of course, and all the white men had guns except the old priest, but in his fevered state, filled with rage and hate, those thoughts never occurred to Manuelito. He was invincible. He would walk among his enemies, slaying them in a frenzy of blood and death, and if they killed him it would be a good way to die.

Rising to his feet as he came up behind the man holding the horses, he lifted the knife in his hand above his head, ready to strike and spill the man's blood.

Then a wave of weakness went through him without warning, and he stumbled slightly, just enough so that his foot hit a loose bit of lava and made it clatter as he kicked it aside.

The white man turned and saw him and said, "Oh, hello. Who are you?"

Manuelito snarled and leaped forward, driving the knife downward.

"Kid, what are we going to do?" Annabelle asked as they stood pressed to opposite walls inside the cave mouth, watching Fortunato and Father Jardine climb slowly up the slope toward them. "You know we can't trust Fortunato!"

"I know," The Kid said. "But he's so anxious to get his hands on that old book, he's made a mis- take. He's given himself to us as a hostage."

Annabelle's eyes widened. "You're going to take him prisoner?"

"That's the plan," The Kid replied. It was a hastily-formed one, he thought, but it was all they had. "We'll keep him with us until we get back to civilization."

"He'll be trying to get loose and kill you every step of the way."

"I reckon."

"And even if we make it, he'll never forgive you for humiliating him like that. He'll hire killers to hunt you down, no matter where you go in the world—"

"I'll take my chances," The Kid said. "All that matters is getting you and the padre and that candlestick back where you need to be."

"Why?" she said. "Why does it matter to you?"

He frowned. He couldn't answer that question. Ten days ago, he hadn't even known her and Father Jardine. He'd never heard of Albrecht Konigsberg or that blasted candlestick or anything called the Twelve Pearls. But since then, he had risked his life numerous times for them and was about to do so again. Why indeed?

"I don't like anybody who feels like he can just take whatever he wants, no matter who else gets hurt along the way. It's not right."

"You want the world to be *fair?*"

The Kid knew better than that. The world would never be fair. He had a hunch that fortune was always going to smile more on those who didn't deserve it. That evil was going to win more than it lost. That the ultimate triumph, if there ever was one, would belong to the barbarians of the world, and despite Count Eduardo Fortunato's cultured veneer, that's what he was—a barbarian.

Most folks would say that he fit that description, too. A drifter, a killer, a man who rode alone. There was no place for him in a civilized world.

But at least he knew that every now and then, a man had to stand up and do something because it was right. He might not have a personal stake in it, but if he could help bring about even a brief flicker of light in the encroaching tide of darkness that threatened to wash over the whole world . . .

Well, that was worth something, wasn't it?

Those thoughts went through his mind in the blink of an eye, and he said in reply to Annabelle's question, "No, I just want to shoot that son of a bitch because he's got it coming. But I'll hold off if it means getting you and the padre out of here safely."

There wasn't time for any more talk, at least between the two of them. Fortunato had stopped about ten feet from the mouth of the cave. He stood there gripping Father Jardine's arm with his left hand. His right held a Winchester slanted across his body with the muzzle pointed at the priest's head. The light from the lantern in the cave spilled down over them and revealed Father Jardine's bruised, bloody features as the priest lifted his head to look at them. Annabelle gasped at the sight of him. The Kid's jaw tightened in anger.

"Padre, are you all right?" he asked.

In a voice tinged with pain but still containing a note of strength, Father Jardine said, "The Lord sustains me, my son. The Lord sustains me."

Annabelle spoke up for the first time, unable to contain her anger. "What did you do to him, Fortunato?" she demanded.

"Ah, Dr. Dare," the count said. "You *are* in there. I was beginning to worry that something had happened to you, since Mr. Morgan was doing all the talking."

"What did you do?" Annabelle said again.

Fortunato shrugged. "I did nothing, Doctor. It was my Yaqui friends who tried to persuade the good father to reveal your destination. But then I realized it wasn't necessary for him to do so. *You* led me here, Doctor. You and Mr. Morgan."

In the lanternlight, The Kid saw the rage on Annabelle's face and knew how close she was to losing control. She wanted to step out there and rush to Father Jardine. She wanted to shoot Fortunato, too. Giving in to either of those impulses might be disastrous.

"Annabelle," The Kid said softly. "Take a deep breath. Settle down."

She glared across the opening at him, but she took his advice, then gave him a curt nod to show that she was all right.

"I'm not sure I believe you about the Konigsberg Candlestick," Fortunato went on, "but we'll leave that for later. For now, I want this book that contains the secret of the Twelve Pearls. Hand it over, and you can have Father Jardine."

"If we do that, what's to stop you from killing us?" The Kid asked.

Fortunato shrugged. "My word? Is that worth anything to you, Mr. Morgan?"

"Not a damned thing."

"Then we won't be able to continue this negotiation. Perhaps you'll feel differently in the morning. Come along, Father."

"Hold it," The Kid said. "What makes you think you're going back down that slope, Count?"

To emphasize his point, he cocked the Colt in his hand. In the close quarters of the cave, the sound was loud, plenty loud enough for Fortunato to hear it outside.

Fortunato's face darkened with anger. "We were trying to strike a deal," he snapped. "That implies a truce."

"It may imply it, but nobody said it," The Kid drawled. "Anyway, I wouldn't lose any sleep over lying to a snake like you, mister."

Fortunato stiffened. "Have you no honor, Mr. Morgan?"

"What I have is six bullets in my gun and you in my sights, Count. You're not going anywhere except into this cave with Father Jardine, and come morning, we're all riding out of the malpais together. Your men will be long gone by then . . . if you want to live."

"You intend to make me your hostage?" Fortunato's voice shook a little with rage.

"That's the idea," The Kid said.

"Never!"

"Well, then, the alternative is to shoot you down right here and now. You reckon those fellas who are working for you will stick around once you're dead and can't pay them anymore?"

The Kid had moved forward enough so that he and Fortunato could see each other clearly. The two men traded cold, level stares.

There was no telling how the standoff would have ended. At that moment, a high-pitched scream ripped through the night. It was such a horrible, blood-curdling sound that everyone looked to see where it came from. The Kid saw a tall, skinny hombre in a dusty suit run frantically into the light. A bronzed figure stumbled after him, slashing at him with a knife but missing.

With Fortunato distracted, Father Jardine moved suddenly, acting with surprising speed for a man of his age, especially a man who had undergone torture at the hands of the Yaquis. He twisted in Fortunato's grip and grabbed the barrel of the count's rifle. He tried to wrench it out of Fortunato's hands, and as he did, he shouted, "Fight, Mr. Morgan! Fight them!"

"Kill them all!" Fortunato yelled as the unexpected assault by the priest made him stumble backward.

The Kid threw himself forward in the cave mouth, calling, "Doctor, get down!" as he did so. He saw muzzle flashes from the guns ranged around him, but the bullets went over his head. The Colt in his hand bucked and roared as he triggered it. He heard Annabelle's Lightning blasting, too.

Fortunato lost his footing and fell, and since Father Jardine still had hold of the rifle, the priest went down, too. The two men tumbled over and over down the slope.

Muzzle flashes lit the night over the malpais. The Kid saw that one of the Yaquis was already sprawled face-down on the lava. The Kid shifted his aim and drilled the other Yaqui through the lungs. That left the other gunman, a lean, lantern-jawed man dressed in red and black. He had a rifle in his hand, spewing lead and flame as he worked the lever. The Kid and Annabelle fired at the same time. The man's rifle flew out of his hands into the air as both slugs, The Kid's .45 and Annabelle's .41, caught him in the chest and drove him back-ward. He crumpled.

That left Fortunato still struggling with Father Jardine, and the other man about to be killed by the Indian who had chased him into the light. The last Apache, thought The Kid as he recognized the leg-gings, the tunic, the bright blue band of cloth around the man's jet-black hair. He had caught up with his quarry, knocked him to the ground, and knelt on top of him with a knee in the man's back.

The Apache caught hold of the man's hair and jerked his head up so that the skin of his throat was drawn taut. He was about to bring his knife across the man's throat in a deep slash that would open it up wide.

Up on a knee now, The Kid shouted, "Apache!", and when the warrior's head turned toward him, he put his last bullet between the Indian's eyes. The Apache's head jerked back as the slug exploded out the back of his skull. He dropped the knife and collapsed, slumping forward over the man he'd been about to kill.

As The Kid and Annabelle started down the slope, Fortunato finally tore the rifle loose from Father Jardine's grip and slammed the butt against the side of the priest's head. Father Jardine rolled across the lava. Fortunato whirled toward The Kid and Annabelle. The Kid hadn't had time to reload. Fortunato lifted the rifle, grinning as he said, "Now all the German's treasures will be mine!"

Annabelle pulled the trigger of her Lightning, but the hammer clicked on an empty chamber. She was out of bullets, too, which meant they were at Fortunato's mercy.

And The Kid knew exactly how much *that* was worth.

Nothing.

Before Fortunato could pull the trigger, Father Jardine lunged at him from behind, grabbed his ankles, and pulled his feet out from under him.

With a startled cry, Fortunato pitched forward. The rifle in his hand blasted as his finger involuntarily jerked the trigger. Chips of lava sprayed in the air as the bullet slammed into the ground.

And Fortunato screamed.

The scream turned into a hideous gurgle. He rolled onto his back, the rifle forgotten. His hands fumbled at his throat, where bright red blood gushed between his fingers. By the time The Kid reached his side, the light was going out in the count's eyes. Fortunato peered up at him and tried to talk, but nothing came out of his ruined throat except incoherent sounds. Annabelle reached Father Jardine and helped him onto his feet, and along with The Kid, they stood there and watched Fortunato die.

"I will pray for your immortal soul," Father Jardine told him.

"I don't reckon it'll do any good, padre," The Kid said. "Fortunato's shaking hands with the Devil by now. He's dead."

Father Jardine prayed anyway, as he leaned on Annabelle.

The Kid turned away from the corpse as he heard a feeble, "Help! Please!" He went over to the dead Apache, who was still sprawled on top of the man The Kid didn't know. The man must have heard The Kid's footsteps, because he said, "Please, could . . . could you remove this savage?"

The Kid thumbed fresh cartridges into his

revolver, then hunkered beside the warrior's corpse and the man pinned underneath it. "Who're you, mister?"

"My . . . my name is Arturo. I'm Count Fortunato's manservant."

"Well, Fortunato's dead, so I reckon that means you're out of a job. How does that sit with you?"

The man closed his eyes and sighed. "That's regrettable."

"Not from where I sit, it's not."

"What I meant to say was, I bear you no ill will, sir. Could you please get this dead Indian off me? And take me back to civilization?"

"Can we trust you?"

"I give you my word."

"All right, then." The Kid took hold of the Apache's tunic and rolled the corpse to the side. Arturo sat up and hunched over, hugging his knees in what appeared to be sheer terror. "Take it easy," The Kid told him. "Nobody's going to hurt you now."

Arturo stared wide-eyed at Fortunato's body. "What . . . what happened to him?"

"That's a damned good question," The Kid said.

Epilogue

It didn't take them long to figure it out. The shot Fortunato had fired as he was falling had exploded one of those bubbles in the lava, leaving an opening with sharp, jagged edges all around it. His head had slipped into that opening, and the lava had slashed his throat wide open. Call it fate, call it justice . . . call it whatever you wanted to, The Kid thought. The important thing was that Fortunato and all his men were dead, except for Arturo, and The Kid, Annabelle, and Father Jardine were alive.

And the Konigsberg Candlestick was going back where it belonged.

A week later they were in a hotel in Santa Fé. The candlestick was locked up in the hotel's safe until Father Jardine and Annabelle caught the train that would take them back east. There would be a stop at Yale, and then Annabelle planned to accompany the priest all the way to the Vatican, where the candlestick would be turned over to Church authorities and eventually make its way back to Spain, where it had come from. Highly efficient guards, paid for by the Church, would accompany the candlestick on its journey.

Annabelle had asked The Kid to come with them. "I'd . . . feel safer with you along, Kid," she had said.

But he had turned her down as gently as possible, saying, "From what I've seen, Doctor, you're plenty able to take care of yourself, and the padre, *and* that candlestick."

Annabelle had Konigsberg's journal to take back to Yale with her, too. It had historical interest, even though it was of no practical value.

"This doesn't seem fair," Annabelle said as the three of them lingered over coffee after having dinner in the hotel dining room. "What have you gotten out of all this trouble, Kid?"

"Some excitement?" he said with a smile. He grew more serious as he went on, "I was able to help out some folks who needed help, and because of us, Fortunato won't be around to plunder and kill to get what he wants anymore."

"Because of me," Father Jardine said quietly. "I'm the one who ended his life."

The Kid knew it had been bothering the priest that he'd had a hand in Fortunato's death. He said, "You didn't end his life, padre. If anything, his own greed did that. You were just trying to protect Dr. Dare and me. I don't pretend to be on the best of terms with *El Señor Dios*, but even I don't see how He could hold that against you."

"I pray that you're right, my son."

Annabelle touched The Kid's hand and nodded toward the arched entrance into the dining room. Arturo stood there, clutching a hat in his hands, and when the servant spotted them, he came across the room toward them.

"Pardon me for intruding," Arturo began as he came up to the table.

"It's fine," The Kid said. He gestured to the empty chair. "Sit down. What can we do for you?"

True to his word, Arturo didn't seem to be holding a grudge against any of them for being involved in Fortunato's death. In fact, in talking to the man as they were riding out of the Jornada del Muerto, The Kid had gotten the idea that Arturo hadn't really liked the count that much.

"I was wondering . . ." Arturo began. "I mean, I don't particularly wish to return to Italy, and I thought perhaps . . . would you be in need of a servant, Mr. Morgan?"

The question took The Kid by surprise. He leaned back in his chair and frowned. "No offense, Arturo, but do I *look* like the sort of hombre who needs a butler?"

"Oh, I'm not actually a butler, sir. I'm a man-servant. What the British, in their inelegant fashion, call a batman."

"Well, I don't need a batman, either," The Kid said, although there had been a time in his life when he'd had any number of servants. A thought occurred to him, and he went on, "You go to San Francisco and see a man named Claudius Turnbuckle. He's a lawyer. Tell him Conrad sent you, and that I said he should help you find a suitable position. I'll stake you to the train fare."

Arturo smiled. "That's incredibly generous of you, sir. If there's ever anything I can do to repay your generosity, please don't hesitate to call on me."

"Might take you up on that one of these days," The Kid said.

When Arturo was gone, Annabelle looked intently at The Kid and said, "Conrad, eh? Conrad Morgan?"

"Not exactly." The Kid took a sip of his coffee.

"You can't blame me for being curious . . . Kid. I'm a historian, and—" she grinned. "—I'd bet a hat you have a fascinating history."

"I don't know that I'd call it fascinating."

"What would you call it?"

That was a good question. Dark? Bloody? Tragic? His history was all of those things and more.

But it wasn't really *his* history anymore, he realized. It belonged to Conrad Browning, not Kid Morgan. Kid Morgan was a clean slate.

"I'd call it forgotten," he said. "As forgotten as old Albrecht Konigsberg will be, one of these days."

They had left the bones in the cave. Father Jardine said they should not be disturbed. And as the years passed, that was the case. No one went to the cave in the malpais. No one bothered Albrecht Konigsberg's bones. No one ventured into the Jornada del Muerto without good reason.

The men who went in 1945 had a good reason. Twenty-two kilotons of good reason, in fact. On July 16, 1945, they detonated it in a place called Trinity Site, two miles east of the cave where the bones of the man who had pinpointed that spot more than two centuries earlier still rested.

No one looked up. No one noticed the twelve stars moving into alignment. Even if it had been night, they couldn't have seen the Twelve Pearls. The explosion was too bright.

The shockwave rolled over the barren landscape, and in the cave, the concussion blasted away the rocks that covered the rest of the bones and then turned the bones themselves into powder and ash.

But in that last split second, as the skull of Albrecht Konigsberg peered into the heart of a power greater than any ever seen on earth, it seemed to wear a grin of vindication.

Even if he *had* been off by two hundred and sixty years.

Center Point Publishing

600 Brooks Road • PO Box 1
Thorndike ME 04986-0001 USA

(207) 568-3717

US & Canada:
1 800 929-9108
www.centerpointlargeprint.com